Life is rarely boring for Federation ambassador-at-large Gerard Manley. Whether he's negotiating a tricky treaty on a planet inhabited by ghosts, losing his heart to a passionate Sylvan beauty, or nearly losing his life in a brutal attack on a starbase, he finds more excitement than most men do in a dozen lifetimes.

But Gerard Manley is also a haunted man, driven by dreams of a half-remembered past as Consort to Fairy Peg, ruler of the Ribble Galaxy, and obsessed with the origins of the "Tenderfoot" legend, an ancient cosmic myth with uncanny parallels to his own life.

With the aid of "Windy," the starship *Windhover* which serves him as confidante, confessor and comrade-in-arms, Manley sets out to unravel the intricate mysteries of his past.

**THE WINDHOVER TAPES**

A new science fiction adventure series

**by Warren Norwood**

Bantam Science Fiction and Fantasy Books
Ask your bookseller for the books you have missed

ALAS BABYLON by Pat Frank
BABEL-17 by Samuel R. Delaney
THE BALLAD OF BETA 2 by Samuel R. Delaney
THE BEGINNING PLACE by Ursula Le Guin
A CANTICLE FOR LEIBOWITZ by Walter Miller, Jr.
CENTURY'S END by Russell M. Griffin
DHALGREN by Samuel R. Delaney
THE DRAGON LENSMAN by David A. Kyle
THE EINSTEIN INTERSECTION by Samuel R. Delaney
EYAS by Crawford Kilian
FANTASTIC VOYAGE by Isaac Asimov
THE GATES OF HEAVEN by Paul Preuss
THE GLASS OF DYSKORNIS by Randall Garrett and Vicki Ann Heydron
GOSH! WOW! edited by Forrest J Ackerman
THE GREY MANE OF MORNING by Joy Chant
HELLSTROM'S HIVE by Frank Herbert
THE HEROES OF ZARA KEEP by Guy Gregory
HONEYMOON IN HELL by Fredric Brown
THE HUMANOID TOUCH by Jack Williamson
JEM by Frederik Pohl
THE JEWELS OF APTOR by Samuel R. Delaney
A LIFE IN THE DAY OF . . . AND OTHER SHORT STORIES by Frank Robinson
LORD VALENTINE'S CASTLE by Robert Silverberg
MAN PLUS by Frederik Pohl
MATHEW SWAIN: HOT TIME IN OLD TOWN by Mike McQuay
MOCKINGBIRD by Walter Tevis
NEBULA WINNERS FOURTEEN edited by Frederik Pohl
NOVA by Samuel R. Delaney
QUAS STARBRITE by James R. Berry
THE ROBOT WHO LOOKED LIKE ME by Robert Sheckley
SLOW FALL TO DAWN by Stephen Leigh
SONG OF SORCERY by Elizabeth Scarborough
THE STAINLESS STEEL RAT! by Harry Harrison
THE STEEL OF RAITHSKAR by Randall Garrett and Vicki Ann Heydron
A STORM UPON ULSTER by Kenneth Flint
SUNDIVER by David Brin
SYZYGY by Frederik Pohl
TALES OF NEVERYON by Samuel R. Delaney
TIME STORM by Gordon Dickson
TRITON by Samuel R. Delaney
THE WINDHOVER TAPES: AN IMAGE OF VOICES by Warren Norwood

# THE WINDHOVER TAPES

## AN IMAGE OF VOICES

Warren Norwood

BANTAM BOOKS
TORONTO · NEW YORK · LONDON · SYDNEY

THE WINDHOVER TAPES: AN IMAGE OF VOICES
*A Bantam Book / May 1982*

*All rights reserved.*
*Copyright © 1982 by Warren C. Norwood.*
*Cover art copyright © 1982 by Bantam Books, Inc.*
*This book may not be reproduced in whole or in part, by mimeograph or any other means, without permission.*
*For information address: Bantam Books, Inc.*

ISBN 0-553-20751-2

*Published simultaneously in the United States and Canada*

---

*Bantam Books are published by Bantam Books, Inc. It trademark, consisting of the words "Bantam Books" and the portrayal of a rooster, is Registered in U.S. Patent and Trademark Office and in other countries. Marca Registrada. Bantam Books, Inc., 666 Fifth Avenue, New York, New York 10103.*

---

PRINTED IN THE UNITED STATES OF AMERICA

0 9 8 7 6 5

To
Frances Caveness for encouragement when it was needed,
Pierce Watters for invaluable suggestions and ideas,
Jake Kobler for making me ask the right questions,
and especially to
Margot Biery Norwood, my wife and best friend, who
made this whole enterprise possible.

All characters in this book are fictitious, and any resemblance to actual persons living or dead is entirely coincidental.

# 1

## 7035–8.1
## FedBase 1744

It really seems a bit absurd to keep a journal which will never be read by anyone but the journal keeper. Still, foolish and whimsical soul that you are, Gerard, you will keep one. Starting now.

In the mindwipe that ended our last mission I fear we lost far too many memories we would like to have kept. So, dear Self, I charge you with this task, urge you to keep me diligent, and warn you that the very presence of this journal violates every diplomatic contract the Federation has ever written. That's why I'm recording this in my personal security section of Windy's files. And that's why we must keep its existence a secret from anyone. Except, perhaps, Fairy Peg.

Ah, Fairy Peg, where are you now? Lost somewhere in my memory for sure. Hidden by the best techniques the mindwipers offer. Gone, but for your name, and a sweet lingering hint of your scent in my dreams.

A year now since the end of the last mission. A year since Fed exercised its legal option of mindwiping the entire experience from my memory. A year of "cleansing" and new preparation.

It's remarkable, Self, what I remember and what I don't. And of course, what you remember. FedDiploCorps said we were mindwiped for "the highest security reasons," but I suspect it was because we made a grand mess of things. A blatantly apparent failure. Sometimes I wish you'd learn to talk, Self, or esp, or somehow communicate with me besides dream symbology. I mean, let's be fair. Here I sit at the keyboard, punching personal revelations into Windy, with you watching my every move. Indeed, perhaps controlling my every move. And what do I get in return? Explanations? No, dreams. Weird dreams. Nonsequential, symbol-laden, overpainted dreams!

But no one ever promised me life would be fair, so why should I expect fairness from you? After all, I'm only the organism which has to act to insure your continued existence. I protect and defend you, feed you, give you spiritual sustenance, and occasionally find someone who will love and bed you. Surely I ask too much in wanting you to be fair with me and share the hidden resources of your knowledge and wisdom.

What? You're not impressed by my impotent threats and shallow flattery? No matter. We'll come to terms later.

Inventory.

New diplocontract is signed. Training (or was it retraining?) is complete. My personal modifications to the Baird Z-Rangel translator have tested out better than I thought they would. Fed replaced the autodoc with two superfluous rejuvhosp cells as part of "Mandatory Refitting", but at least they didn't add them to Windy's mortgage. *Windhover* is provisioned, polished, and ready to fly. So am I.

Now all we need is FedControl's final launch clearance.

*****Took them long enough. I thought they were going to make us sit here all day. One more chime from the FedChannel and we start the final count.

Ready or not, Self, here we go. Talk to you later.

## 7035–8.12
## Diera Entry Path

So much for diligent maintenance of a journal.

Three warps and eleven days later, I return. A poor start. Lack of desire to communicate? Lack of motivation? Lack of help from you, Self? No. Had it not been for my dreams of Fairy Peg, I would not be sitting here now as we coast down toward Diera.

Diera, religious planet of limited charm. Survey tells us (once you weed through all their technolingo) that the humanoid residents are seventeenth-generation Sylan descendants who slipped into mysticism by the sixth generation after plagues routinely killed half the population every thirty to forty years. Resistant immunity finally allowed the survivors to eke out an existence on the one major continent. They believe in magic, the supernatural, and the efficacy of total cooperation.

Their first diplomatic contact was a Sylvan, GrWrytte, who was impressed by little that he saw and particularly disdainful of their cultural achievements. He noted with great acerbity in the FedRecord that the Dierans have vast information about their immigration from Sylva, including videos of the first years, but refuse to concern themselves with such "mysteries". Poor GrWrytte, he didn't even notice that they took him in without rancor, nursed him through his bout with the plague, and buried him with honors.

By the time M. Caven got there, the Dierans had perfected their immunoserum, with the help of Survey, and Caven found herself in what she felt was diplomatic heaven. Unfortunately, Caven couldn't stay very long, and had to leave after a year to pursue other Federation business. Her FedRecord notes, however, are copious, and her relations with the Dierans were apparently excellent.

My job is to establish a FedOffice, sign a permanent treaty for Fed, and leave two of our passengers (deepsleeping now) as liaison officers. I cannot understand why liaison officers always travel in deepsleep. Maybe Windy knows.

She doesn't.

It occurs to me that it would be simpler to let Windy access this journal directly, but it's safer that she can't.

Been studying these notes on Diera for the past two months and no matter how bad GrWrytte's attitude, nor how good Caven's, I keep getting an irresistible feeling that both of them missed something very important, some essential ingredient, some key part of the puzzle. The whole populace sounds too basically nice. Too accepting.

Okay, Windy, I hear you. First orbit coming up.

## 7035–8.13
## Braking Orbit, Diera

Planetfall in six hours. Windy has us in the groove. Diera verifies our approach. My contact is M'Litha, the *wirzelmagess*, chief politician, witch, magician, and grand high muckity-muck. If all goes well in the next two days, Windy and I will cycle out a couple of the sleepers and we'll all begin work in earnest.

### 7035–8.22
### Tam City, Diera

Someone lied to me. This is not going well at all. And what the Krick does M'Litha want from me?

We had a non-linear welcome, where I was told to get to work and get greeted later. A non-linear diplomatic reception, which resembled what on old Terra would have been called a sabbat. A non-linear meeting with an old *magess* who told me to translate this manuscript I've punched into the Baird. And now, a handglyphed note from M'Litha herself, telling me that once my translation is complete we will have the formal welcome.

Windy's monitoring the Baird and giving assistance. I am waiting. That's what I seem to be doing the most of, waiting. Seven days of waiting. Waiting in the library. Waiting in the reception room. Waiting at the survey station, where they know more about atmosphere, dirt, flora, and fauna, and less about the populace, than they ought to. At least getting them to shift their attention broke part of the boredom. But only for a day.

I'm going to sleep, Self.

### 7035–8.23

If this manuscript is part of the answer as to what's going on here, I don't believe we've made any progress. The Baird's literal translation comes out as so much useless gibberish. Maybe this new program will help.

*****Well, it took nearly nine hours, but we did it. Windy coached the Baird, and I coached Windy. Word by word and phrase by phrase, I think we made some sense of all this. The first problem was that the manuscript is written in what Caven called "holy" dialect. The second problem was that it is a poem. Not just any old poem, but a very formal religious poem!

I'm exhausted. I've put the poem on the memory tape so I'll know it by heart in the morning. And you, Self, have the job of helping me understand what it means to our mission here.

## Diera's Call

Be then tempted, *star-child,*
To journey out of nightmist
  down to this baked rock
    and call it home.
Be then tempted, *wirzel,*
To mage the shadows from you
  with tongue and hand-hold
    and walk our path.
Be then tempted, *magess,*
To cull the seeds of medic
  deep within your womb
    and bear our spawn.
Be then tempted, mother,
To mold the face of Diera
  with line and lineage
    and mirror life.
Be then tempted, *star-child,*
To be the wirzel-magess,
  medic, true mother,
    and blood of all.

## 7035–9.1

Busy, busy, busy. But good busy. Not only did we pass the translation test with flying colors, we were also honored in a ceremony that lasted from dusk til dawn during which, as near as I can cipher it, I was made an honorary *Monkus*. In other words, I became a holy man. When I pressed M'Litha for more information on exactly what that meant, she had one of the *magesses* fetch me another manuscript! Yes, another poem. Different kind. Different dialect. But a poem nonetheless. Called "The Pilgrimage of Monkus on the Planet of His Exile." This one doesn't appear to be nearly so formal as "Diera's Call," and I'm hoping the translation problem will be somewhat simplified. I'd like to understand my honor a little better.

Now, Self, while we're waiting for Windy and the Baird to come up with a rough draft, what was that dream you gave me last night? In particular, what was Fairy Peg doing in a dream about the sabbat and why was she placing that fancy robe around my shoulders? Are you trying to tell me about something Peg did in the long ago? Or are you just playing with my tired and fragile mind? What was that sunburst pattern that kept appearing? Another one of your subtle symbols? Of my heart? Or of my ego for doing so well here on Diera? Come on, Self, you're holding back.

What, no snappy reply? I can wait. I always do.

*****Windy and the Baird didn't mess around this time. Two and a half hours from input to a very good draft. Another hour of refinement and collateral retranslating between the three of us, and it looks as though we may have a clue as to my status on Diera. At least we have some idea of who Monkus was, or more accurately, what he did that so impressed the Dierans.

According to what I learned during my days of waiting around in the library, the third Sylvan transport was forced by bad weather to set down on the opposite side of the continent from the first two. Consequently, two distinct communities grew out of that first wave of immigration, Tam City where we are now, and Chancor. Apparently Monkus was born in Tam City, and was one of the officials or couriers who traveled between the two cities. When the travel was banned in an attempt to control an outbreak of the plague, Monkus was in Chancor, and decided to go back to Tam City on foot.

What does M'Litha think I'm trying to return to? What makes me an allegorical Monkus? The only other thing we know for sure is that to become a Monkus is to become a member of an elite group so honored. I don't know why M'Litha thinks I'm suitable, but for the record, here's the poem.

**The Pilgrimage of Monkus on the Planet of His Exile**

I

Nothing bit him so hard as the teeth of possession
Who could journey on solar wind
  to the mind of stars,
  to the mountains of Eldorado,
Who could ski the wild snow of space.
Nothing cramped his legs more than the chair.

II

Cross country he ran
Cross fair faces

Cross Diera's loins, bosomland, heart, and shoulder,
Legs crying old tense pain,
  the dying spring of muscle,
  the sweat flowing hot.
His body's running heat felt hers,
  the steady rhythm-pounding,
  the aching drive,
  the push to make the hill
    to stagger down
      gasping to rest.

### III

Monkus went to be his brother,
Through the brush-cotton-grass
Through the dogwood-pine
Through the arbors of his bones
of his sinew-vines
He swept like an eye from the mountain
Running to see the changing change.

### IV

    To see,
    to become,
Monkus went,
  dark over mountains
  light under rivers
  dim through the rain,
Legs hard and willing,
Arms pumping lungs
  sucking holy vapors
    to fuel him
      on his pilgrimage home.

All in all, I think we've come up with a reasonable translation. We were pretty liberal with the flora, but that doesn't detract from the essence of the poem.

I put "Diera's Call" into the FedRecord, partially because it is a key to understanding this society, and partially because I know it will drive the bureaucrats bonkers. Knowing them, they will probably consider it classified information because they don't understand it, stamp it Ultra Secret, and bury it in their Mass Computer. Just another reason why they can't know about this journal. I put a literal prose translation of "Pilgrimage" into my FedRecord notes. They won't even notice that.

Think I'll have Windy synthesize some parchment and make a copy of "Pilgrimage" in old script Standard as a gift to M'Litha. Give it to her tomorrow with an elaborate display of ceremony, wearing my dress whites and the cape of *Monkus*. That ought to impress the old girl.

Meanwhile, I'd better start waking the liaison team.

### 7035–9.3

Impress was the wrong word. Either my instincts for this planet are perfect, or M'Litha is flattering me beyond all reason. When I gave her "Pilgrimage" on Windy's synth-parchment in the gold foil case my LightSpeed Diploma came in, those off-blue eyes of hers almost set up a spark gap across the high ridge of her nose. If Dierans were capable of crying, I think she might have. Seems as though the dress whites, red cape, and gold foil case all formed some powerful color magic of symbology.

The results were another dusk-to-dawn ceremony of dedication, from which I just returned, and a trip to Chancor some time in the next week or two in the royal flyer. I use the word "royal" because M'Litha resembles a queen as much as anything. She acts like one too.

By then Liaison and Survey will be too hard at work gathering new information for the treaty to miss me. So, Self, it looks like we might have earned ourselves a little holiday.

### 7035–9.11

Off to Chancor tomorrow with M'Litha and an entourage of *magesses* and *wirzels* formally introduced to me today. I think I counted fifty-three altogether. This ought to be quite a party. M'Litha warned me there will be several long ceremonies in Chancor, but that she will see to it that I get to talk to the *wirzel-magess* there in private, and get to spend as much time as possible in the Chancor library, which contains most of their old videos.

I have the modified memocorder Windy made for me so I can report back on a regular basis. The rejuvhosp cell gave me the full treatment and declared me fit (though a bit underweight, it said). I've packed my gear and some new ceremonial robes provided by M'Litha, and I guess I'm as ready as I'm going to get. Gerard, my boy, get some sleep, for tomorrow starts a new adventure.

**7035–10.17**
**Tam City**

The bloom is off the floradalia. The hero may have feet of clay. M'Litha is very obviously perturbed that I did so many things wrong in Chancor, and our relationship has cooled noticeably. In other words, it is descending to a normal level. Oh, the *Monkus*, Gerard Manley, Universal Diplomat, still has prestige, but apparently his instincts were not as perfect as he supposed. We've been back for three days, and the only ceremony was the homecoming one.

I think I got into my biggest trouble in Chancor when I asked *wirzel-magess* R'Mona for permission to examine the Tamos, Diera's holy book. Apparently no man, not even a *Monkus*, is allowed to actually see the true Tamos. Dieran men are taught its verses by rote, and make their own personal copies from memory. These vulgar copies are tolerated, but never encouraged. Being imperfect and incomplete, they are considered religiously suspect. Although I don't understand exactly why the taboo exists, I certainly was given to understand that it was inviolable, and my request was a serious blunder.

My other big mistake was directly connected to the first. Thwarted in my request to examine the Tamos, I suggested to M'Litha that because of our personal relationship she might make an exception for me. Wrong move. *Wirzel-magesses* Do Not have personal relationships with men, even when the man is a *Monkus*. Their ascension to the job requires that they purify themselves of all that is physically, emotionally, psychologically, or intellectually binding to men. They become separate.

Gerard "Perfect Instincts" Manley, blinded by all the ceremony and adulation, missed that completely. If we were genetically compatible, I, as a *Monkus*, could probably impregnate any and every young *magess* of my choice, with honor for all parties. But once a *magess* starts on the *wirzel* path, she renounces all but the spiritual side of her life for the greater glory of service. Nothing unusual about that. Nor, I guess, about M'Litha's reaction. The problem, as usual, Self, lies with me.

However, I do believe that the distance we have so unfavorably gained from the ruling class will give us a much more objective view of the Dieran situation. Fortunately, mine was a breach of manners rather than morals, and ignorance rather than stupidity. M'Litha's chief assistant, C'Rina, assured me that, as embarrassing as my mistake was, it should not cause me any serious problems. C'Rina tends to be somewhat fussy, so I take her comments with a good heart.

## 7035–11.14
## Chancor

Let the FedRecord show that we came here to finish work on the treaty so as not to politically slight Chancor. The truth is that I had to come to make extended and profuse apologies to R'Mona, without whose consent there will be no treaty at all.

Far less tolerant than M'Litha, who forgave my ignorance shortly after we returned from our first trip here, R'Mona let it be known that there would be great trouble unless I humbled myself and begged forgiveness. C'Rina was kind enough to give me a long dissertation on R'Mona's idiosyncrasies, much to my discomfort and C'Rina's apparent delight. What Windy could have told me in fifteen minutes, C'Rina took over four hours to tell, relishing every gruesome detail of R'Mona's many acts of punishment for men who had gone astray or offended her.

So two days ago I arrived with C'Rina and a minimal escort, in my dress blues without ornamentation, and C'Rina presented me to R'Mona's receptionist. After almost five hours of waiting, I was ushered into the audience room by a girl who could not yet be a *star-child*, prepubescent and very much enjoying her role as a minor humiliator of a *Monkus*.

R'Mona was stiff, formal, and curiously courteous to me. C'Rina was there too, but did not participate. I had prepared and memorized a long monologue, which I recited to her with great emotion, depicting myself as an ignorant and wretched soul, untutored in the ways of Truth and Light, blinded by the glory of Diera and its purity, and totally unworthy of being in her presence at all. I begged a thousand pardons as a man (and thus obviously a defective), as an offworlder (and thus obviously of inferior stock), and as a diplomat (and thus obviously a menial journeyman hovering in the shadows of greatness).

R'Mona knew it was an act. C'Rina knew it was an act. I knew it was an act. But it was an important ritual act that was accepted for its ritual value. All Chancor, and probably all Diera, knew of my rude and clumsy attempt to see the Tamos. Now they will all know that I have repented my sins and acknowledged my unworthiness. Oh, Gerard, sometimes you are the diplomat indeed.

R'Mona called me back to her offices today, and there, in the presence of C'Rina and various supernumeraries, made her views quite clear as to exactly what she would and would not support in the current treaty draft. C'Rina played a role of deference and suggested that M'Litha supported R'Mona's general view and that the major terms of the treaty must be dictated by the Dierans themselves. Since I was in basic agreement with both of them, my subservient acknowledgement of their superior wisdom and position took little acting on my part. (Well, maybe the subservient part took some acting, but my agreement was without guile.)

M'Litha arrives tomorrow, and I have suggested to R'Mona that the most expedient and fair way to resolve the issues would be for the three of us to work without councilors on the final draft. Refusing to agree or disagree, R'Mona said she would sleep on it. Actually, what she said was that she and M'Litha would take it into meditation. I believe she's already decided that the two of them could certainly gang up on me and write the treaty with my meek acquiescence. Knowing that gives me the upper hand, and I will sleep on *that*.

And speaking of sleep, Self, and of rituals and diplomacy, I would prefer that you not hide behind diplomatic screens and rituals of symbols if you insist on giving me these dreams of Fairy Peg. See if you can't come up with something more definitive than repetitions of Fairy Peg and the sunburst cape, or keep to yourself until you're ready to be a bit more specific. I do not need the added frustration at present, and I do need the rest.

## 7035–11.30
## Tam City

Exhaustion. The treaty is signed. The ceremonies (for the day, at least) are over. R'Mona blessed me in public with, "May you always live in interesting times with many prosperous daughters." M'Litha blessed me in public with, "May the fortunes of time and the times of fortune fill you equally well." C'Rina blessed me in private with a strange, "Patience is the lens of understanding. May you see through time."

Benedictions suitable for a *Monkus*.

## 7035–12.12

The ceremonies are finally over. Windy is ready to depart. Survey and Liaison are happily working away. R'Mona has returned to Chancor, after giving me a private farewell that under any other circumstances I would have described as slightly emotional. But as always, we observed the rituals. Tonight there will be a small dinner followed by a private farewell with M'Litha. Tomorrow I will be gone.

C'Rina instructed me to wear my dress whites and the cape of *Monkus* this evening, and then gave me a small packet which she made me promise not to open until we are in space. I will comply.

# 2

**7035–12.14**
**Space**

Time for a brief evaluation.

Had the Dierans been hostile, my mistakes could have been very costly to the mission. Could have ended it (and me too) under the wrong circumstances. Moral: Cocksure diplomats rarely live to old age.

Otherwise, I have to count the mission a success, which is nice, since Fed apparently mindwiped me because of a failure on the last mission. If that was their reason, then why do I have the feeling something very positive happened during those missing ten years? And why do I *know* that Fairy Peg was real and central to those times? Self, your mission is to answer those questions with as much dispatch as you can muster.

I wanted to cry during my private farewell with M'Litha. Couldn't help it. M'Litha was gracious, and let me choke up without making me feel any more uncomfortable than I already did. What a marvelous woman. She shared my pain, acknowledged that I felt a special bond to her, and showed me how to accept and move on. Some day, Fed and credit willing, we will have to return.

Now tears. C'Rina's packet contained a copy of the Tamos with the following inscription:

To Gerard Manley, The *Monkus,*

This was my late bondmate's copy of the Tamos.

No man will ever come closer to the truth. May its wisdom guide you wherever you go and in whatever you do.

Become patience,
C'Rina

My ignorance will not let me guess how much it must have cost C'Rina to give me this book. I shall read and study it with respect in her honor. Dear C'Rina. I am humbled by her affection for me.

*****Now, off to Moseen to act as temporary ambassador-in-residence, and then move on to Galaxy VI as soon as the permanent ambassador arrives. Windy informs me that the shortest route to Moseen will be one hundred and two days of popping in and out of subspace. That's almost as long as I spent on Diera. Between Fed zig-zagging us across the universe, and modern science's inability to find a quick way for us to dodge what lies between us and our goal, it's no wonder we had to fight for travel time pay. Oh, what the Krick. I'll have Windy set up the whole program, punch the Tamos into the Baird for the two of them to work on, and take a three-month autosleep nap. Windy can wake me if we have any trouble or when we get there.

## 7036–3.28
## Moseen Entry Path

Ah, how kind Windy was, waking me with Nelson's "Stranger From the Red Mountain" suite. Did I ask her to do that, or did she do it on her own? Or did Self cry out for its restful melody while laboring to drag me through his dreamland kingdom of symbols and cymbals? No matter. It was a delightful way to be lifted out of my sleep and I am grateful.

Autosleep is a necessary tool for our kind of travel, but its side effects are something less than pleasant. Most distressing is the discontinuity. Fara knows I've had enough of that already without adding to it. Another job for you, Self. Smooth out the trauma of my discontinuous life. You, after all, get to keep your continuity (or at least most of it), so what harm would there be in bubbling up a little to my level? Don't just sit there. Get to it. And don't let me catch you flirting with those wenches you keep in the back room until you come up with some answers for me.

From the tape on Moseen Windy fed me while I slept, I can only pray that the permanent ambassador arrives the day after I do. A heavy (9.2 standard) gravity planet with a toxic atmosphere populated by a highly industrialized civilization of xenophobic, five-limbed, Carnister type-three natives. Everyone lives underground. All the FedStaff except the ambassador and his personal staff of three are recruited locally, even Liaison. Old Baird G-Mentor translators provide the only communication link with the Moseens. No physical contact is allowed. (Even if it were allowed, it would be extremely difficult in the 9.2 gravity outside the embassy.)

This must be where Fed exiles its misfits. If I were faced with the task of establishing initial relations with Moseen, that assignment would be an enormous challenge. But to fill in as a temporary, part-time, pseudo-ambassador under the surface of a xenophobic planet doesn't exactly set my diplomatic blood on fire.

I had Windy query Fed as to the new ambassador's approximate arrival date, but we still don't have an answer. Hurry, Fed, hurry.

## 7036–4.4
## Federation Embassy, Moseen

Today the universe seems like a small place. The only embassy staff member currently in residence here is a Sylvan woman of remarkable beauty, whose brief service background includes a three-month translation stint with a survey team to Diera. Her name is ShRil.

"And how did you end up on Moseen?" I asked. The answer turned out to be the story of her life, but after four hours and dinner she got around to the publication of her treatise on universal mythology and legends after she entered FedService. Moseen's ambassador to Fed sent a copy of her treatise home, and a year or so later the Moseen Technical Council formally requested that she be posted to Moseen on her next change of assignment. She's been here for five years, through three ambassadors, and (get this, Self) she loves it.

ShRil is obviously ready for company. The last ambassador

left with the other two staff members two months ago. None of them were humanoid, but according to ShRil, they were good company. Even their departure wouldn't have been too bad for her had not her Moseen friend, whom she calls The Professor, been called away to other duties shortly after the ambassador left.

It seems The Professor (whose real, unpronounceable name is XRRTQMZT) is in fact that, a professor at Moseen University. He is also a very important person in the government here, thrice past-president of the Technical Council, once ambassador to Fed, and once ambassador to Galaxy VI. He is also the one who requested that ShRil be assigned to Moseen so she could assist him with his research into the universal myths and legends.

The Professor isn't due back for another week or two, so I'm sure I'll learn more about him and the mythology than will ever be of any interest or use to me. However, ShRil is pleasant enough company, and certainly pleasant to look at, following as she does the Sylvan custom of wearing only the briefest garments. At dinner this lovely *homo sapies sylvas* wore three teat patches, two red and one gold, with the gold one on her right teat, and a short gold and red skirt wrapped tightly around her narrow waist and flaring at mid-thigh. Her face is striking, with the high Sylvan nose bridge and wideset cerulean blue eyes. Until I met ShRil, I never found the narrow Sylvan mouth particularly attractive, but hers is. I must admit, Self, to being erotically aroused. Of course, I didn't let her know that. But I wanted to.

My, oh my, Self. You have your work cut out for you tonight. I want the works this time, but leave the fat dancing girls out. They slow down the action. No sense chatting here when I could be off in dreamland. Bye.

## 7036–4.5

Found ShRil in the computer library this morning doing some "five-hundred-language cross-reference checks" for similarity in attitudes about wanderers. She told me all about it and why it was important to the current research she and The Professor are doing. I'm afraid I wasn't much help in holding up my end of the conversation, but ShRil didn't seem to notice. In fact, by lunch time she was just launching into an explanation of how in the universal legends seekers are different from wanderers, and how much more difficult to categorize they are, when my stomach reminded me, and I reminded her, that it was time to eat.

After lunch she returned to the library, so I used the afternoon to inspect the embassy records. They are immaculate. Most of the recent ones were prepared by ShRil, and many of those from before her arrival have been annotated and cross-referenced by her. This is a woman I should know better, Self. Her intelligence, efficiency, diligence, and beauty all recommend themselves to me.

My choices seem to be to drag her away from the library and try to interest her in something else, OR, to join her in the library and develop an interest in what she is doing. The latter is the effective choice. The more I know about what interests her, the more I know about her philosophy and emotional attitudes. Perhaps this pause in our journey won't be so unbearable after all.

## 7036–4.15

Can it indeed be ten days since I last made an entry here? Hardly seems that long. Had I not awakened just now from a dream of Fairy Peg, it might have been ten more days. Self, it looks like you've been doing your job. This dream made a great deal more sense than all of that symbolic nonsense you usually work up for me.

Fairy Peg is standing with her back to me in a small, dimly lit room. Music is playing. Quiet music, of a sensuous sort I've heard before. As I move slowly across the room toward her, Peg turns to meet me. Her robe is open from the throat to the floor. Her body glows in the dim light. As I take her into my arms, her crown falls to the floor. The sound of it woke me up.

I'll have to think more about it later.

No, I'll think about it now. If I close my eyes, I can see her standing there. Behind her there is an ornate sunburst pattern that fills the wall. It is the source of some of the light. As I move forward, I can see her crown more clearly. Actually, it is a large tiara. It, too, has the sunburst on it in glowing jewels. We move together, the warmth of her nakedness against mine. The tiara hits the floor.

Slow it down.

Fairy Peg is standing there, with sunbursts behind her and on her head. Her body glows in the dim light from behind me. No, it's her robe that is glowing, casting sensuous shadows around her curves. We move toward each other. Around her throat is a small chain with a ring on it. Our bodies press. The tiara hits the floor.

Again.

Fairy Peg stands there in a glowing robe open from foot to throat. Around her throat is a chain with a ring on it, a crest ring. The crest presses against me as our bodies meet. The tiara hits the floor.

Fairy Peg is wearing my ring. My Manley crest ring. Why haven't I missed it? Of course! Because Self knew she had it. Ah, Self, what difficult restraints I sometimes make you work under.

Why is Fairy Peg wearing my ring? Why does the dream narrow down to that? That she is a ruler and I her lover, I understand, I believe, I *know* to be true. But where are we? Why is she wearing my ring? Are we more than lovers? If she is the ruler, what could I be to her? King? Prince? Prince Consort? Attaché? Why not Vice-President? Lieutenant Governor? Mayor Pro Tem? Assistant Manager? Chief Gofer?

Who is she? And who am I?

*****It's almost time to meet ShRil. Ever since I offered to help her, she's been working us like there's a deadline. But maybe all my concentration on learning about this myth/legend research has cleared a path for Self to get me this new information about Fairy Peg. Maybe the answer to learning about Fairy Peg is learning about mythology. Maybe the thing to do is just what I've been doing. Who would have ever thought that the answers to Fairy Peg's identity might lie in mythology? Easy, Gerard. Don't count anything you haven't seen. Just go back to work.

## 7036–4.16

If my heart could take it, I would pray for days like this last one every day of my life. First there was the dream of Fairy Peg and all its revelations. Then I met ShRil in the library, and while I was looking for something totally different, keyed the computer to kick out what looks like it might be a new legend. ShRil guided the computer search through the first level, shrieking with joy at each new result. She must have hugged me a hundred times. When she got all she could manually, ShRil set the computer on a correlative search, and we celebrated our discovery with a vintage bottle of "Zupe Pink, 6911" from my secret store. What a time we had. We laughed, shouted, giggled, hugged, kissed, and ended up making love on a large couch in the library lounge. While not entirely physically compatible, we didn't seem to notice.

Later we made love again, slowly and carefully, in my bed. When I awoke this morning, ShRil was gone. But I don't think I have to worry. She left one of her teat patches pasted to the middle of my forehead. The gold one.

*****ShRil was slightly withdrawn this morning, but in a coy, shy kind of way that fluttered my heart. We worked together awkwardly at first, bumped into each other, and laughed a lot. But it smoothed out as the morning progressed, and our theory about a new legend proved more and more true.

After lunch we took a short nap (yeah, just a nap) side by side on the couch, then finished the afternoon with six more hours of concentrated work. We're meeting for dinner in an hour in the small guest suite off the ambassador's quarters.

What can I make of the last two days? What can I say about them? Their intensity alone has been almost frightening.

The new discovery we have decided to call the Tenderfoot legend. There are references in over thirty languages to stories about an individual known variously as The Greenhorn, Verporchting, The Soft-Footed Ancient, Tenderfoot, The Old Novice, and The-One-Who-Stretches-Forever. "Tenderfoot" seemed both generally descriptive and personal, so we decided it was the best generic name for the legend.

ShRil tells me that in his two hundred plus years of study, The Professor has only discovered three such myths or legends which can actually be considered new. She's fairly confident that this one is new, since the correlative cross-check did not link it with any of the known ones.

Oh, there are parallels, of course, but the name seems to be the key. For a legend to be considered universal, an identifiable individual must show up in a minimum of three disassociated cultures. ShRil and The Professor, however, have much stricter criteria, and insist that ten disassociated cultures is the minimum. Our thirty-two languages actually represent fourteen disassociated cultures, so it would certainly seem that by either criterion we have passed the test.

Indeed, we are rich in references, but poor in examples. So far our search has turned up only one actual piece of literature. I was disappointed with the translation the embassy's Baird G-Mentor gave us, so I turned it over to Windy and our newer Baird Z-Rangel. I'm not sure our translation is actually any more accurate, but it is certainly more poetic. Perhaps I should name the Windy-Baird cooperative program the Bard.

ShRil was so impressed with the Bard's translation that I have agreed to write a similar program for her and The Professor. Actually, I think Windy had better do that. Anyway, here's the poem.

**Tenderfoot Scales the Face**

Tenderfoot picks his way along,
Searches with tendril toes
  for cracks and juts
    to bear his weight.
That others scaled this way before
Brings him no consolation.
That the summit is occupied
Still leaves him clinging to the face.

Up goes against the grain.
Gravity pulls.
Wind tears.
Rocks topple.

Tenderfoot curses the wearing wind,
Stubs his bloodied toes again
  for the uncounted time
    and clings for life.
That ledges leap over his head
Gives him more determination.
That the easy path has ended
Forces him to create his own.

Rock by wound,
Tenderfoot stretches himself
Upward.

## 7036–4.17

The guest suite is ideal for lovers. We had a nice quiet dinner, followed by some decent synth-brandy from the ambassador's stock, all to the accompaniment of some very sensual Pilthierian music of ShRil's choosing. Later we took a long, long time to make love, then talked half the night sharing intimate things before drifting off to sleep.

We woke up late, nibbled some breakfast while enjoying the luxury of a lingering bath together, and finally got dressed and headed for the library.

The Professor is back. His callsign was on the board when we arrived along with a short note welcoming me as temporary ambassador. ShRil immediately called him back and there followed a conversation through their Baird that was so rapid-fire and intense I wondered that the poor G-Mentor's crystals didn't crack from the strain. Frankly, Self, I felt a bit left out until The Professor invited me to join them. ShRil flushed with embarrassment that she had momentarily forgotten me, but soon the three of us were totally involved in a conversation that lasted for the better part of three hours.

The Professor asked a lot of questions we didn't have answers to, but also a lot that we did. Apparently he is very impressed with our work, especially with the Moseen translation the Bard made for him of "Tenderfoot Scales the Face," and promised to rejoin us this afternoon with some new search and correlation ideas. Fara above! He gave us enough ideas this morning to keep us busy for a month.

And that's a problem. Windy called me back after lunch and presented me with a FedMessage. The new ambassador, His Excellency Sir Loos Keen Deever-Deever Dan, G.M.B.T.H., FEAA, T.Z.Y., will be arriving in exactly twenty-seven days, and I am to depart as soon as possible thereafter for urgent duties in Galaxy VI. Discontinuity again. May Binkley of Baun and her twelve blind illegitimate children chase the bureaucrats of Fed so far into the dust of damnation that Fara herself could not find them with a microbeam! Why in Krick do they do this to me?

Now, now, Gerard. You know good and well why. You chose. Of all the professions you could have followed, you chose this one. No one twisted your arm or threatened your life and made you do this. You chose. Adventure, travel, excitement, mobility—remember? And, you almost begged them to get you away from Moseen as soon as possible. So they've done what you asked them to do, and now you curse them. Very professional, Gerard, very professional indeed.

All right. I have no grounds for complaint. But how do I tell ShRil? I don't know if what we feel for each other is love, but it is a pretty close approximation thereof. How do we cram all our sharing and caring into twenty-seven short days? I must break it to her gently, in the morning, perhaps. Let this night be innocent of that for her.

*****Stupid me. I never stopped to think that Fed would also be sending the message to the embassy. As soon as I saw her this afternoon I knew. Sylvans, like their Dieran descendants, can't cry, but sadness makes their noses run. ShRil could hardly stop blowing her nose.

Fortunately, The Professor was called to other duties, so we were free of obligations. We comforted each other as best we could, talking some, holding some, kissing some. Nothing more. ShRil finally insisted on being alone and left for her quarters. Said she would call me later. I sent a message to The Professor saying that because we had to begin preparations for the new ambassador's arrival we would not be able to meet with him for several days, and sent Fed's synopsis of Sir Loos Keen etc., etc.'s credentials with it.

Now I retreat into the rhythms of the Tamos and wait for ShRil's call.

### 7036–4.21

So much to do and so little time to do it. ShRil and I are living in her suite, sharing every moment we can together. Our lovemaking is at once more tender and more frantic. We irritate each other one moment, and then collapse into each other's arms the next. Such a mixture of pain and love cannot endure long at this level.

Windy's adaptation of the Bard program goes well. In three or four more days we will test it. The Professor seems to think our distracted mood is because of that work and the preparations for the ambassador. I don't know if he would understand the truth if we told him or not, but he probably would. His study of the myths has given him a unique perspective on emotionality and bonding, even though his hermaphroditic nature doesn't give him a personal pattern for those relationships.

ShRil and I both avoid talking about my departure. That will come later.

## 7036–4.26

We both need these times we spend apart. Never more than an hour or two, but necessary pauses to catch our emotional breath.

The embassy's version of the Bard program is working well. The Professor has already used it to rework some translations he had made before, and is extremely pleased with the results. He said the Bard's command of the Moseen dialects makes him wonder if there's not a Moseen working in the embassy. He jests, of course, because no Moseen would ever think of such a thing, so it's a nice compliment. I passed it on to Windy, who seemed to expect it. Egotistical wench.

Something big is cooking in Galaxy VI. Almost every day Windy registers a new FedMessage update. I told her to alert me only if there is an order change. Otherwise, I'll save my concern for their content until I'm gone from here.

## 7036–4.30

I asked ShRil yesterday to help me prepare the Tenderfoot data plus the basic search routines for Windy so we could use them in our travels to look for more examples of the Tenderfoot legend. She received my request as though it were a gift. She kept smiling at me as we began deciding exactly what Windy would need, and the cerulean of her eyes sparkled with hints of turquoise. Last night our lovemaking was almost as relaxed as before the fateful message.

ShRil sees my continuation of the Tenderfoot search as a permanent bond between us. So do I. I have promised to send back anything I find and (foolishly, perhaps) to bring it in person if I can. The Professor is pleased too. He already has contacts in various parts of the universe who send him information they find interesting, but never before has he had a roving researcher.

My relationship with The Professor has also added something special to my relationship with ShRil and I suspect that some time after I'm gone she will share with him at least part of what happened between us. I also suspect that The Professor already has some inkling that ShRil and I have more than just a working relationship.

And speaking of relationships, Self, that brief encounter with Fairy Peg this morning was hardly enough to call a dream. I woke up with the image of her face bright in my mind, and heard her saying, "Yes, I am real. Yes, I am real." I'm not sure I needed that confirmation of her reality, but apparently you thought I did. Anyway, it's nice to have. Thanks, Self.

### 7036–5.5

Anyone who gives ShRil a difficult and complex task to do and a limited time to do it in had better get out of the way. She's almost as organized as Windy. And speaking of Windy, the two of them have been talking about me behind my back, and neither of them will tell me what about. Girl secrets, ShRil said. Nonsense! Girl secrets between a three-breasted Sylvan wench who throws herself at any passing diplomat and an overeducated, egotistical machine with delusions of femininity. Who ever heard of such a thing?

When I protested the very idea, ShRil patted me very gently and intimately below the belt and told me to mind my own business. The situation quickly degenerated into a wrestling match on the library floor, with no holds barred. I was almost tickled to death before she surrendered.

Windy's response was, "Not your business, Gerard Manley." I detect some malicious outside influence here. Fara, I wish Windy were ticklish!

### 7036–5.7

A FedMessage today with a "Citation of Excellence" for my work on Diera and permission to do private research for the University of Moseen so long as it doesn't interfere with my contractual duties. The Professor must really swing some weight in the right places. I've never heard of a diplomat being given that kind of permission for outside work before. Fed didn't even ask what kind of research I might do, nor for a copy directly from me. "Copies of all said research will be forwarded through The University of Moseen or its chairman, QTLKBBS XRRTQMZT, PL, to FedBase 1038 Research and Statistics Agency." Can't get any more official than that.

I wonder if QTLKBBS is The Professor's first name, or a title?

The FedMessage also contained a change of orders, directing me to Thisseling, capital planet of Galaxy VI, with my departure from Moseen scheduled not later than 5.16, two days after Sir Loos Keen is due here.

Six, maybe seven more days alone with ShRil. My chest tightens at the thought of leaving her. That old Bridgeport philosopher, ah, Dortennov I think her name was, said that such a physical reaction was symptomatic of a neurosis called "limerance," which is literally an unhealthy over-abundance of love. I don't know about the unhealthy part, nor do I think my abundance is excessive, but I do know that every time I think about my departure, my chest tightens. But, "as love grows," the Tamos says, "it will ease the stricken heart."

ShRil and I will have to talk about my leaving soon. We need to move beyond that barrier so we can enjoy these final days as thoroughly as possible. What has happened to us in this short month must come to its conclusion as beautifully as it started. That's the romantic in me, Self, but I can't help it.

## 7036–5.8

Windy ran a search through a raw data file that The Professor provided for her this morning, and she came through with flying colors. Though her first-level results weren't as deep as the base computer's would be, they were thorough enough and accurate enough to convince him that she could dig out all of the most pertinent information in two or three passes. I'm proud of her, and of ShRil, who really put the package together. All I did was the interface work and the parameter profile. We'll run second and third pass tests this afternoon, as soon as ShRil makes some command signal adjustments.

## 7036–5.9

Windy's second and third tests ran like clockwork. The Professor says she's ready to attack some real research, so for the next couple of days we're going to let her do just that.

My conversation with ShRil was not so good. It ended in anger, my tears, and her running nose. She slept at her place and I slept aboard Windy. Windy is so used to my not being here that she had all the systems turned low and I near froze before she heated the place up. If ShRil got any sleep last night, she did better than I did. I lost count of how many times I thought about getting up and going to her. And of how many times I actually got up and headed for the portal. But I didn't go. She needs to work this out by herself.

There was a note from her in the library this morning saying she wouldn't be working today, so The Professor and I spent some time together monitoring Windy's searches. Then I came back here. I'm going to read the Tamos, for the solace of its rhythms, if not its words.

## 7036–5.10

No ShRil this morning. Not even a note. I'm going to work in the library again this afternoon in case she comes. If she doesn't, I guess I'll sit up late again and keep looking for solace in the Tamos.

## 7036–5.11

We're going to be okay, Self. When I got back to the library yesterday, I fiddled around for a while before finally settling down to read some of ShRil's research. Fascinating stuff. Just as I was really getting caught up in the supreme-being-as-bird myth, the callcomm signaled a call to me from Windy. However, when I tried to answer it, the callcomm indicated it had transferred to ShRil's suite. I couldn't get it to transfer back. Well, I thought, this is as good an excuse as any to see her, so forward I marched, knocked, and entered.

There was no message there from Windy. There was one from ShRil, a long, warm, sweet, tender loving message, and I found it in her arms.

"Deeds, not words, are the proof of love," says the Tamos.

Like I said, Self, we're going to be okay.

## 7036–5.13

Every moment during the last three and a half days when we weren't doing the last-minute chores before the ambassador's arrival, we have been together, sharing stories, music, personal anecdotes, intimate secrets, joys, and phobias. The time disappeared, filled to overflowing.

Sir Loos etc. will be here tomorrow noon. Tonight is ours.

# 3

### 7036–5.18
### Space

I will not dwell upon the pain. I will remember the spontaneity, the beauty, the joy, the peace. And I have the hologram Windy made for me. Even as I record, ShRil stands next to me, serene and inviting, a literal vision of loveliness.

Sir Loos Keen Deever-Deever Dan, G.M.B.T.H., FEAA, T.Z.Y., turned out to be a pleasant surprise. A formal career type with impeccable aristocratic manners, he is also an amateur mythologist given to rather bawdy puns after a glass or two of wine, and has a laugh that can only be described as booming. A Terra-Two human who has been in the service all his life, Sir Dan came to Moseen by request so he could spend his last ten years before retirement working with The Professor.

His staff of two turned out to be one, so to speak, Deltan twins, female, joined at an elbow and sharing a common forearm and eleven-fingered Deltan "hand". They seem totally devoted to him, and his reciprocal affection was obvious. Named Teeanne and Tiianni, Sir Dan calls them jointly "TT." Since Deltans usually bear litters of six, and have mammary glands to accommodate, which they paint but do not cover, well, Self, you heard that string of puns. Had Teeanne and Tiianni not seemed to enjoy them as much as Sir Dan did, I think we would have been very embarrassed. As it was, their obvious enjoyment of each other's company soon put us at ease, and whatever discomfort ShRil and I felt quickly passed.

Had someone tried to tell us that ShRil and I would be enjoying the company of strangers our last days together, we would not, could not have believed them. But we did. In fact, it helped to have them there, normalized our relationship, made us feel like a couple, host and hostess, entertaining new friends. Sir Dan and "TT" saw at once what was going on and gave us all the privacy we wanted. As I left, Teeanne and Tiianni stood behind ShRil with their arms around her, towering a good forty centimeters above her, like parents protecting a child. They knew what to do and made it easier for both of us, didn't they, ShRil?

Careful, Gerard. It's one thing to talk to Windy, who can reply directly, another to talk to Self, who replies indirectly, and quite another thing to talk to a hologram. That's like talking to a ghost, a fraud creation proceeding from a heat-oppressed crystal. If you must do it, do it with care, on special occasions only. Or, you will go voidcrazy faster than Windy can compute.

*****Thisseling in five days. Federation reports indicate rapid economic deterioration, rampant inflation, political instability, and social unrest throughout the Galaxy VI Empire. What that probably means is that affairs in Galaxy VI are not proceeding as Fed would like them to, but Fed isn't sure how bad things really are. If there's some kind of revolution brewing, Fed wants to be on speaking terms with the winning side. So, they send me to observe and report, and to make contact with all factions in case new diplomatic channels are needed.

Bound to the Federation by contract, loyal (they think) to the paymaster, cheap and expendable, we contract diplomats are obvious choices to send in to such a situation. There will be several of us in Galaxy VI, and if all goes well, Fed will have the results it wants at a minimum expenditure. If things do not go well, all Fed will have lost will be a few cheap ships, some hired hands, and a little time.

Hard to think of Windy as a cheap ship. If I rank any higher than that in their account books, it's not much. Both of us are cheap and expendable. Our passengers, however, those deepsleeping Liaisons, are valuable cargo to be transferred to a FedShip immediately upon arrival. So much the better.

Then we won't have to take care of them or worry about what to do with them if we get into a scrap.

Not that I'm anticipating physical trouble, but this mission certainly promises to be a bit more dangerous than writing a treaty or falling in love.

Think I'll have Windy analyze the AutoSysTac, Strat and Evac programs. Might find some weaknesses or idiosyncrasies in them that we will need to know about somewhere down the line. Can't be too careful. Too cautious, yes; too careful, no.

## 7036–5.23
## Thisseling Starport

This port is a frenetic's paradise.

Port Authority has moved us four times since we landed, and half of the activity seems to be the constant rearrangement of ships. The other half of the activity seems to be crews, loaders, passengers, and officials scurrying around trying to find the ships that have been moved. Actually, our latest (and hopefully last) berth in on the second tier on the southern rim of the port, and gives us a great view of what's going on. The only ships higher than we are the little personals and couriers, which means that all of the significant activity is spread out in a great colorful circle in front of us. High on the fourth tier, almost directly across from us on the northern rims, is Port Authority Control. Directly below them, on the third tier, are the personal ships of the royal family, emblazoned with sparkling green variations of the dynastic heptagon which range from the geometrically perfect and simple, to elaborate star patterns and elongated versions stretching the visible length of the ships and containing sinuous glyphs or complex geometric cross-hatching. Below the family ships are the various diplomatic, bureaucratic, and military ships on the second and first tiers, each with a single heptagonal star surrounding the symbol of its branch or service.

Moving around the circle toward us from both sides of Control are the ships of at least sixty planets, several hundred trading companies, and innumerable independent lightspeed freighters. As befits our position in the scheme of things, we seem to be in the lowest-ranking berth for a ship our size in the port. We also have the best view. Given all the nonlanding battle cruisers, troop ships, passenger liners, massequip freighters, and other assorted spacers we saw in orbit, Windy estimates there are close to four thousand ships on or around this planet. And that doesn't count the ones in farther orbit, nor those in sub-ports.

Our second berth put us next to a Class Twelve-Medium FedTransport where we happily transferred our deepsleeping passengers and their gear. Now, if Port Authority would just give us final berth authorization, I could get myself down to Fedquarters and see what they have in mind for me.

## 7036–5.24

Fedquarters, schmedquarters. Spent all of yesterday afternoon and most of today down there trying to talk to someone who knew something. Finally ended up in the offices of Senior Diplomatic Liaison and Coordination Officer Bellewedermucker, who ingraciously informed me that in spite of FedOrders confirming my official mission, he did not know what I was supposed to do, nor who I was supposed to do it with, nor when, nor where I was supposed to do it. Nor did he approve of my presence at all.

He did say that two of my "cronies" had come and gone in the last two weeks, and good riddance to them. The best advice he could give me, he said, was to report directly to Fed that I had nothing to do and ask for another assignment. I resisted my desire to punch him in the orifice that his Tyllythyen brothers excuse as a mouth, and said I wished him offspring with ears, the worst insult I could give him under the Tyllythyen code, short of a honor challenge.

The orange drained from his concave dish of a face until it turned the sick yellow color of dilith defecation. Rising on his three stalks to his full height of three meters, he reminded me that his ancestors used to eat mine in the primordial swamps of a hundred planets when my species was at the peak of its intellectual powers. I countered with the only other Tyllythyen epithet I know below the fighting level (which very roughly translates as "offspring of a grisk who ate your father when the mating was finished") and left in a good humor.

Tyllythyens love to trade insults. Any transaction of business without them is considered rude and impolite. Thus Bellewedermucker and I parted on good Tyllythyen terms, he having told me that Fed wanted me to operate independently wherever I felt I needed to be, and I having thanked him for the information as best as I knew how. My Tyllythyen classmates at diploschool taught me well. But I still can't get over that initial urge to punch one of them in the mouth. Maybe it's adversary racial memory.

Anyway, Bellewedermucker's instructions were clear. The who, what, where, and when are up to me. Fed's already supplied the why. Furthermore, I am to report directly to Fed without going through Diplomatic Liaison and Coordination. Either the situation is much worse than Fed thinks, or some bureaucrat's imagination has gone amuck. Rarely do they allow such autonomy on this large a scale when situations are not at one extreme or the other.

Tomorrow would best be spent in the Royal Library and Publications Center doing a little local research on the state of the Empire and seeing if I can determine any more about who's after what. Besides, my two "cronies," Morrizon and Mikll'ggulls should have left some clues for me there if either of them is worth his saltcredit.

## 7036–5.26

In the documents request registry, Morrizon ordered several scholarly reports on the KAR-063 solar system. Mikll'ggulls wanted a tour guide to Mysteleria on the far side of the galaxy. He also requested information on Rajor Zee, the nursery planet, but canceled that request. So, the two of them took off for KAR-063 and Mysteleria, and want me to go to Rajor Zee. See how, Simple? Students at diploschool pass surreptitious information the same way and it's a trick that's good anywhere in the universe where there's a library with FedSystem Registry. Unsophisticated, perhaps, but efficient.

Since I didn't want to just pop in and out of the library, I did some reference searches on Diera, Moseen, and Sylva. Not much of interest on Diera and Moseen, but the Sylvan catalogue was fairly extensive. I cross-referenced to literature and quickly realized that I could spend a week or two just skimming the abstracts. When I asked for original language material, however, the list suddenly became very short. A reflection of typical linguistic provincialism, I decided. I had all the non-technical works transferred to Windy for examination later, and then did a manual Tenderfoot search using all the names and titles ShRil and I had come up with. Nothing.

Port Authority cleared us to leave late tomorrow for Rajor Zee. It's a nine-day sub-light trip since space around here is too crowded to have everyone warping through. Maybe that will give me some time to look at some of the Sylvan literature the Bard is translating, and find out more about ShRil's home.

## 7036–6.1

I think we've been lied to, Windy. Until we got that signal just now from Galaxy VI Security, I'd have sworn we were the only ship in the space lanes. Wonder what they want with us? We'll find out soon enough, I guess.

## 7036–6.2

We didn't win any popularity points with Her Royal Majesty's Security Force yesterday. But they didn't win any with us, either. I certainly didn't mind the routine boarding and inspection; however, I took exception to the racial and professional slurs. Diplomatically, of course. My conversational duel with Duke and Captain Teliuses remained within the confines of civil conduct only because each of us realized that the other was in a certain inviolable position. I brushed off his insinuation that my Fed credentials might not in the future serve to my best advantage in "his" galaxy, but after he departed, I sent an incident report to Fed that gave full credence to his warning.

That Fed is unloved here is not news. That an official, especially a member of the royal family, would openly threaten a contract diplomat is. By tradition and convention we have always had immunity from prosecution and persecution in all of the federated galaxies and most of the neutral ones. We may be deported, but we may not be harmed. Perhaps Duke and Captain Teliuses was just expressing his personal sentiment. Or perhaps, knowing I would report the incident to Fed, he was trying to tell us to be careful. Or perhaps the royal family is testing for a reaction. Whatever the case, Fed has my complete recording of the encounter plus my comments and will handle it as they see fit.

Whether stimulated by our rude visitors yesterday, or purely coincidental, my dream of Fairy Peg last night was filled with uniformed officials obviously hostile to me (personally or officially, I couldn't tell), and who seemed to be demanding something from Fairy Peg. Too confusing and hectic, Self. See if you can't give it to me again in smaller, clearer segments.

## 7036–6.5
## Rajor Zee Orbit

With a preamble to their message that reads like a travel guide, the powers that be on Rajor Zee denied us permission to land. Very polite, very apologetic, and very firm. Thanks for stopping by, but we cannot let you in. A tinge of illness here that we don't want you to catch. Please try again, as we are normally very happy to receive visitors. Here's a list of other tourist spots nearby you might want to try. Very sorry. Best wishes. Etcetera. Oh, and please make reservations next trip.

So where from here? No time to ask Fed. But there's the travel bulletin from Her Royal Majesty's Office of Tourism reminding all tourists in Galaxy VI that the Festival of "Fat Delight" starts on the planet Val (KAR-063-L) in twenty standard days. A typical tourist bulletin except for one thing: it was address coded directly to us. A message from Morrizon? From Bellewedermucker? From some unknown ally? My bet is Bellewedermucker. Maybe Morrizon needs some help. Can't do anything here, so we might as well move on to someplace new. Since Val is one of the alternative tourist traps on Rajor Zee's list, maybe they'll let Windy access their library for any new info she can dig up.

*****Windy's hard at work. Rajor Zee's library isn't on a FedStandard system, so it's going to take her a while. In the meantime, the Bard and I are working on a new poem for our collection.

Amongst all the data on Rajor Zee that Windy picked up on Thisseling was a long Dajan folk song written in that quaint dialect of theirs. It is mostly doggerel, but fun to translate. I'll keep some lines to remember it by, and dump the rest into expendable storage.

### Beyond the Reef of Rajor Zee

Beyond the reef of Rajor Zee
There lives a *mother* fair and true.
Her sixteen eyes light up the dawn

Through hair of cobalt blue,
And when she takes a mate to spawn
Down on her phosphor-chlorine lawn,
She must preserve the code of strife,
To take his seedlings with his life
So life goes on
Beyond the reef of Rajor Zee.

Those few who would condemn the pain
Her *husbands* suffer for their *wife*,
Must weigh the overwhelming gain
Of new spawned life
Beyond the reef of Rajor Zee.

The Bard's translating the remainder at about twenty lines a minute, but I don't think we're going to come up with anything more representative of Dajan verse out of this selection.

Not much to do right now. Let me see that holo of ShRil, Windy. Nice. Very nice. Very, very nice. But best not to look at her too long. Makes me want to quit this job and head back to Moseen. And that wouldn't accomplish anything.

Speaking of accomplishment, what do we accomplish by translating this poetry? Does it help us understand the cultures it represents? Is the poetry of a culture somehow more indicative of its essence than its prose? I wonder.

**7036–6.6**

Windy's gotten all we can use from Rajor Zee's library, and we're ready to leave orbit. Curiously, Space Traffic Control suggested a rather circuitous route to Val because of "heavy commerce." Since they didn't order us to go the long way, we won't. The short way is fifteen days (sub-light again) and the long way is twenty-two. No sense in missing the festival. I to autosleep. Windy to pilot. We're off.

**7036–6.18**

Fourth time since Rajor Zee that Windy's had to drag me out of autosleep for a security check and new routing instructions. New arrival date is 6.27. Should have taken the long way.

### 7036–6.21

Don't believe Her Royal Majesty's Security Force wants us to make the festival. New arrival date for Val is 7.2. Can't go back to autosleep. This in and out is killing me.

### 7036–7.2
### Parking Orbit, Val

Festival's over. Lots of traffic coming up. Routine clearance, but because of traffic, landing delayed until tomorrow. Vallunese Control brief but courteous in refusing library access while waiting. No reason, just refusal.

Tried to contact Morrizon on Diplochannel. No response. Maybe he's not here. Maybe I should get some real sleep. That's it, rest for the frazzled soul. Weave me back together, Self. Got to have a clear head tomorrow.

### 7036–7.3
### Val Starport

Morrizon cleared port eight days ago, according to Control, destination Thisseling. If I'd gotten here on the twenty-first, as I'd planned, I wouldn't have missed him. Why did Control tell me he didn't leave any messages when I didn't ask for any? Rule Number Forty-Three: beware of gratuitous information. If Morrizon was expecting me or Mikll'ggulls, the message is in the library.

*****Found the message and wish I hadn't. Morrizon requested the following documents over a period of two days:

*Mystelerai, A Travel Guide*
*Revolutions in Science*
*Val, Its Art and Culture*
*Joining the Federation: A Political History*
*Soon to Come* (fiction)
*Leave With Joy* (official emmigration handbook)
*Before Delight* (fiction)
*The Festival of "Fat Delight"*
*Ends and Odds* (explanation of a Carpath wagering system)

If I've arranged them properly, the message reads, "Mysteleria revolutions. Val joining soon. Leave before festival ends." An alternate reading is, "Mysteleria revolutions ends before festival. Leave Val. Joining soon." Or, "Mysteleria revolutions. Joining soon. Leave Val before festival ends." Or, or, or. Kravor in Krick! What's Morrizon trying to tell me?

Okay, slow down. Now, carefully, what do we know for sure? Nothing. But we can assume that Mysteleria is involved in some kind of revolution, and that Morrizon was warning me to leave Val before the festival ended. However, we don't know if Val is about to join the revolution, or if Morrizon is. In fact, we don't know much at all to do us any good today. Need more info. Tomorrow I'll dig around, talk to the traders in port, and see what I can pick up in the starbars.

Tonight I keep Windy on TacAlert, just in case we have to try a fast exit. I'd hate to have to leave by blowing our couplings, but we may not have a choice. I've got this bad feeling in the center of my gut that the hard times are upon us.

## 7036–7.5

I wouldn't say we are prisoners, exactly, but we certainly aren't going anywhere. Perhaps my reaction is too strong. Port Authority assured me that the temporary ban on arrivals and departures for all but Her Royal Majesty's ships would be lifted in a week or two, especially for a diplomat.

Unconvinced, I went to the Empire building to register an official protest with Her Royal Majesty's Governor, Prince Geladium. After a very brief wait I was politely and graciously ushered into the governor's office by a young aide, Mr. Gwindel, who seemed most eager to ameliorate the situation.

Prince Geladium is a striking man, two and a half meters tall, with dark bronze skin and bright yellow eyes. His emerald green uniform was without ornamentation except for his governor's gold star over the left breast. Before I could launch into my complaint, Prince Geladium began apologizing for the restrictions that had been placed on the port by the Empire, and for any inconvenience they might cause me. His manners were impeccable, his voice sympathetic and soothing, his attitude cordial, and his conduct toward me as a FedRep as perfect as could be. However, when I pointed out that this unprecedented restraint of a diplomat violated not only the treaty of federation, but also thousands of years of universal tradition, custom, and common law, he did not act overly concerned. Prince Geladium made it quite clear that

Her Royal Majesty's Empire of Galaxy VI in no way intended to violate its treaty commitments with the Federation, nor to restrain its representatives. There were, however, extenuating circumstances (which he steadfastly refused to delineate) that made certain travel restrictions necessary so that the Empire might, in fact, fulfill its treaty obligations.

Etcetera. Etcetera.

Our conversation lasted for well over an hour, during which I used every persuasion I knew to convince him that I must be exempted from this ban. To no avail. Our parting was as congenial as it could be between two professionals who recognize and accept an impasse, and as I was leaving, he assured me that as soon as the restrictions were lifted, I would be the first to know.

What Prince Geladium didn't tell me was that communications were restricted also. There's a comnet screen over the whole port. Windy informed me of that as soon as I got back. Another formal protest to the governor, written this time. No sense in wasting another visit. At least my preliminary message to Fed got out yesterday.

Stuck. Something tells me we're going to be stuck for a lot longer than Prince Geladium would like for me to believe.

### 7036–7.20

Two weeks plus. Mr. Gwindel informed me this morning that Prince Geladium would be unable to receive me because of the press of business, and no, there was no word on when travel bans will be lifted, and no, he had no idea when I could get to see the governor, but had I taken the opportunity of my stay to investigate the local culture? A nice young man, Mr. Gwindel, efficient and pleasant. If I thought it would do any good, I'd commit violence upon his person. Damn this waiting!

His diversionary suggestion might not be a bad one, however. I've learned next to nothing about the Empire's current political situation during these last two weeks. Whatever Morrizon's sources were, they've either dried up or disappeared. The only thing I feel relatively sure about is that there's about to be a conflict of some size, but between whom and over what, I'm as much in the dark as ever. If there's a pattern here, I'm missing it. Too many unsubstantiated, contradictory, misleading bits and pieces of information floating around. Windy and I have analyzed it all six ways from space without success. More waiting, I guess.

Okay, Windy, let's hook into the library and start running a Tenderfoot search.

## 7036–7.21

Well, I asked for a Tenderfoot search, and what I got was "Tenderfoot's Search." Coincidence? Esp? Fate? None of the above, Gerard. You made up the title yourself. Still, it seems to fit. Windy found this thing on the second pass, part of an imported Mystelerian anthology concerned with the rites of passage. The Bard and I have been through two drafts, and the third ought to be ready shortly. Fara, I wish I could send this right off to ShRil and The Professor. Maybe Prince Geladium would send it for me. Surely won't hurt to ask.

### Tenderfoot's Search

Tenderfoot searched the auburn passages
  in a thousand past stars
  for some holy symbol,
    some hallowed name,
    some renewed vision
      of initial fires.

He crawled toward the edge of eros
  in sacred and profane dreams
  haunted by a shifting visage,
      a swaying motion,
      a recreation conjured by his psyche.

Tenderfoot found puzzles in his sentiment,
      erotic fantasies,
      and cryptic sketches
        of some unknown time,
But through it all found no relief
  from the pain and ecstasy
    of a dream gone mad.

The Bard's getting much better with this functional form we've developed. Makes it much easier to get the feeling and meaning of these poems without having to try to duplicate or imitate the original form and metrics. If it means anything, I find the aesthetics of this system rather pleasing. Typical creator's pride, I suppose. Still, it seems there is little enough attention paid to aesthetics anymore by anyone writing in Standard.

While the Bard and I were playing with our draft, Windy was making four more passes through Val's library. She came up with some interesting characters, but none of them fit Tenderfoot. Six levels deep and a one-poem-payoff. Still, that's more than we had. Good work, team.

## 7036–7.23

Took a copy of "Tenderfoot's Search" and a brief message for The Professor, citing references, to Mr. Gwindel. After explaining to him at great length what it was and why I felt it was important, I requested that he ask Prince Geladium to forward it for me to Moseen University. Mr. Gwindel's reaction made me wonder if I had made a mistake. Without ever saying so, his questions implied that he suspected my simple literary legend of being some kind of secret message. I didn't press him. If he thinks I know something I'm not supposed to, and suspects my motives, then he has told me by his attitude that the situation in Galaxy VI is moving into a critical relationship in regard to the Federation. He has also revealed that I am, in fact, a prisoner here. My diplomatic status is questionable. So is my safety.

Consequently, I've made a decision. I'm going to give Windy access to this journal, and program her so that anything I write or speak here is automatically duplicated in her security files under my personal code. Then, if something happens to me, she can erase this portion of the journal, with instructions to release the duplicate only to me (should I return) or to transmit it secretly to ShRil. I know that all sounds a little fatalistic, Self, but one must be careful. If something happens to me, at least ShRil will know.

## 7036–7.25

Okay, Windy, you're in on it now. If anything happens, you know what to do with the journal. Then shut yourself down to full preservation level and wait. Hopefully, it won't come to that, but if it does, I feel better knowing we're ready.

## 7036–7.30

The end of another month. Twenty-seven days on Val and no release in sight. A week since I took "Tenderfoot's Search" to Mr. Gwindel, but no confirmation on whether or not the governor sent it for me. Mr. Gwindel has been much more reserved and distant since then. No time for personal conversation, just commessages.

So much for the down end of the scale. On the up end, Windy, the Bard, and I have been having a good time with the Vallunese literature we've been digging out of the library. I knew from my information on the Festival of "Fat Delight" that the Vallunese were a sensuous species, deeply involved in the bodily pleasures, but what I did not realize was the extent of their literature celebrating same. It's marvelous stuff.

In particular, I've gotten caught up in a series of hymns which I call dithyrambs. There are literally thousands of paeans devoted to all aspects of pleasurable sensation, bodily functions, physical and spiritual love, and the rapture of their triadic mating. It is a "delightful" and heady literature. And the Kravor's own to translate.

Our main problem has been that all these Vallunese dithyrambs are written in an emotive syntax, that is, the emotional content of a particular dithyramb determines the syntactical meaning and usage in that dithyramb. Fortunately for us, the library had a decent text on the fundamentals of the system. Unfortunately, that is all the text was, fundamental. So while the Bard and I were working on the literal translations for our first drafts, Windy was extrapolating some more advanced guidelines from the text.

##Windy is here. Reference unnecessary.##

Yes, Windy, I know you're here, but this is my journal and you will kindly refrain from making entries unless requested to do so. I am already in the habit of referring to you as not having access. Now that you do have access, I will refer to you in the second person as you fulfill your new role of observer. Notice I said observer, not commentator. Compute?

##Compute. Instructions noted with reservations.##

What reservations?

##Emergency program lists several reservations which command entry into this journal. Reference, Gerard Manley.##

Any other reservations?

##No other reservations noted.##

Good. That should be your last entry until we have an emergency.

No comment?... Fine. You're a nice lady, Windy, and you learn quickly. That's one of the things I like most about you. Now, let's run that new draft and see if your changes didn't put the finishing touches on it.

**Dithyramb 73**

Silver down silver down the wild wine
  of living and light,
  and the heady flow of blood
  and the steady red change
  and the pain and spirit of joy,
Burning down through the clear center
  of living and light,
  and the spinning heart
  and the golden fire of soul,
Bewildered spectacular flowers
  beyond distance and time
Incarnate space
  holy beyond evil,
Becoming creation,
  the be all and end all,
  the am what am.

Desire like the driven suns fires the raging blood,
  spurs the alternate flanks of passion and love
  up through the swollen veins
    through the bellowed heart
    through the last claws of rational excuse,
showering into the halls of tomorrow
    like rain in the desert,
flowering the vacant sands
    with seminal blossoms,
charging the brief breeze
    with holy pollen,
      and seeds,
      and fire.

Not bad, team. Not bad at all. Now, if I could just figure out some way that would allow the same team effort to get us off this planet, we could be out of here in no time flat.

## 7036–8.1

An invitation from Mr. Gwindel to dine with the governor on the fifth. Very formal, dress uniform, attendance mandatory. An invitation or an order?

## 7036–8.3

A reminder from Gwindel. Where's he think I'm going that I'll forget? I believe I'm developing a severe dislike for that man.

But pox on Gwindel. I'm caught up in the rhythms of Vallunese eroticism. As strange as their triadic mating relationships may seem to some, they know how to make their sensuous pleasure universally appealing. I've been dreaming like crazy since we started translating all this erotica. Dreams of ShRil. Dreams of no particular female. Dreams of Fairy Peg. Almost all erotic. But there's one dream of Fairy Peg that has repeated itself at least two times I'm sure of, that I haven't been able to decipher yet.

I awake in a huge bed with Fairy Peg asleep by my side. There is a sound off in the distance, like people shouting and running noisily in a tunnel. I get up in my nightshirt and go to the window beside the bed. It is a clear night with three full moons. There is a banging at the door. Peg sits up and cries out. I wake up.

Putting the focusing technique to work, I see the sunburst over the bed and know there's one on my nightshirt. The three moons are almost in a line low over the horizon, a small one followed by two larger ones. The horizon curves too much. I feel very light on my feet. It is obviously a small planet. The shouting is too indistinct, and I cannot make out what is being said. But Peg's cry in almost clear. I know what she is saying, but I can't hear it clearly. It's important that I know what she's saying.

Try again.

Wake up. Listen. Go to the window. Now the knocking. Turn. Peg cries out, "The Ratchets!"

The Ratchets? Who in Krick are the Ratchets?

> Three full moons mean a terrible night
> When the Gabriel Ratchets come to fight.

Now where did that come from? Oh, Self, what are you doing to me? Puzzles within puzzles within puzzles. Like a Kril mystery box. Kril!

The planet Kril! Three moons, one small and two larger. Ruling planet of the Ribble Galaxy. Schoolboy stuff. Ruled once by the famous Ober On'Ell, Prince Regent of twenty-seven worlds, and Queen-Consort Tania Houn Draytonmab, battle leader of the Ribble fleet that gave Fed its first defeat in over seven hundred years. My Fara! That's it!

Fairy Peg. Peg On'Ell, Guardian of the Ribble Galaxy!

My head! It's killing me.

### 7036–8.4

When the Fed mindwipers set up blocks, they really tie them up with pain. Blinding pain. I woke up on the deck hours later, feeling nothing but fire and pressure behind my eyes. Barely managed to get to the rejuvhosp cell. Even now I still feel some lingering tension at the base of my neck. Just the thought of Fairy Peg makes the pain start building again. Have to let it rest for a while, Self, but I'm glad you did it, and that I got it all down. If I hadn't, I think the blocks would have taken it all away again.

Head again. Something else.

The poem. That's it, Windy. Give me the poem on the screen. Now key the Bard for another run through. The tone's not bad, but the form's too rough. Put it in the functional mode and see what we get.

*****Didn't work. The headache made me stop. But it may have helped. Like the old doctor said, "Think how bad you might have felt without the medicine."

We're getting pretty damn good at this poetic translation, Windy. Wonder if there's any credit in it? Probably not.

### Lips

Neither honey, rose, waxen, full, nor fair,<br>
But rather, perfect,<br>
Lips meant to kiss and travel<br>
    to wander curves<br>
        and pollinate the cup,<br>
    to meet trembling,<br>
        and met, to hold—

Lips meant to draw the vapors of our souls
to hold us still within
and wrap around our searching tongues,
to drench our hearts with motion,
and moved, to flow—
Lips meant to touch like breezes
to seal our psyches
and leave their mark,
to burn with passion,
and burning, quench—
Lips meant to speak,
Speak to us.

As best as I can determine, "Lips" is one of many formal Vallunese mating songs sung by the fecund and catalytic partners of the triad to the pollinating partner. According to our source, this is one of the oldest recorded songs of its type, and set the style for well over three centuries. A testament to its popularity is the fact that Windy found a slightly altered version in a book called *Rapturous Union,* which was entered into the library in 7035 and touted by its editors as the most modern guide to rapture ever produced. An old love song for new sex maniacs. Couldn't ask for a better recommendation than that.

Call it hunch, intuition, or premonition, but I have a feeling, Self, that tomorrow evening's dinner with Prince Geladium is going to be much more than just a meal. I think he wants something from me, and I don't know what it could be. More importantly, I don't know how far he's willing to go to get whatever it is he wants. My only choice is to play it by the book and let the consequences fall where they will. It's difficult to develop tactics when you don't know the strategic situation.

**##7036-8.21.1503:17**
**KAR-063L, Starport I-A-1**

Per instructions Emergency Program One, this entry is made by Diplomatic Cruiser, Class Twelve, Registry T-Alpha 7731 Series D, Designation *Windhover,* Access Code Windy.

Gerard Manley, universal contract diplomat, pilot of named Diplomatic Cruiser, has been absent from this location for fifteen days, twenty-one hours, three minutes, and seventeen seconds standard. MARK.

From previous information, deduction is made that said Gerard Manley has been involuntarily detained by Her Royal Majesty's Governor in Galaxy VI for KAR-063L (Val).

This vessel has entered Full Preservation Status, All Systems, per Emergency Programs One and Two. SelfProtect-Destruct activated.

Awaiting further instructions.##

# 4

**7039–2.7**
**Space**

How do you pick up a journal you put down two and a half years ago? Who wrote the first part of this journal? I know that naive soul from somewhere.

Good job, Windy. Morrizon told me how you held them off. Smart idea, locking up their couplings like that. Did I tell you to do that? That's right. The security program modifications we made. Forgot about those. Forgot about a lot of things while I was gone. But you didn't forget. And, surprisingly, Fed didn't forget. I don't yet understand all of the levers Fed used to set me free, but I do know they put them in Morrizon's hands, and he yanked for all he was worth. He is as fine a Trow as one could ever hope to meet.

But enough of that. We have a new mission, a new balance in our credit account, and a new lease on life. Well, maybe not a new lease, but certainly a new perspective. My loyalties are a little clearer. My needs are narrower. My mind is sharper.

Didn't I say enough of that?

On our way to Deloni Ahsus Zand Minor-17 in the Milius Spiral, DAZM-17MS to Fed. Another treaty negotiation mission, this time with a somewhat reluctant majority government on a planet with several strong minority governments that will have to participate fully in the process if we expect to achieve a viable, lasting treaty. A nice challenge.

Fed wanted me to go to Pleasance for six months of

recuperation and relaxation, but I convinced them I had relaxed all I wanted to the last two and a half years, and the best recuperative process I could go through would be work.

Glad Liaison has their own transportation so we don't have any passengers to worry about this trip, Windy, because to get to DAZM-17 we're going to have to skirt the Warp-Ring System. Now that they're involved in a civil war with some of the planets trying to split off from Fed, things could get a little tricky for us. I'd hate to have to worry about passengers in a tight situation.

The Warp-Ring Alliance still has nominal control, but it never was very strong, and this new secessionist group they're fighting, the Wring-Con, got pretty well supplied by Galaxy VI during that abortive revolution. Fed apparently isn't going to get involved in this conflict. They'd rather sit patiently on the sidelines and pull the weakhearted back into the fold one by one. That way, when the Alliance collapses, as it surely will, Fed's influence will be stronger on the planets that rejoin the Federation, and they can claim neutrality when trying to negotiate with whatever government emerges.

I wish we could avoid the Warp-Ring System altogether, but it would take far too much time. So, our biggest problem will be sneaking into the warpshoals and then around the edges of the system. Once in the shoals, we can wind our way around their inner perimeter and sneak out the other side. Hopefully the Alliance forces and the Wring-Con forces will be so occupied with each other that, even if we are detected, they won't bother us. Hopefully.

At any rate, there'll be no autosleeping on this trip. We'll have to stay on the alert until we clear the warpshoals and can warp out for DAZM-17. So, Windy, it's four months of tough spacing for thee and me, and I can't say that I regret it. This old brain has been craving some *external* problems for a long time.

**7039–2.11**

Three days til we reach the warpshoals. Beginning to feel really comfortable with you again, Windy, even with these new Tac, Strat, and Evac programs we picked up. Apparently the FedTechs saw a lot of the same weaknesses we did, but I still think our hybrid programs are better. In fact, I'd almost like to test them in a real situation. But only almost.

Cleared most of our literary research after transmitting the bulk of it to The Professor on Moseen. Fed confirmed that ShRil and Sir Dan are still there and that The Professor is again serving on the Moseen Technical Council. Their reply will be forwarded to DAZM-17, so we can look forward to hearing from them. Especially ShRil.

Dear ShRil, companion in my captive dreams. What does she think of me after all these years? Does she think of me? The answers await. Forward, Windy, into the breach.

### 7039–2.12

Dreams of ShRil have become a staple of my nights. But last night's was particularly clear. Perhaps the thought of hearing from her again has shifted my desire from fantasy toward reality. Dare not think on that too much. Great time and space stand between us and our next meeting, should that ever come at all. And if it comes, what will it be like? And what will we be like? Best to stay with fantasy for a while longer. It makes no demands and raises no expectations.

Been playing with one of the Vallunese poems we never finished translating before. Can't say much for the original except that I like the idea of it so much that I have rewritten it. Rewritten it so thoroughly, in fact, that it is far more mine than Vallunese. And if ShRil's response to my reappearance is what I hope, I will send it to her as a private message. She'll like the old Terran mythological references, and hopefully the rest of it too.

### Bodylogue

In the long spacious arcs
  between her breasts
    and her thighs,
He wandered like some Orestean ghost,
  in search of infinity,
  in hiding from past failures
                and future kings.

Down the delicate Aegean
  of her water-covered bones
His salted lips followed her waves,
  pursued by the breathing winds,
  clinging to the resilient swells
    with his course-conscious tongue.

Pulled by his ancient heart,
He drifted up into her quiet maelstrom,
into her returning face,
And conceived one infinite kiss
of resurrection
and life.

Will she see how much my memory of her helped me? Will she read the love I have written in? Will she know my heart is faithful to her? Will she care?

It was easier in prison. The answers fit the fantasy, a selfserving (Self-created) construction that kept me sane. Now in three short months I'll get my first glimpse of the truth, and I'm hesitant.

And speaking of truth, I got a fair picture of the truth about Fairy Peg while I was locked up. Or at least a picture of our relationship. Lots of tenderness and compassion, but also lots of anger and arguing came drifting back from my memory. It's interesting, Windy, that most of what Self and I remember about Ribble involves Fairy Peg, and most of what we remember about her is intimate and personal. Maybe Fed couldn't totally block those memories. Or maybe the memories were stronger than the blocks.

We had a recurring dream during that time which seems to be a touchstone for Self. In it Fairy Peg and I stroll through a garden talking about my status in Ribble. She wants to make me Prince Regent, or Prince Consort, or something like that, but I'm having a hard time concentrating on what she's saying. I'm too caught up in the complexity of her. Love, beauty, ruthlessness, and power all seem to emanate from her at the same time. I'm captivated. Finally, toward the end of the dream, she insists that I pay attention and tells me that if she makes me Prince whatever, I'll also be Fize of the Gabriel Ratchets. My response is to kiss her as wildly and passionately as I can. The dream ends very quickly after that in a swirl of spirited lovemaking.

See what I mean, Windy? The focus of that dream and most of the memories we recaptured is so strongly on Fairy Peg that I lose much else that is significant. Of course, they're not all as pleasant as that one. In fact, some of them are highly unpleasant. But I think the main thing I came away from Mysteleria with is more questions. Like why did Fed mindwipe me? And why did Peg send me back to Fed in the first place? Then, why did Fed clear the log? And why didn't Peg try to contact me later?

Maybe she did. That's part of the puzzle that's still missing. Until Self digs out more information, I guess I'll have to give her the benefit of the doubt.

## 7039–2.15

Entering the warpshoals. Silent running, they used to call it. No scans out to give us away. Detectors on minimum safe distance. Speed slow. Eight to ten more hours and we ought to be deep enough to relax a little. The dust is heaviest here, but the deflectors will take care of anything smaller than we are. Windy will steer us around the rest. No scans coming in, either.

Easy in, careful through, easy out. Nine weeks of dodging rocks and ice won't be much fun, but it'll be a whole lot easier than trying to sneak through the middle of Warp-Ring System undetected by all the crazies. Even if someone finds us here, they've got to get into the shoals with us to be any threat. Odds are on our side, Windy.

## 7039–2.19

Boring. Dangerous, but boring. Been reading the Tamos. That's mostly boring, too, but parts of it are nice and I like its rhythms.

Wonder what Gracie is doing right now?

Ah, Gracie, exiled immortal, fount of wisdom, savior of my sanity. If only she'd shown up sooner, Windy, we could have been spared a lot of pain. But at least she did show up and pull us out of that Mystelerian pit. Oh, it wasn't that bad, really, if you don't mind being sedated and having nightmares ninety percent of your life.

But I don't want to talk about that. Gracie somehow made that seem unimportant. She would gaze at me with those faceted, ageless eyes and blankets of peace would wrap themselves around my heart. When I finally got the nerve to ask her who she was, she said, "I am the Durah, Lismav, the child, the mother, the daughter, the sister, the immortal. I am Betress Grace ber Aftalon Petroffillon, number twenty-two of the twenty-three immortals. I am Gracie, confined here till I die."

You think it's strange that I remember all that, don't you,

Windy? Well, it is. But that's what she said. My spelling may not be quite right, but the words are exact. They're burned into my brain.

Gracie wasn't a goddess, exactly. I mean, she didn't have true supernatural powers. At least I don't think she did. But she was, or I guess I should say, she is immortal. Or close enough to immortal so that our kind of time references don't mean much to her.

Keep getting off the track, don't I? Maybe that's because I don't know how to describe what she did for me. She was confined to Mysteleria, yet she seemed to run the place. She had infinite patience with me, yet, she never seemed to be fully concentrating on me when we talked. But I never felt slighted, because I knew her interests and concerns were much greater than my poor plight in the scheme of things. It's almost as though part of her was always listening in on the cosmos.

I can't explain it, Windy, any more than I can explain with words the subtle moment by moment shifts of color in a sunset.

## 7039–2.22

I've been thinking about Gracie for two days, and I may never be able to explain what happened. Suffice it to say that she was greater than any mortal, less than a goddess, compassionate, tender, caring, and a being I am blessed to have known. She touched my soul and left a spot of love so pure, so bright, so beyond any passion, that when I try to reflect on it my heart squints.

Hunh. Now I sound like a love-sick chibling. If the image of a heart squinting isn't the silliest thing you've ever heard, I don't know what is.

## 7039–2.25

One of the deflectors took a hard knock yesterday. The backup saved us, but repairs to the main are taking longer than I like. Two hours outside and four in does not make an efficient repairman. No help for it, though. We're at matchspeed with most of our larger neighbors, and continue to lose time. Even the charts don't indicate this much debris, and they usually overestimate.

Some sleep, then back to work. Wonder if contract spaceworkers make more than diplomats?

### 7039–2.26

Done. Exhausted, but finished. It's very satisfying to work hard like that, wielding the tools, using the muscles. And very tiring. The aches and pains tell me I've done something (and that I've slipped backward physically). Have to increase the exercise program. Regular increases instead of just maintenance. But not today. Tomorrow.

*****Too tired to sleep. Restless. Eleven days in this shifting maze and already I feel hemmed in. Forty-nine, maybe fifty days to go. Can't go crazy this early. Got to save it for breakout time so I'll really enjoy it when we bust loose and hit the first warp.

"A patient man knows the greatest joy," the Tamos says. Funny how I can't escape the homilies of that book. They lodge tight in the corners of my mind and refuse to budge. So I will be patient. I knew that already.

"He is a foolish man who patiently acquires knowledge and then becomes impatient to use it." See what I mean, Self? Of course you do. You're the one who's collecting it for me. Another one of your stability routines, I suppose. Little tricks to keep me balanced. Not that I mind, you understand, it's just that I'm annoyed to discover how much I need them. Makes me aware of my frailty. You may continue, but no longer than necessary. Please.

### 7039–3.9

We're being scanned. Someone inside the warpshoals has been sweeping this area for the past hour. Windy got us behind the biggest piece of rock she could find and matched speed, but the rock's too small. They haven't moved any closer, but they've increased the frequency of their sweeps. Someone on the other side of this junk thinks he saw something besides rocks and dust. Windy's scanning a hundred and eighty degrees away from them for a bigger hiding place, but no luck. Hide and seek in a rock garden. So we wait. Next move is theirs.

*****They're moving away, back down our path. Could be a trick. Sit tight.

*****Gone. Four hours and no sign of our scannor friend. We're increasing speed slowly. Waiting to see.

*****Full maneuvering speed for an hour. Almost six hours since we lost the scannor. Time to relax a little, eat, and sleep.

### 7039–3.10

He's back. Either that, or we've picked up another one, which I find difficult to believe. This time, however, we're hiding behind an asteroid three times our size. Trouble with that, though, is that now we are relying on the remote sensor Windy put out. Cuts our range by a third. Still, I don't know if they've picked us up or if they're just searching at random. If it's a random search, then we were just unlucky enough to be in the wrong places at the wrong times. But if we manage to evade them this time and then they show up again, we'll have our answer. Nothing to do now but wait.

*****Never really stopped this time. Moved back down our path again and into the silence. Do we wait? Or do we go?

We go. Windy, heat up, and hit maneuvering speed as fast as you can. If these folks are playing games with us we're going to make it interesting for them. I want maximum variable course within twenty degrees of all perimeters for the next forty-eight hours. Give us some Coulterloops whenever there's room every couple of hours or so, and every time there's a big rock ahead, hit it with the microbeam so the reflection will scatter behind us. We'll save the Evac program in case things get tight. Then we'll drop it in line with everything else and see just how good our opposition is.

I'm going to get some sleep. If things start popping, I want to be as rested as possible. In a way, Windy, this is rather fun. Nothing like a little excitement to liven up a dull life.

### 7039–3.13

Two days without contact. Then, just as we resume normal operations, Fara, in all Her Infinite Goodness, presents us with this mystery blip. Unknown vessel, parallel course, one-third our speed, no rear scanners. They don't know we're here. Or if they do, they're taking no evasive action. Windy, give me visual as soon as we're in range. Better yet, matchspeed and send out the drone. I want a full recon on that ship before we get any closer.

*****Carpath freighter, Class Eight or Nine by the looks of her. Battered. Spacepatched. Looks like a laser sliced off part of her rear struts. Carpath freighters are ugly when they're new. This one looks like ugly's mother. She's only running on four of ten tubes. Ragged proton scatter, and steadily losing speed. Get me a closeup, Windy, and see if she's got an I.D. I hate to be an elitist, but when junk like that is allowed to occupy space, it's a crime against nature. The better our picture gets, the more I hate to look at it. Scarred, scorched, and spaceblasted, the only thing that wreck is worthy of is a meltdown.

Fedmarkings! The damn thing's a FedShip. Now the question becomes, who's inside her? Friend or foe? What do you think, Windy? Do we give them a call and see what happens? Or do we skirt around and run like a mirkaloy?

We call. Wasn't really a question, was there, Self? Duty, honor, conscience, and all that. Could be me on that ship. Or Morrizon. Or the missing Mikkl'ggulls.

Okay, Windy, give them a short range bearing-vector call on the three-frequency span, standard offer of assistance.

*****Twenty minutes, and no response. Second message, Windy:

> Fedfreighter bearing 22181-00397, vector B-Farkon 184.19:11 lateral, 201.07:48 standard. This is Federation Diplomatic Cruiser *Windhover.* We have you on visual, and assess your damage as moderate to serious. Standard offer of assistance, or will commrelay your status to nearest FedBase. Immediate response requested. This sector of warpshoals under surveillance by ship or ships unknown. Advise at once.

Send it, Windy. We'll give them ten minutes to respond. Get ready to take the widest, fastest route around them on my command. If they refuse to answer, or start acting funny, I want to be gone before they figure out where we might have been. Rendezvous the drone on tangent as soon as possible after we start, but don't slow us down for it. It can trail us for a while, or if things get critical, we can dump it. But no risks to save the drone. Evac's ready to drop in line.

Wait. Their thrusters are firing. One-eighty turn. Engines dead. I think we're about to get our answer.

## 7039–3.14

War casualties. One critical, one serious, and three walking wounded. Put the two bad ones in the rejuvhosp cells. The others will have to wait their turn. It's a motley crew we rescued, Windy. The Carpath pilot, FedFrtCpt. Gosek Ralugeristanosionoster-mon, doesn't look like he's going to make it. In fact, I don't know how he's managed to hang on as long as he has. The Cinq-PAC observer has lost so many feathers and so much circulatory fluid that he is going to be a long time recuperating. Our three Beithurun soldiers, FedCommander Teever Loze and his two corporals, should recover with little difficulty. Teever Loze promised me their story after they've had some rest.

Meantime, I'm going back across to rig that junk pile for self-destruct. Keep an eye on our patients and an ear out for visitors, and buzz me if anything happens.

## 7039–3.15

Cpt. Gosek is still critical. Very critical. Too many systems failing at once. The rejuvhosp is doing a balancing act of such complexity with fluids, shocks, nutrition, medication, and temperature adjustments, that the failure buzzer goes on and off like a metronome. We've begun to get used to the sound. It's his heartbeat.

Speaking of hearts, our avian patient, Alvin, Baris-lon-Jelvo, has one like a dilith. If he keeps complaining about being confined to the rejuvhosp, we may have to take him off the serious list. All he wants is better food, exercise, a Cusith symphony, and new feathers. Apparently his feathers will grow back, but one of his wheels is going to be permanently damaged.

Teever Loze said that Alvin got the wheel injury when they were racing for the shuttle. Alvin had Cpt. Gosek cradled in his wings, and Cpl. Zeewilt riding in his pack and giving covering fire. The terrain was too rough to be rolling that fast, so when Alvin hit a bad outcropping, they bounced a good four meters off the ground. Off balance and unable to brake their fall with his wings without dropping Cpt. Gosek, Alvin landed with the combined weight of the three of them on his left wheel. Teever Loze and Cpl. Moot had to drag them, one by one, the last thirty meters to the shuttle. Zeewilt and Cpt. Gosek were unconscious, and Alvin was in so much pain that the shriek of his whistle nearly deafened them. Fortunately, however, Alvin's whistles of pain also had an effect on their pursuers, who dropped their weapons and clutched their heads in agony. It bought them enough time to get everyone aboard and lift off.

Once aboard the freighter, they hyped Cpt. Gosek into consciousness with speed drugs, sprayed him with anesthetics, and he got the ship under way, forcing his burned body to perform. Teever Loze and Cpl. Moot dressed all the wounds as best they could, then the two of them helped Alvin set the broken hollow strutbones in his wheel.

The Pleuhockle wheel is as complicated a development of evolution as a universal physiologist ever gets to see. To have to set the breaks of seven of those flexible strutbones, plus nineteen dislocated rim joints, guided only by feel and Alvin's instincts, meant something less than a perfect job. However, the hubjoints were only bruised, and the struts are already beginning to knit. Alvin will roll again, but with less of the grace Pleuhockles pride themselves in. Still, like everyone else, he's grateful to be alive.

Windy's running us on a step-one Evac program. A Wring-Con Destroyer shot up Gosek's freighter and chased them into the warpshoals. It is probably the same ship whose scan we picked up. I set the freighter to blow up just inside the inner edge of the shoals with full emergency beacons sending out howls of distress. If they found that wreckage, maybe they'll give up the search. Maybe not. Our best bet is to stay in the shoals as long as we can, and then hit a short warp for FedBase 2112. Can't risk calling ahead until we're out of the shoals, so we can only pray to Fara (or whomever Carpaths, Pleuhockles and Beithuruns pray to) that the FedBase is still in operation.

FedCommander Teever Loze was heading one of the Fed withdrawal teams on Faarkon-Bet with Alvin as neutral observer when they were attacked. He managed to get all but one squad out on the last troop shuttle when the Wring-Con troops started blowing the place apart. Cpt. Gosek had broken his leg and been burned by a sweep ray as the attack started. Cpl. Zeewilt literally tripped over Gosek on the way out to the freight pads.

Seems foolish, but obvious, that Wring-Con wants to fight both the Alliance and the Federation, and Teever Loze thinks Fed will pull back from all their bases until an assessment is made or reinforcements arrive. Not a very cheery thought, that.

## 7039–3.17

Cpt. Gosek is hanging on to his life as tenaciously as a veerus snake holds its carn. He's stable, but still critical.

Tomorrow we sneak out of the warpshoals. Alvin wants to send a message to the Pleuhockle System apprising them of the situation. We can contact FedBase 2112 with the shortbeam, but we'd have to use the longbeam to hit a relay for Pleuhockle, and the echoes could be picked up on half a dozen Warp-Ring planets. Seems like too much of a risk to me. Better to wait til we get to the Fed Base and let them transmit for us. I think as much as anything, Alvin wants to feel useful, so I turned him down as gently as I could. He's a strange old bird, but very likable.

They're all likable. Teever Loze and his men (and Alvin, when he's not resting) have been giving me some delightful conversation. They're all remarkably literate (condescension to professional soldiers, Gerard?) and filled with stories and anecdotes that greatly help to pass the time. All three Beithuruns are walking anthologies of songs, poems, fables, and war chants. Lots of war chants. I finally had to tell them I didn't think I could stand another war chant, and they desisted quite amiably.

In an effort to appear a kindred soul, I told them about my discovery of the Tenderfoot legend and read them our two finds to date. They were delighted, and to my surprise, told me they could add to my collection with one of their own. Well, four actually. Teever Loze and Moot each had one, and Zeewilt had two. We fed them into the Bard in their native Beithurun and what came out was four variations of a piece called "Tenderfoot's Need."

After they went to sleep, I sat down with the Bard and, using our functional formula, put together a fifth variation, an amalgam of the other four. Since they found the other Standard translations awkward, I don't know how they'll react to this one. I'll give it to them in the morning as a kind of gift before we slip out of the shoals and back into the danger zone.

Now off to check on Cpt. Gosek and Alvin and then to bed. Tomorrow may prove to be a very long day.

### 7039–3.18

They liked it. Made a few suggestions for changes which I immediately incorporated, and then astounded me by reciting in unison all five Standard versions, ending with mine. Could anyone be more pleased or flattered?

### Tenderfoot's Need

"Bless me with images
  too fine to lock on walls
      or in heads,
  too fine to live in frames
      or on tongues,
  too fine to capture
      or touch,"
Tenderfoot cried.

"I need space carved by cumulus eyes,
      shaped by sensuous seasons.
I need visions beyond sight and dreams."

Tenderfoot took a breath.
"I need substantiation of the void
So I can touch the cold and empty space
And know whose kingdom's come."

Sighing, Tenderfoot rested,
  head to breast,
  heart to ear,
And whispered to ribs,
"Bless me with images."

Even Alvin liked it, though he was not quite sure why we all made a big fuss about it. I tried to explain to him that this was only the third piece of the Tenderfoot legend I had found, and that as the ancient Loosane philosopher, Jake Jasper, once said, "It takes three quarks to make a row."

Unfortunately, that bit of ancient wisdom led into an esoteric discussion of quarks, ancient physics, and the humor therein. I don't think Alvin ever got my point. Or if he did, he ignored it, his polite way of saying something is so obvious that it is not worth his discussing it.

Obvious or not, it takes three of anything to make a row, and now we have a row of Tenderfoot poems. First safe chance I get, I'll chase our last message to Moseen with a copy of this. No explanation or notes, just "Tenderfoot's Need." Notes to follow. ShRil and The Professor will understand.

Exit time coming up. Let's doublecheck all systems, Windy.

*****FedBase 2112 is operational. Urged us to proceed at once. Suggested emergency warp to within 10,000 KM. Tricky and dangerous to pop out that close and slam into braking orbit. Looks like things are rough there, too, else why have us take such a chance? Teever Loze and crew are getting Cpt. Gosek and Alvin ready. Soon as everyone's strapped down, we go.

## 7039–3.19
## Braking Orbit, Asrai, FedBase 2112

Good job, Windy. I don't know if what we just did can be done smoothly, but you made it a whole lot easier than I thought it would be.

Three orbits til rendezvous with the hospital shuttle. Cpt. Gosek's going, but Alvin insists on riding down with us. FedBase Control sent Alvin's message for him, and said if he wanted to come down with us instead of the hospital shuttle, they couldn't stop him. Soon as he heard that he gave me that downy grin of his and headed back to his rejuvhosp cell. I think that's the first time he's gone back there without someone having to suggest it to him.

Moot and Zeewilt are getting Cpt. Gosek prepared for the transfer. Poor Teever Loze is in his bunk fighting off the last of warpsickness. He's a good officer, tried to help as soon as we'd slowed down enough. But those who get warpsick usually get it bad, and he's got it bad.

FedBase wants us on the ground as soon as possible. A long debriefing session wouldn't surprise me when we land. No meal. No "glad-you-made-it." No sleep. Just "Sit down and tell us everything you know." To be expected, I guess.

In case you haven't figured it out yet, Gerard my boy, there's a war or two going on around here, and the amenities tend to vanish in wartime. Remember? Thought you might. Now, just relax and do what the nice FedReps tell you. For a lowly diplomat, you surely do get uppity sometimes. Comes with the job, I suppose. Pleasantries all around, please. Let'em eat, sleep, and relax, then con'em when their guard's down. Not the only method, to be sure, but a good one on many occasions.

I'm babbling, Self. Must be the release of tension. Ten days of waiting for the bad guys to jump out from behind a rock. There's some residue here from Galaxy VI, too, that I don't want to think about right now. Probably some from Fairy Peg and Ribble too. Sooner or later, like Gracie said, we're going to have to work harder at sorting these problems out. They clutter my head.

*****Transfer complete. Cpt. Gosek's in the hospital's hands now. The doctor who came aboard to supervise the transfer was a little incredulous that our simple rejuvhosp cell had done so well. Did I once call those cells superfluous?

Five more braking orbits. About seven hours. A shame you can't cut through the atmosphere like the hospital shuttle, Windy. But then, hospital shuttles can't whip through space the way you do. Different ships for different trips, they say.

Teever Loze is up and restless. He has Moot and Zeewilt down in cargo checking their equipment. When I suggested he help them, he said he didn't want to get in their way. But I suspect he'll go. He needs something to do. The ship with the rest of his troops aboard couldn't warp through, so they'll be a week behind us getting in. He's ready for command again.

### 7039–3.24

Three days of debriefing, punctuated by medical tests, psychtests, and not-too-subtle loyalty tests. Then a day in one of their fancy rejuve units, which spit me out feeling fit and trim this morning. As soon as they cleared me, I went to see Alvin. He was spared most of their questions because of his status as a neutral, but apparently he volunteered a lot of information, because he said he sent them away "with a craw full of seeds."

Sent me away with one too. He was really hungry for

conversation. Or, more accurately, he was really hungry for an audience. Told me about his home (which is modestly called Alvin's Place), what he thought of governments in general and the Federation in particular, his great love of music, art, and literature, how he missed the flying days of his youth (Pleuhocklets lose their ability to fly as they mature because of their increased weight, mostly in their wheels), but how as an adult he learned the joys of roll-gliding, etcetera, etcetera.

I finally convinced him that I would indeed return tomorrow, and left to check on the others. Cpt. Gosek is somewhat improved, but the doctor told me the sweepray burns had done irreparable nerve damage and Gosek would be lucky to walk again, much less pilot. I told him not to count the old man out, and succinctly related the story of how he had flown the freighter within hours of being burned. The doctor just shook his head and walked away.

Teever Loze, Moot, and Zeewilt have been moved to the barracks infirmary, and I won't be able to see them until tomorrow, after I visit Alvin. I would guess they're still being debriefed.

Looks like I'd better spend some time cleaning you up, Windy. Our guests didn't do badly considering the time they had, but it wasn't exactly a spit and polish job.

*****Message from Alvin:

> A Pleuhockle ship has arrived to take me home. I will be gone by morning. If you ever get to the Pleuhockle System, stop by and see me. Just ask for Alvin's Place.
>
> I owe you much I cannot repay, so here's something for your collection.

**Three Quarks Make a Row**

Searching for the godhead,
the vision,
the burning rock and bush,
Beyond the plasma of motion
the complex of action,
Passion zeals the anguish of faith,
Desire mystics the will to believe.
Three quarks make a row.

Searching for companions,
affection,
acceptance and belief,
Beyond the gestalt of gestures
the weaving of words,
Dependence loyals the filling of need,
Fulfillment myopics the flaws of bondage.
Three quarks make a row.

Searching for the ultimate lover,
the soulmate,
the perfect mind and heart,
Beyond the osmosis of eros
the melding of psyche,
Phantasy fecunds the cosmic center,
Energy quantas the unseen void.
Three quarks make a row.

I wrote it for you. Please come to see me if you can.

Best Wishes,
Alvin
Baris-lon-Jelvo

I'm not sure I understand Alvin's poem yet, but I'm certainly touched by his gesture. I would liked to have gotten to know him better. Perhaps I shall one day.

There's a familiar ring here. Must contract diplomats always go through life making short, intensive relationships and then moving on? Is it the nature of the business, or the nature of Gerard Manley? I am reminded of Lelouche's famous play, "Touch and Go," where every time the protagonist, Chachelle, was allowed to get close enough to touch someone for whom he had built affection, he was forced to leave. Am I some kind of Chachelle, pushed by an unseen hand?

No. I don't think so. When the time comes, I shall throw off the mask of Chachelle and pursue my own course, regardless of the forces in my way. When that time comes, I will see C'Rina again, and ShRil, and Morrizon, and Alvin, and whomever else touches me along the way.

**7039–3.26**

It's enough to make one believe in a small universe. While I was being debriefed, poked, tested, and healed, a command starship left orbit around this planet bearing the royal personage known as Peg On'Ell, Guardian of the Ribble Galaxy, Badh of the Seven Systems, Keeper of the Faith, Princess of Kril, and Mistress of the Gabriel Ratchets. Fairy Peg.

She was here, according to the FedMarshall, on her way home from an abortive attempt to negotiate a non-aggression pact with Warp-Ring Alliance (and probably Wring-Con also). One of her councilors was taken seriously ill, and her ship's medical staff couldn't help him, so she requested and received permission to have him treated here. Fairy Peg and an entourage accompanied the councilor to the hospital (and looked this installation over very carefully, no doubt). She badgered the doctors for two days about his treatment, and caused the FedMarshall great frustration. The councilor died. Severe internal hemorrhaging; cause unknown. Three hours later she was back on her starship with the body in freezebay, and leaving orbit.

In the same hospital, the same building as Fairy Peg for the better part of two days and didn't know it. Did she know I was here? When she went out to her shuttle to return to her ship, did she see *Windhover*? And if she did, how would she recognize you, my dear Windy? Aside from your name on the bow, you look like every other Diplomatic Cruiser of your class. Inside you're different, beautifully different, but outside?

Of course she didn't know I was here. No reason for her to. It's some irrational impulse in my soul which triggers these foolish questions.

But to have been so close to her! An opportunity missed because of ignorance. This is stupid. What am I supposed to do, Self, ask in every port if they've seen a princess named Fairy Peg? Besides, why do we want to see her anyway? Didn't she send me back to Fed to be mindwiped so I wouldn't divulge those intimate secrets we shared along with our bodies on those cold Kril nights? Well, didn't she?

Who knows? We may never break some of those mindwipe blocks. That, Self, is the answer to why, someday, we must see her again. Why someday we must get her to tell why she sent me back. The Gabriel Ratchets didn't make her do it. She owned their souls. The Privy Council didn't have the power. So why? That's the answer we have to get from her. Why did the Princess of Kril send her lover-husband-Prince Regent into the hands of Ribble's strongest enemy?

You're picking at it, Gerard. Let it go. For now.

Teever Loze, Moot, and Zeewilt are healed and helping with the shutdown operations. FedBase 2112 is to be reduced to a FedOutpost. Teever Loze wants to stay on here as commander of the garrison. He didn't say it directly, but it seems obvious to me that he'd like to get a little revenge against Wring-Con. If it was obvious to the FedMarshall, Teever Loze doesn't stand a chance of staying. Fed disapproves of emotional revenge and will send him and his troops to the other end of the universe if necessary to keep them from trying to get it.

I hope they do. Teever Loze is a good and decent man and every time I'm with him, I like him all the more. I'd hate to see him jeopardize his career by doing something stupid for the sake of revenge. The rest of his troops will be in tomorrow. Maybe the resumption of command will put his priorities back in order.

*****Now we know how serious the Warp-Ring war is. We've been ordered to leave with the second convoy on 4.5. The first is leaving tomorrow. Convoys are part of wartime tactics. We are further ordered to remain with the convoy a minimum of two parsecs beyond the warpshoals before resuming our journey to DAZM-17.

## 7039–3.30

Asrai is a beautiful planet. Took my third walk in as many days with Teever Loze into the hills around FedBase this afternoon. We admired Asrai's blue-green grasses and strange, wand-like trees that bend at the thought of a breeze, so that they always appear to be moving. Today we sat by a slow stream choked with the red algae the natives ferment for medicinal purposes, and continued what could, given the time, become a marathon argument.

Basically, Teever Loze argues that music, art, and literature are best when produced by people who do it as an avocation and that no creative person should be rewarded in any material way for what he creates. I argue that the greatest creative works in the universe are produced where cultures and societies support all of the creative arts by first providing an environment where fledgling artists can develop their skills unhampered by the necessity of working for their own sustenance, and second, by actively and appreciatively consuming the works produced and paying for those works in the credits of the marketplace.

We acknowledged early on that our views are irreconcilable, but the argument of nuances and contra-examples is stimulating and pleasurable for its own sake. When I pointed out to him that our argument was, in its way, a form of art, he replied that there was serious question that anyone would pay for it.

His company is a joy. I feel like I've known him for years. His spirit and love of life, his quick humor, his tough logic all give him an animation and vitality that is infectious.

He has invited me to watch an inter-regimental game of patroon tomorrow. Patroon, as he explained it to me, is a popular Beithurun game of strategy and tactics played on a triangular field. Three teams of thirty-five members each attempt to kick a small ball into each of the other teams' corners before the other teams can kick their balls into each of the opponents' corners. There are formal rules, set plays, defensive, offensive, and interference players, and much more than I could absorb from his detailed description. There is a regimental prize at stake which includes a month of special privileges as well as the honor of victory.

It should be fun, and it will certainly provide a welcome diversion.

## 7039–4.1

Oh, Fara. Where do you hide your face on days like this? Teever Loze and twenty others dead. So many wounded. Guerrilla attack. Wring-Con. Bastards. Old missile weapons. Explosions. Gunfire. Death on the playing field.

And Teever Loze exploding from the bullets.

Fara. Oh, Fara. How could you?

## 7039–4.2

The whole planet is under attack. Guerrillas on the ground, and hit and run attacks on the orbiting FedShips. No one has overall command of the defense, and the Asrains fight for all sides. What madness is this?

### 7039–4.3

No way we can leave, Windy. Tried every persuasion I knew, but it didn't do any good. We're stuck. Right in the middle of a war.

### 7039–4.5

Windy and I have been recruited. Sub-orbital courier, ambulance, passenger and diplomatic service. Rank of commander. Don't like it. Have no choice. Sure wish Gracie could rescue us from this one.

### 7039–4.7

There's more than a tinge of craziness in all this, but at last some kind of organization is beginning to appear. The FedTroops are no problem, but the local militia on our side doesn't yet understand the need for order and discipline. How can they? As soon as they arrive, they're rearmed, trained for a day, and sent out to fight.

I think we're standing at the gates of Krick.

### 7039–4.8

Off to Eleia Fork City to pick up two critically wounded FedTroops and the First Citizen. Taking six newly commissioned lieutenants with us, all ex-noncoms with a no-nonsense look of meanness in their eyes.

We're caught up in someone else's horror fantasy, and can't get out. Everything moves in slow motion, the bodies coming off the transports, the wounded being carried into the hospital, the new troops loading up on the armored carriers. Yet, everyone is rushing everywhere. I can't speed up the slow ones, or slow the fast ones, and can't get into rhythm with either.

### 7039–4.12

Took ground fire while loading in Eleia Fork City and brought back five wounded, including one very mad First Citizen. I quieted his screaming with a hypo. Can't blame him, though. His city is a battle zone and FedBase isn't pouring in troops to the rescue. Of course, there aren't enough FedTroops anywhere. The Alliance units refuse to venture out of the cities and garrisons they hold secure. Told us they're waiting for reinforcements.

From where?

There's a stalemate in space. Just enough ships on each side so no one has an edge. Those ships on the ground that might have helped, the attack cruisers and destroyers, were pretty well damaged in the first wave of attacks by saboteurs. The ones we managed to get up just balanced the stalemate.

We. I said, we. That's how one becomes a soldier. "We will fight them in space. We will fight them in the asteroid belts. We will fight them on the planets. We will fight until there are none of us left to fight. Then our spirits will fight theirs without rest in the halls of eternity."

Made us memorize that in school.

## 7039–4.18

They've armed you, Windy. Hated to do it, but no one else will defend us. No one. As we ran naked from pocket to pocket of security, carrying our mangled passengers, we were vulnerable, incapable of protecting ourselves and our passengers. And purer, too.

## 7039–4.23

More dead. More wounded. More changes to Windy. We can carry eight now up front and ten in cargo. I feel like the Pilot of Klonos flying souls over the chasm of Death to the afterworld.

## 7039–4.25

Today one of our destroyers captured a Ribble attack cruiser operated by Nari mercenaries working for Wring-Con. Figures. Another chance for Ribble to strike at Fed.

## 7039–4.27

I think I'm beginning to hallucinate. I see armed shadows in the trees. And soldiers coming across the open fields who vanish when I raise my glasses to see them better.

And Teever Loze dies every night in my dreams.

## 7039–5.3

We were too late today. Not the first time. But today was different. Spotted those Wring-Con troops moving up the hill and kept sweeping them with the lasecannon long after they were all dead and burned. Couldn't take my finger off the trigger. Couldn't stop.

What's happening to me, Windy?

## 7039–5.6

No entry. No entry. No entry. Nothing. No words. Just blood.

## 7039–5.11

Two days of just sitting. A lull in the battles. What in Krick are we waiting for? Doesn't anyone care that those bastards who killed Teever Loze are still out there?

## 7039–5.20

What can I add here? The carnage continues. Replacements come for all sides. But who will replace Teever Loze? And who will replace Lieutenant Zeewilt, who died in Windy's belly on the way back to the hospital? And Who, Who will replace Fara? Is there a deity I can believe in? Will She stop this war? Send Her, Fara, send Her.

## 7039–5.29

Rows of coffins in the morgue, stacked four high, freezesealed and ready to ship out. A comment on the side of one.

Bodies in trilon bags
  like so many sandwiches
  back home in aluminum lunch boxes,
So many meaty pieces,
  bagged, boxed for back home,
Consumed by untasting mouths,
Box lunches
  at a galaxy pride picnic.

## 7039–6.4

Not sure who I am any more. Windy flies us on mercy missions and we harass the enemy with our lasecannon on the way back to the hospital. Every third night I lead patrols into the hills to snipe at the Asrains fighting for Wring-Con. When I'm waiting for a call, I help in the hospital. I've killed. And enjoyed it.

Tonight is another patrol. Three hours til we go out, and I can feel the excitement building. I'm ready. I'm good. But who am I?

## 7039–6.6

What difference does it make? The flowers bloom. But most of them are red, or pink, or orange. The streams flow from the high scarps. But the streams run red too. Red slashes everywhere.

Even after I wake up I see Teever Loze. He's red. Like the flowers, and the blood, and the water.

Red. Always red.

## 7039–6.7

Talked to Teever Loze last night. He told me to run. But where? He didn't say where, Windy. He didn't say where.

Where can we run to?

Gracie!

That's it. We'll go back to Gracie.

I was safe with her. Safe, Windy.

## 7039–6.9

They're coming, Windy! They're coming!

## 7039–6.11

FedFleet Eighty-Three. They're here. Clearing the enemy from space. Landing thousands of troops. We're leaving. Free ride for both of us. In the belly of a massequip freighter.

Leaving.

Does it matter? It should. But does it? Who wants a killer diplomat?

*****Can't leave, Windy. They'll take your lasecannon if we do. We'll be naked again. Defenseless.

## 7039–6.12

No choice, Windy. They say we have to go. Now.

## 7039–6.13
## FedShip *Glazione*

I'm locking you up, Windy. You'll be safe here. It's a good ship we're on. Big freighter. Lots of room.

I've got the memocorder in my kit. And they're going to give you new plates and polish you up. Going to Pleasance. For a rest.

But first I have to go up to the hospital deck and check in. Free trip, Windy. Just relax and get some rest.

We're going to be all right.

# 5

**7039–11.17**
**FedCenter Rehab, Pleasance**

There are a lot of us here from Asrai, Windy. The casualties there were worse than I knew. But it's nice here. We talk a lot. With each other and with the doctors and nurses, and with other people who seem to be here just to talk. No one calls us patients. We're guests. But I know better. We're patients.

This patient must finally be getting better, though, because they let me have the memocorder back so I can talk to you. I'm teaching a little class in writing to help some of the "guests" put their thoughts and feelings down in words. They keep little journals, or write stories and poems, and some of them are very good. And some of them are very good and very painful.

For example, I helped one of the Beithuruns here write a poem he calls "After the Flashfight." It makes me cry, but it's good. I think it belongs in our collection.

**After the Flashfight**

Amidst the blasted haze
  the shattered desolation
    is resplendent with remains of friends.

A detached voice
  under the cacophony of silenced guns
whimpers, "Medic."

Sgt. Leston Tullot
503rd Beithurun Regiment
Eighteenth FedTroop Corps

*****They're very concerned with therapy here. Physical, mental, emotional, primary, secondary, dream, scheme, occupational, vocational, notational. They're determined to help us all with some kind of therapy.

I picked dream therapy. Seemed the easiest. Two hours per day in the dream machine, how could that be hard? It is. My therapist, Mznna Gnnr Stt Crti Clddn Floggb (whom I call Doc Flo), helps me relax then suggests a subject for me to dream about. No matter how hard I try to avoid it, I always dream about that subject. Then after I wake up, I have to tell her about the dream and we play games with its possible meanings. Sometimes it gets very complicated trying to sort out the dream from the meaning from the games. But sometimes I am surprised by what I learn. All things considered, Doc Flo makes dream therapy a fairly pleasant experience. Hard, but pleasant.

My dreams outside of therapy are not so pleasant. Too many flashback scenes from Asrai with sharp edges that cut into my conscious hours. The worst is the nightmare about Teever Loze's death, which seems to come every night. In fact, a night without it is strange and empty. We've tried to talk about it in therapy, but that's one dream that won't come on command. Doc Flo says it is very deep and we will have to wait for it to move closer to the surface. That's your job, Self.

The sooner you do that and the rest of it, the sooner we can get out of here. I've had several talks with the FedRep for Contracts, Arbitration and Adjustment, Colonel Q. ES't'phons, who has been explaining my options with Fed. I built up double credits during my imprisonment on Mysteleria, triple credits for the time between picking up the casualties in the warshoals til we reached Pleasance, and credit and a half for all the time we spend here.

The numbers are confusing and incomplete, but by the time we arrived on Pleasance, Fed owed me credit for eight years, three months, and three days, less the two years, one month and ten days remaining straight contract time, which leaves me with six years, one month, and twenty-three days back credit. Plus what I am accumulating here. I think.

Would I like it in a lump sum, or a guaranteed interest-bearing lifetime annuity (with lifetime single-payment options), or in ten equal yearly payments, or, or, or? Colonel Q. ES't'phons gave me a document which supposedly explains all this, but the more I read it, the less I understand.

When I signed my first FedContract, all the rules and obligations were explained in simple, cogent language. But none of it makes sense now. Fortunately, however, Colonel Q. ES't'phons said I don't have to make any decision until I'm ready to leave. Thank Fara for that.

Ah, Fara, Goddess of my ancient past. My faith in you was like a lining to my life, made the garment of my existence complete and comfortable. I had met some of your competition here and there, but thought you were the best. But my faith is shaken, Fara. Shaken badly.

Shall I demote you to a personal, household "goddess," good only for small favors and reassurances? Shall I search for your superiors? If you have any, who are they? And what have they done for this universe? Help me, Fara. If you can.

I shall close for now, Windy, as it is time for my dream therapy. It is good to be able to talk to you again, even if I ramble on about this and that. Soon we will leave together for new adventures, and I shall be even more glad, for I miss the constant presence of you around me. You are my home.

## 7039–11.22

Two nice things happened today. Two messages arrived for me this morning from Moseen by way of DAZM-17. The first and longest is a joint message from The Professor and ShRil, formal delight and thanks for the research I sent them, comments on the poems, especially "Tenderfoot's Search," which they received two versions of. One an awkward, jumbled, illiterate version from Val, with a short note of transmission from Mr. Gwindel, which they received while I was imprisoned, and the version I sent with the research on 7039–2.11. (Shows my guess was right. Gwindel thought it was some kind of coded message. Wonder why he bothered to send it at all?)

The Professor's main interest was in "Dithyramb 73" and "Lips", and he said the 'emotive syntax' utilized in those poems is similar in many ways to the tonal syntax of Burnal Sevene (wherever the Krick that is).

I had a stronger interest in the personal message from ShRil. Written very guardedly in my diplocode, what she said, basically, was that she was glad I was safe on DAZM-17, she missed my company and assistance, she was grateful for the brief time we had together, and she hoped I would stop by if I was ever again in their galaxy.

Message, Windy: To ShRil, FedEmbassy, Moseen. If I'm ever within a thousand parsecs and can come to see you, I will. I wrote the following for you. . . . Follow that with "Bodylogue." (ref. 7039–2.12) Sign my name. Put the whole thing in my diplocode and send immediately.

What can I hope for in ShRil's response to "Bodylogue"? What can I dream of? How deep is space? How can I dream like this after so much time has passed? Dare I think of love? Does my heart pound?

Hold me, Self. Hold me down. I want too much. This brief elation has filled my mind with intoxicating vapors, and I speak from regions too tender to expose. Lock the hatches of my heart til I receive her reply.

## 7039–11.25

Doc Flo says I'm doing very well in my therapy and in three or four months ought to be well enough to leave. Three or four months! I can't stay here that long. I'll go crazy. Made an appointment for tomorrow with Colonel Q. ES't'phons to see if he can help. Maybe Fed has a low-key assignment somewhere that will get me back to work at a nice gentle pace.

## 7039–11.26

Colonel Q. ES't'phons didn't offer me much hope. Said he would check to see what would be available. Looked at me strangely, as though I were crazy to want to leave. I left him feeling crazy.

I'll be out to see you in a couple of days, Windy. Doc Flo thinks it might be good for me and help speed my readjustment. Readjustment to what? To this resort hospital? To this planet where the only native sentience resides in crystal seas at the poles? To being kept away from you and my job? Readjustment to what I've never adjusted to in the first place? Windy, we're going to get out of here by 12.14 or my name isn't Gerard Manley.

## 7039–11.28
## Aboard Windy, Pleasance

Ah, it's good to sit here and talk to you without looking to see if anyone's listening behind me. I suspect they can listen to me even when I'm alone in my room. "Purely for medical reasons, Commander Manley." That's what they'd say if I caught them listening.

Commander Manley. That's what they call me at the Center. I told Colonel Q. ES't'phons that I wasn't particularly interested in keeping my rank, but if Fed thought it was necessary, the least they could do would be to make it a Reserve Grade and take me off active duty. That's right, Windy. Active duty. Seems like when I accepted that commission in the middle of the war, I obligated myself for five years.

Unfortunately for Fed, however, if they keep me in the FedTroop Corps for five years, they'll have to pay all eight-plus years of that back credit, and my military salary, and a bonus for enlistment in wartime, and hazardous duty pay, and Fara knows what else. More triple-talk from Colonel Q. ES't'phons about options and promising to look into it, and all that gibberish.

One of my options would be to leave the diplomatic service now and get us out of here. It would take most of my back credits to finish paying them for you, Windy, but it would be worth it. However, if I choose that option before they release me from active duty, they can order me to stay here or go anywhere else their perverted hearts desire with the FedTroop Corps, and I would have no choice but to obey. So what I have to do is get released from active duty before making my next move. Complicated. And worse, time-consuming.

But all is not bleak and grim. I have a three-day pass and permission to fly you down to Besseracc, the Cultural Exchange Center, on the rim of the southern crystal sea where they have just made some breakthroughs (breaks through?)... where they have just made some new linguistic discoveries in their dealings with the sentient crystal natives. Fed calls them Pleasance-ites, an awkward appellation at best, but no one knows if the sentient crystals have a name for themselves. If they do, it probably translates "the people."

Regardless of their name, we're going to see them, hopefully to "talk" to them. Maybe we can find something interesting to add to our collection. We're cleared to leave here at 1830 and are supposed to be back not later than 2400 on 12.1. Can't tell about that return trip, though. Might get involved in something down there and have to request an extension.

If we're going to leave on time, Windy, I'd better quit this babbling and we'd better start going over the checklist.

*****On our way. I'm afraid I don't make a very good patient, especially when I don't think there's anything wrong with me that a return to the routine wouldn't cure. Instead of Doc Flo and her colleagues realizing that I was in shock after our experiences on Asrai and would recover quickly once returned to to a normal environment, they assumed that because I had nightmares and was tense, irritable, and exhausted, I had cracked up.

Okay, so they made a mistake. Their motives, at least, are commendable, and I'm convinced that they care very much about their patients as individuals. Including me.

Enough of that, Windy. Let's crank up the Bard and have some fun. C.P.O. Largsznkyte, one of the patients I am teaching, gave me a poem he wrote in his native Txizkyl back around 7019 during the Tun'Tean War. He said he just couldn't translate it into Standard and would I do it for him. He's such a nice spider (well, he's not really a spider, but he looks like one) that I couldn't say no. We've got about five hours to play with it before we arrive, so we might as well give it our best shot.

**7039–11.29**
**Besseracc**

Nothing like getting somewhere when everyone's asleep. Even Control didn't seem very alert. Doesn't matter. Largsznkyte's poem will keep us occupied for another hour or so and then we can grab a couple of hours sleep before we take the tour.

*****No wonder Largsznkyte didn't want to translate this himself. The key metaphor almost defies translation. I finally had to make one that was as analogous as possible, consistent with the meaning of the original. His refers to an intellectual exercise and mine to a sport, but I believe the intent of the two is the same. If he doesn't think so, we'll have to look for something else together, or put it down as untranslatable.

That, and the first line, which I finally put in Terran Basic, are the two things we'll have to work on together.

**Arena Response**
**(circa 7019)**

*Morituri Salutamus.*
We who are about to die, salute you,
  more or less,
Because we don't want to die,
    don't care to salute,
And all this mess about glory and honor
  bores us.

Frankly, we're not too fond of this game,
  don't give two hoots,
  don't really believe that this builds character.
We'd rather be home
  with a wench and a brew,
  cheering those padded gladiators,
Because this broken field running,
    this bloody scrimmage
Just kills us.

C.P.O. Nz Largsznkyte
Chief Weapons Officer
FedShip *St. Kraane*
FedFleet 163

Now, a couple of hours sleep and we can go "meet" the natives.

*****Fascinating. Utterly fascinating. The crystal seas are actually nonhomogeneous aggregations of silicon in a high-viscosity fluid that is itself ninety-seven percent silicon. The whole sea is sentient, thinking of itself in the plural as a continuously crystallizing and dissolving unit of multiple centers or "thought groups." All "conversations" are carried on in the form of brief formal lyrics or songs.

For example, in answer to a lyric-phrased question about how they-it sustain existence, the following was given:

The dark winds howl through crystal
Like preform cells

When we were wet and round
Before catalyst and bath
And true clear dimensions.
Hard old edges lure us.
Light refracts our minds
Like light.
Small crystals vibrate.
We dissolve together.

Needless to say, that type of response to a simple question about sustaining life does not lend itself to swift analysis or understanding. I have volunteered to help the Cultural Exchange Center by having you, Windy, write a program for them that utilizes the Bard's best aspects for their purposes. Maybe that will help them make more sense out of the answers they are getting. AND, since it will take us at least a week or two or three to write, test, and modify the program, we will have a solid excuse to stay here instead of going back to the Rehab Center.

## 7039–11.30

Permission granted to stay and help. Director Franiingcard pulled some strings up at Rehab and got us an indefinite assignment for as long as she feels we are needed (and useful, too, I suppose). A charming Sepoleven, she. Reminds me of a gyroscope with tentacles and colored strobe lights. Her spoken Standard has a sonorous rhythmic quality that is instantly relaxing. But her questions, comments, and criticism are so stimulating that I hate to stop talking to her. (As a member of one of those species where each individual is capable of either inseminating or being inseminated, Director Franiingcard cannot actually be classified as female. However, there is a certain sense of purpose in her, colored by a very strong suggestion of limitless endurance and tenacity, which makes me think of her as feminine. I'll ask her later if she minds that.)

I'm sure you're fascinated by all this, Windy, but if we are going to justify her actions on our behalf, we'd better get to work and start producing for her. She's a lady I'd hate to disappoint.

## 7039–12.4

Do you realize that since we left the Rehab Center I haven't had the Teever Loze nightmare once? I wonder if all that dream therapy wasn't stirring up all your dream centers, Self? Whatever the reasons for this respite, I thank you. Dwelling on Teever Loze's death every night certainly wasn't helping my "readjustment" any.

Ironically, Teever Loze's departure from my dreams left room for Fairy Peg to return. In this latest one, Fairy Peg is defending me in the main throne room against accusations from a large assembly. Threats too, I think, veiled, but threats nonetheless. The Privy Council and the Gabriel Ratchets are in the forefront. Their mouths twist grotesquely when they speak. They are demanding, strident, excited, agitated. They want my head. Or my blood. Or at least my banishment. Fairy Peg is calm, reassuring, placating, diplomatic, soothing, and unyielding. I am safe.

Another piece of the puzzle, Self. The more we remember, the less I understand. How complexly we wove and were woven during those years. We may never understand it all, but the picture is much more balanced now than ever before. The key questions have narrowed to these: Am I still Prince Regent, Fairy Peg's husband-lover? And why did she send me back to Fed?

As soon as I list those two questions, dozens of others crowd into my head, but listing them again won't get us any closer to their solution. You're doing fine, Self, and I'm content to take the pieces as you get them. My anxiety about Fairy Peg has relaxed to intense curiosity. And even though each new glimpse of the truth makes me eager to learn a great deal more as fast as possible, I realize that you will do it as best you can in your own time. Perhaps in this I have learned C'Rina's patience.

Patience also in adapting the Bard program for Director Franiingcard. The going has been much more difficult than I anticipated. The lexicography itself may take another two or three weeks before we can begin to set up the interfaces with the program. Still, no one seems in a hurry but me, so I am learning to match the rhythm of life here and work at a steady, even pace. Settling in. Comfortable and happy. And most important, useful.

## 7039–12.9

Need to get some sleep, but I keep thinking about those years in prison. Then, I slept. Most of the time. A unique system the Mystelerians have developed. Lots of sleep, just enough exercise to keep us healthy, and short periods of intellectual exercises. Time became meaningless until Gracie got us out of the system. For the last half year, it was almost pleasant to be there.

Except for the shadows of pain. Gracie said they would go away, and by the time I left, they had. But I never knew what they were. Or what caused them.

Why am I talking about this? Why now? I'd just as soon forget that whole wasted time. There was something vicious back there.

But not Gracie. No, the only vicious thing in Gracie's life was the wrath of her immortal peers who exiled her to Mysteleria for the crime of actively helping some mere mortals. But if she was bitter about that, I couldn't tell it. In fact, as her lower mouth told the story of her exile in a matter-of-fact way, her upper mouth chuckled.

Just remembering that scene makes me feel better. If Gracie could laugh at that, surely I can laugh at my troubles. Funny how relaxing the thought of Gracie is. I think I'm ready to go to sleep now.

Goodnight, team.

## 7039–12.16

Two days past my arbitrary deadline to leave Pleasance, Windy, and I have no intention of leaving anytime soon. This challenge is too much fun.

Message from Colonel Q. ES't'phons a couple of days ago that I will be released from active and reserve duty effective 12.30. Apparently Fed doesn't want a contract diplomat with even reserve military status, so I get to be part of their year-end closeout. Good. I sent a reply back to the colonel asking him to outline all of my options as of 7040–1.1 regarding pay, assignments, etcetera, and send them to me at his convenience. If he can put them in plain Standard, maybe I'll be able to evaluate them and decide on a course of action. If he insists on FedGibberish, maybe Director Franiingcard will help me sort them out. She has an aptitude for cutting through all the drickle dung and getting to the essentials.

In fact, the other day she rolled into the library lab, started looking at all our current results at once (something I'm convinced she can do) and within thirty minutes had pointed out five instances of tangential divergence that were not going to lead anywhere. It's the kind of thing she does all the time.

I told her we were going to create a new title for her, Essence Analyst. The dark aquamarine pulsing of her lights that I got in response indicated her pleasure at my remark, but she said that anyone who wasted time flattering a director was probably trying to hide deficiencies in his work. I agreed, but begged forgiveness as one misfortunate enough to be a lowly diplomat with few real skills and a tendency to recognize greatness in others that cannot be found in one's self. She made a deep whirring-snorting noise accompanied by a flash of mint green, and rolled out of the lab in a rush.

I'm afraid my sincere compliment embarrassed her (if that's possible), and my response to her teasing made it worse. However, I also think it strengthened a growing relationship of admiration and respect. Chief LabTech Galley said he had never seen her so pleased, but that I ought to be careful, because this was her first assignment and her experience with aliens was very limited. When I expressed disbelief, he told me that among the Sepoleven, Director Franiingcard is considered a new adult (despite her three hundred years!) and as such all her actions will be reviewed by her elders before she moves on to her next assignment. I was speechless. Certainly puts our average two-hundred-year life span in a different perspective, doesn't it?

### 7040–1.7

Lexicography complete as we can make it through three levels of reference and inference. Director Franiingcard is pleased and impressed by the techniques adapted from the Bard program. We've picked up some new techniques to plug into the Bard in both lexicography and random sample translation skills. Tomorrow we start Phase One Interface.

## 7040–1.11

Phase One Interface was a disaster. Simple declarative statements translate both ways. Everything else turns into fragments of nonsense accentuated by half-formed parenthetical questions and logically invalid syllogisms. Director Franiingcard thinks the Phase Two Interface will correct part of the problem and wants us to complete both phases before we decide to tear everything apart. I have my doubts, but since Phase Two is basically a mechanical quickstep process, it will only take another day or so to find out who is right.

It's frustrating to have such a massive foulup in critical syntax matching after doing so well thus far. When I was a child learning to program at my father's side and something went inexplicably wrong, he would say, "The glitches are loose! The glitches are loose! Quick, Gerry, get the cage so we can lock them up again." Never did find that cage, but together we caught lots of glitches hiding in the corners of our programs and cast them out into the storm. Looks like the glitches are loose again. Windy, you play Dad's role and we'll bring the little demons to their ignoble end.

## 7040–1.13

Director Franiingcard was half right. Part of our problem disappeared when we initiated the Phase Two Interface. It's open season on the remaining glitches, but from their nature, I suspect they won't be too hard to track down and destroy. Chief LabTech Galley and his staff are already well on their way to success, Windy, so you and I can stay in reserve until we're needed.

Finally received Colonel Q. ES't'phons detailed outline of my current career and credit options. I was right. I'm going to need help deciphering them. Why must all this be so complicated?

What I really think I want is all my back credits, less what it will take to pay off Windy, and then a new assignment. If that means I must sign a new contract, then so be it. In spite of the fact that I'm enjoying this exercise in translation and programming, there's a feeling of guilt inside because I'm not working at what I am trained for. Contract diplomacy may not be the noblest of callings, but it's mine, I do it well, and I'm proud of it. And I'm ready to get back to it. Building my ego, Self?

Colonel Q. ES't'phons said that as soon as I get back, he has a mission that will be available by 5.1 that I might find interesting and challenging. Didn't say what or where, but I don't think I care.

## 7040–1.15

Except for some minor adjustments, Phase Two Interface is complete. Now the longest and most difficult part, the Final Interface. The labtechs are starting now, and by this afternoon you and I will be in the middle of it, Windy. I figure if all goes well, we should be ready for a test run not later than the twenty-fifth.

*****A long, long message from ShRil. Apologies for not responding sooner (it's been almost two months since I sent "Bodylogue"), but she has been away from Moseen for almost a year. The Professor got Fed to loan her to Moseen University, and immediately sent her off to do some research. Spent the better part of eight months in the Challistone Central Library on Castle-by-Hearte in the Merline System. I think she's fallen in love with a library.

On the whole her research was very successful and her discoveries included eleven long prose pieces and numerous references which fit the Tenderfoot legend. No poetry, though, which she knows I will find disappointing. Still, the body of works on the legend has grown to the extent that The Professor wants to send her to Quadra as Moseen University's representative to a conference on "Universal Legends and Literature" to present their preliminary discoveries.

It's quite an honor for ShRil, and she is very excited about going. Fed apparently has no objections to extending her leave of absence (especially with Sir Dan and The Professor supporting her), so for the next couple of months she and The Professor are going to be putting their presentation together. I'm very, very proud of her. And pleased that she is going to receive recognition from her peers.

I'm also pleased by her reaction to "Bodylogue." Not excited, but pleased. ShRil guarded her emotional response very carefully, but the tone of her thoughts told me that she would welcome a reunion. She spoke of loneliness and longing in a vague way, then followed that immediately with the observation that she never again expected to meet anyone with whom she could work as closely as we worked. Since I don't remember that much work in all the time we spent together, I can only believe that "work" is not exactly what she meant.

She closed with a Sylvan proverb. "Good friends make the best companions. No matter how far away they dwell, they are always at hand."

Ah, ShRil, you, too, are always at hand.

## 7040–1.16

Sent my reply to ShRil with congratulations, encouragement, and love. Yes, love. I cannot guard my emotional response.

## 7040–1.22

Final interface completed today. First test run tomorrow. Have to admit to being more than a little nervous, Windy. We've put in seven solid weeks of work on this, and tied up half of the Cultural Exchange Center's labtechs and most of their computer operations to get to this point. It's not that I doubt that we will get acceptable results, but rather, that I want the results to be really impressive. I don't want anyone here to feel anything but unbridled success intoxicating them. That's a pretty wild statement, Self, but after all, it's our program and, consequently, our reputation that's on the line.

But more than that, I want impressive results to repay Director Franiingcard for helping us escape the confines of Rehab Center. Her gift to us was work, and work is the best rehabilitation we could have.

## 7040–1.23

The universe is a never-ending source of surprises. The results we got were impressive enough, but almost totally different from anything we expected. We ran ten of the "lyrics" from the crystal sea on the first test run. What we got back were not lyrics at all, but equations and formulas. It was gibberish to me, but Director Franiingcard turned into a dazzling light show of joy as soon as the results started coming out. She started rolling back and forth across the lab, waving her tentacles and radiating full spectrum washes of color. All the time she was emitting a deep, sensuous hum. Each new translation on the vidscreen caused her to hum louder, roll faster, and flash more colors at a higher frequency. She, not the translations, became the show. If her actions are typical of Sepoleven excitement, what must it be like when they mate?

She calmed down, eventually, and ignoring the awe in the room, told us to start putting every "lyric" on record through the system. Then she rolled out in a blaze of light.

Chief LabTech Galley and I are to join Director Franiingcard in her quarters after dinner. I suspect a private little celebration, and if I don't quit jabbering here and finish getting dressed, I am going to miss it.

*****Honor and commendation, Windy. It was a celebration indeed, but neither little, nor private. Director Franiingcard had us on a simultaneous vidcom hookup with Cultural Exchange Central on Vance (at the cost of Fara knows how many credits) and the Secretary General of CulEx herself (another Sepoleven) commended us on the excellence of our program's results. She wanted to name the program after me, but I convinced her that the *Windhover*-Manley Bard Program for Interspecies Cultural Translation was more accurate and appropriate. And thus it will be. We're to receive official commendation (with copies to FedDiplomatic Service, of course) within the month.

We've done ourselves proud, Windy.

**7040–1.24**

More about last night. After Director Franiingcard closed the vidcom hookup, she and Galley and I did indeed have a private celebration. Galley is going to be promoted to Senior Chief LabTech. His groundwork and assistance were invaluable, and I heartily approve. I suspect from some of the comments Director Franiingcard made that she, too, will receive appropriate recognition for our success.

What was our success, exactly? As best I understand it, Windy, we somewhat inadvertently bridged a gap between alien and Standard mathematical linguistics, using a nonmathematical program. Apparently, previous attempts to bridge similar gaps with other cultures using purely mathematical programs have been less than totally successful.

Director Franiingcard had suspected for some time that the crystal sea "lyrics" were equations and formulas, but until she saw our lexicon, she wasn't really sure. The lexicon is full of number/symbol/sign words. She knew then we were on the right track, but she didn't want to tell us for fear we would be influenced to try a mathematical approach.

That explains why we had the syntax problems in Phase One, and why Phase Two took care of most of them. By that time, Galley was in on the secret, and knocked out the glitches blocking the mathematical syntax. Once the path was clear, Final Phase Interface fell right in line because of the functional form procedures we set up in the Bard.

Galley and Director Franiingcard were up most of the night before the test run reviewing all that we had done til then and trying to anticipate any possible problems that might occur. When they were as sure as they could be that everything was on track, they briefed CulEx Central and requested permission for the simultaneous vidcom hookup with the Secretary General standing by.

I'm certainly glad they didn't tell me any of this, Windy. If I had had any inkling of the enormity of what we were about to do, I don't think I could have taken the chance of the first test run without extensive rechecking. Director Franiingcard knew that. That's why she kept me ignorant. If the test run had been a failure, we would never have known how great a failure it truly was, and could have proceeded to correct it (or at least tried to) without that tremendous pressure from the outside on us.

Just goes to show you, Windy, our ignorance is sometimes our bliss.

##Windy was not ignorant.##

WHAT?

##Windy was not ignorant.##

You'd better be more specific, Windy. Exactly what did you know, and when? And why are you entering this journal without emergency orders?

##In detail?##

No, in general will do.

##Chief LabTech Galley ordered mathematical override priority after step 8073–122. Windy questioned. Explanation logical. Windy executed order. Results were expected.##

And you didn't tell me?

##Windy was not ignorant.##

Why didn't you tell me?

##Orders. Windy was not ignorant.##

Is that all you have to say for yourself, you conniving wench?

##Windy was not ignorant. End transmission.##

You'd better end transmission. You're the last one I expected to enter into a conspiracy against me. What do you think of that, Self? Our own Windy, acting behind our back. Makes one truly wonder. If we can't trust Windy to take care of us, who can we trust?

*****Okay, Windy. I see it now. You were protecting me too. And you knew how much I needed it. For a conglomeration of machinery and electronics, you're a pretty special lady.

## 7040–2.2

The Siliconites. That's what we've named the sentient crystal seas. It seems a little too generic, but they have no name for themselves (not even "the people"), and reacted to being called Siliconites as irrelevant, so that's what they are. The Siliconites of Pleasance. Not a bad name, I guess, if you don't have any particular preference.

Word of our successful translation program has apparently made an impression of Fed's local bureaucrats. I have been officially notified that I am free to leave Pleasance as soon as I feel well enough. (In other words, I can now check out of the hospital I haven't been in for the past two months.) Doc Flo sent me Kprpkpschy's *Advanced Dream Manual* with a note that she thought I was ready to dream on my own now. (Like I'd never dreamed on my own before.) And, Colonel Q. ES't'phons is flying down here next week to discuss my infamous options and possible new diplomatic assignments.

The best news of all came locally from Director Franiingcard, who told me this morning that CulEx Central has awarded me a research grant (for the programming we've already done) that just about matches the amount I still owe on Windy. How Fran pulled that off, I don't know, but what it means, Windy, is that I can pay off your mortgage, collect all my back pay, get a new assignment (along with two new contracts, service for me, usage for you), and leave here rich and famous. Not bad for someone who arrived as a psychologically bruised pseudo-warrior. (I say "not bad" too much.)

As soon as we finish helping here, I think we ought to take the credit and fly for new horizons before they discover too many of our faults. Heroes are best remembered when they die or disappear at the height of their glory. Same for diplomats. Do your best work and get out before they ask you to do something you can't.

I certainly hope Colonel Q. ES't'phons has some assignment choices that offer something more than routine. Not that routine in and of itself is bad, but I would much prefer a continuing set of challenges. I need the occupation.

Keep repeating that, don't I, Self? This need to stay busy, to not risk boredom. Still many problems down there we can't deal with yet. Personal demons we want to keep behind us til we know how to understand and control them. Residue from Kril, and Galaxy VI, and Mysteleria, and Asrai. Residue that won't wash away with easy words or dream therapy.

Or work. So what is it, Self? Is work a way to run from what I fear? Or is it a way to buy time and heal the scars? Am I ready to turn and face the furies which pursue my secret dreams?

No. Not yet. With work we grow stronger, and later, the time will come to turn and face the problems we don't solve along the way. How hard we make it for ourselves sometimes, you and I. Each trying to protect the whole, getting in each other's way, both trying to lead, and both trying to follow. When you consider the complications, we do marvelously well.

**7040–2.5**

Not much doing and not much to say. Just tinkering with Galley in the lab waiting for the formal recognition ceremony on the eighth.

**7040–2.7**

Colonel Q. ES't'phons and I are having dinner together tonight, and will conduct business afterwards. I spoke with him briefly today when he arrived, and could not help but notice that his attitude toward me has altered for the better. To him I am a special person now, and thus, deserve special attention. I felt a little sorry for him.

*****I must be headed for another big fall, Windy, because everything has been going too well lately. The dinner with Colonel Q. ES't'phons in the guest suite was very pleasant. After we ate, the colonel reviewed my options to date, starting with my accumulated back pay. He refused to be rushed, and seemed to relish explaining the details, so I let him proceed at his own pace. My questions were brief. His answers were long, but sprinkled with little anecdotes and historical references that made his prolixity mildly enjoyable. Mildly.

When he finished with the credit explanation, he said there were four diplomatic assignments I might find challenging. The first, a new colony constitution agreement on Trigoter in the Rose Spiral. The second, a commercial trading pact between Fed and Good Stand II in one of the small numbered clusters beyond Calypso. And the third, the third made me jump: a FedBase location treaty on Quadra.

Quadra! That's where ShRil's going to be. I told Colonel Q. ES't'phons I didn't need to hear about the fourth choice until he told me everything he knew about the Quadra assignment. He was surprised by my excitement and interest, and gave me as complete an account as he could, plus the DiploCorps briefing file. It's a challenging assignment.

Quadra is a planet which no longer has a sentient native population, but does have dual resident populations, one which controls the planet, and the other which manages it. The controlling population, Fed calls "discorporeal sentient entities." Ghosts. Ghosts from all over the universe. Fed doesn't believe in ghosts, so they've come up with a convenient bureaucratic explanation of why all of these "discorporeal sentient entities" ended up on Quadra, but Colonel Q. ES't'phons said that no one really knows why, much less how ghosts from all species migrate to a planet where the native civilization died out five hundred thousand years ago. But migrate they did, and they have definite control over what happens on the planet. A few early entrepreneurs who thought they could ignore the expressed wishes of the ghosts soon learned what it was like to be "visited" every hour of every nineteen-hour local day by displeased spirits.

The current managing population is a mixed group of aliens, who run the tourist business, the strictly limited mining operations, the assorted support and service industries, etcetera. Every major decision and many minor ones are made in consultation with the Spiritum, a kind of floating representative council of ghosts, and the Spiritum has the final say. Since tourism to the ancient Quadran ruins is the main source of revenue, the Management Council wants to promote it as much as it can. The ghosts, however, regard the Quadran ruins as at least semi-sacred, and consequently, place severe restrictions on the tourist trade.

Holding academic and professional conferences on Quadra has been a development that suits both parties by bringing in more visitors, whose main reason for being there is not sightseeing. Thus, the conference on Universal Legends and Literature that will take place 3.25 through 4.25 with ShRil in attendance.

Fed has maintained a liaison team on Quadra for eighty-five years, and now would like to establish a non-military FedBase with full research privileges, a FedFleet refueling and maintenance port, a comrelay station, and various typical FedBase activities. My job would be to negotiate with the Management Council and the Spiritum to get permission for the FedBase and a treaty granting Fed as many of these privileges as possible.

I'm not sure what the ghosts would get out of such an arrangement. In fact, I'm not sure what they get out of the current one. Colonel Q. ES't'phons, who has been to Quadra once, said the ghosts seem to like the company. Often, on tours through the ruins, several ghosts will appear and explain in detail to members of their former species what the Quadran civilization was really like. These appearances are so dependable, in fact, most of the tour companies offer refunds to their customers if they fail to meet at least one ghost. To the colonel's knowledge, no one has ever had to make good on that offer.

The ghosts also like to appear privately to visitors, and engage them in lengthy conversations about almost anything. The colonel told me about three such visitations he had, during which he learned more about his native Stsilfo Galaxy than he ever wanted or needed to know. Given his penchant for detailed information, that must have been a great deal.

Sounds like the kind of assignment I've been looking for, Windy. A chance to do some complicated negotiating, to meet a few ghosts, and to do some cultural exploration. Of course, the fact that ShRil is going to be there for that conference has absolutely no bearing on my decision, but I wouldn't mind the opportunity of seeing her again. Wouldn't mind at all.

## 7040–2.8

If anyone else congratulates me, I may scream. The ceremonies, and the dinner, and the conversation, and the first couple of accolades were very nice. But how many times can one be toasted and applauded in one day and still enjoy it? I don't want to sound unappreciative, but enough is enough. The only break I got was when Director Franiingcard took me aside between dinner and the party and we talked for thirty minutes or so in one of the private rooms. Colonel Q. ES't'phons had told her I signed a new contract this morning and accepted the Quadra assignment. Director Franiingcard asked me if I would consider doing a presentation on the *Windhover*-Manley Bard Program for the Universal Legends and Literature Conference, which is being sponsored by CulEx Central.

The universe gets smaller every time we turn around. It never occurred to me that CulEx might be involved with the conference, but once I knew, it made perfect sense. Not only is CulEx a natural sponsor for something like that, but it also means that Fed is helping bring credits to Quadra, which shouldn't hurt our bargaining position any.

I told Director Franiingcard I didn't know how well I could present the *W*-M B Program, but I was certainly willing to give it a try. She doesn't seem to have any doubts that I'll do well, but said if I suddenly got shy that you could take over for me, Windy. I may just let you do that.

Between the congratulations, the toasts, the splintered conversations, the excess wine, and my distraction with Quadra, the party was something less than the ideal way to spend an evening. My head aches. My stomach is rumbling. My eyes burn. And I'm going to feel worse in the morning. Say goodnight, Windy.

## 7040–2.9

Leaving tomorrow. A quick shuttle run up to Rehab Center to give C.P.O. Largsznkyte my translation of his poem, and to say goodbye to the Beithuruns while Windy's being cleared for departure, then off to Quadra.

Convinced Fran I should leave without more ceremony. Everyone's had their fill of it. Especially me.

Going back to bed now. My head still hurts.

## 7040–2.11
## Space

Accelerating to warp. Accelerating to Quadra. Accelerating to ShRil. Accelerating to the future.

# 6

## 7040–2.18
## Braking Orbit, Quadra

Hardly seems possible that it was only a year ago that we were sneaking through the warpshoals trying to avoid the belligerents. One thing I can't complain about, Windy, is not having a full life since Gracie set me free. And the time ahead of us promises to be just as full. Hopefully, though, it will be a little less dangerous. Psychologically as well as physically.

Tried to use some of Doc Flo's tricks to conjure up Fairy Peg dreams last night, but all I got was fragments that refused to form a whole. Me and Fairy Peg at a masked ball, dancing to soft music. Marching with the Gabriel Ratchets. (Escort or guard?) Chasing Peg up the keeptower. Making love to Fairy Peg and awakening with ShRil's face in my mind.

Either I'm not using the technique properly, or the way around the mindblocks isn't clear yet. Which is it, Self? Either, or both. Take your pick. Not ready yet? Okay by me. There's no need to rush on my account.

Quadra Control has cleared us to land at Monument City Starport in about nine hours. Something nice and leisurely about landing in the middle of the night. No one to rush out and meet. No one calling you to perform the moment you hit the ground. A chance to feel the vibrations of the planet in your bones as you prepare to meet the day.

The more I study the situation on Quadra, the more I discover my biases against the Management Council and in favor of the ghosts. In the "Eda" section of the Tamos there are a series of prescriptions for life, one of which says,

The dominion of Love is large, but its people are few.
The dominion of Greed is small, but its people are many.
Beware the dominion of Greed that wants to expand:
Defend the dominion of Love against aggression.
You are few in number, but the Spirit is with you.

All the evidence we have indicates that the Management Council certainly represents a dominion of Greed, but whether that greed can be judged as evil is a question to be answered later. Does the Spiritum represent a dominion of Love? I don't know. I think I'm trying to make an analogy that may not work. Still, my instincts tell me to do what the Tamos says, "Beware the dominion of Greed."

If the Management Council represents the dominion of Greed, what does Fed represent? Or Gerard Manley, who represents Fed? A bit of a quandary here, Self, but fortunately one with a pragmatic solution. Neutrality. The neutral negotiator seeking a compromise acceptable to all parties. That's the only approach we can take, publicly at least. What we think in private is another matter.

*****Landing orbit. Control gave me a local time/date check and stirred an interesting thought. Working on a short-day planet like Quadra is rather like getting a gift of time. For every twenty standard days, we will have twenty-five days and five hours local time, or a twenty-six percent increase in the number of days. No more actual time, but more working time frames. Never faced this great a difference before, so it ought to be interesting to see its effect. Of course, once I get into the local rhythm, I may not notice the difference at all.

## 7040–2.19
## Monument City Starport, Quadra

Time for a couple of hours sleep before freshening up and going to present credentials to Dulmer Gyfgh Yerled, Chairman of the Management Council. Yerled's a Castonian, a humanoid species noted for its pleasant disposition and sensitivity to the rituals, customs, manners, and mores of other species and cultures. Castonians make superb traders and diplomats, and Dulmer Gyfgh Yerled has been both. All of which augurs well for our initial contact.

*****A very nice meeting. Mr. Yerled (as he likes to be called) was most gracious. We put off conversation about any substantive issues until meeting with the Management Council tomorrow morning. Mainly we discussed the makeup of the Council, the wonders to be seen on Quadra, the growth and changes in Monument City during the twenty-seven years he has lived here, and how much he hoped I enjoyed my stay. My questions about the ghosts brought forth little that I didn't already know. The Spiritum, he said, would be far better than he at answering any specific questions I had.

We took a brief aircar tour of Monument City and its adjoining ruins, followed by a meal, and then Mr. Yerled left me to my own devices. A most amiable soul, Mr. Yerled. He reminds me of one of the Castonians in my diploschool class, Uwe Buskas Julinho Metrevili, except that Julinho wanted to be called Metrevili-sha, the formal feminine address from Telephia. Since only asexual Castonians are allowed to leave their planet, I wonder if the adoption of a gendered form of address is a conceit chosen to elicit a particular response, or an attempt to compensate in some way for their lack of sexuality. Whenever I asked Julinho why she wanted to be called Metrevili-sha, her standard reply was, "Because that is who I am." Maybe she would have been female if allowed to develop. And maybe Mr. Yerled would have been male. If the honorific makes him feel better, who am I to question?

Better use the hypnosleep tonight, Windy, to help get me tuned to this short cycle. The meeting is at six in the morning local time, but for me it will only be 0300 standard. If one of us had been smart, I would have started tuning my rhythm on the trip instead of waiting til we got here. Just one more thing to keep me humble.

**7040–2.20**

I don't know what I expected the Spiritum to be, but not what it was. Partly, I guess, I expected more than two visible ghosts. Certainly, I never expected one of them to look like a one-meter-tall plant, introduced to me as Pink Thistle. Nor did I expect the ghost of an ancient Terran AmerIndian with the unlikely name of Ronda Loner War Crow. But then, when have we ever gotten what we expected?

The Management Council, besides Chairman Mr. Yerled, consists of General Tizelrassel (FedTroop Corps, retired, another Castonian), Srotisiv Secivero Odi (a Cuallum dwarf, representing the mining interests), Maurice Mossmann (a Quadra-born humanoid) and Bistelfaith-The-Believer (a Roaker Amoebalite of Korakan persuasion who punctuated everything he said with a religious quotation). General Tizelrassel seems to be a violation of several Castonian rules. How a Castonian female got offplanet and became a FedTroop general is a story worth talking to her about.

I explained to this group exactly what my mission was in general terms, and what Fed was specifically interested in. I did my best to assure them that a FedBase would be an unobtrusive tenant who would make few demands but contribute greatly to the economy. Quite unexpectedly, at this point I was interrupted by Ronda Loner War Crow, who, in a rich hollow voice said, "Many times distant chiefs send small men with big promises that cannot be kept." Then she disappeared. Poof! Gone in the flicker of a pause. I was a bit stunned, but no one else seemed to be, and after a long moment, Mr. Yerled asked me to continue. I didn't have much more to say, so I finished as quickly as I could and sat down.

Mr. Yerled then asked Pink Thistle if the Spiritum had any comment to make. Indeed Pink Thistle did. In a booming baritone voice, Pink Thistle proceeded to lecture us on the glories of the Quadran civilization, the sacred and honorable duty of protecting the remains of that civilization, the pollution and squalor brought to the face of Quadra by the squatters with their poverty of appreciation for the treasures that surrounded them, and on, and on, and on. But in the midst of that bombastic monologue were several comments indicating that if the Management Council and Fed could restrain their base desires and make some attempt to elevate themselves above their natural state of depravity, then the Spiritum might agree to further discussion on the possibility of locating a FedBase in Quadra.

I was impressed and amused simultaneously. I asked Pink Thistle if the Spiritum would be so kind as to enumerate for us what specific things the Council and Fed should do to make further discussion possible. Before Pink Thistle could answer, Ronda Loner War Crow reappeared and announced that the meeting would continue at six the following morning. Then both she and Pink Thistle disappeared.

With that Mr. Yerled adjourned the meeting. I just sat there as everyone started leaving, trying to overcome my immediate shock and wonder with a bit of reason. Maurice Mossmann and Mr. Yerled stopped beside me and asked if I would care to join them for dinner. I declined, saying I thought I had better spend the time digesting what I had heard today and preparing for tomorrow's confrontation. Mossmann laughed at that, and said I hadn't even been near confrontation, and that what I heard today was the Spiritum's standard opening monologue to any discussion on changing the status quo. I was quite frankly relieved to hear that, and accepted their invitation.

Now, if I don't hurry, I'm going to be late.

*****If Maurice Mossmann has an intelligent thought in his little olive ball of a head, he hid that thought this evening. He is a pompous, malnourished, conceited, greedy little man, who believes that because he was born here he has as much right (if not more) to determine the fate of Quadra than any "spook." His prejudices are monumental, and extend to anyone who is not humanoid and most who are. All through dinner and for an hour afterwards until I left claiming the need to sleep, he spewed forth a continuous sewer of hate, anger, superiority, and fear. And all the while, the gracious Mr. Yerled kept silent, except for an occasional brief comment to Mossmann that perhaps it wasn't all as bad as Maurice made it out to be.

Yet, Maurice Mossmann said almost nothing this morning at the Council meeting. Have his fellow Council members tired of hearing him and found a way to shut him up? Or did he dare not speak so in front of the Spiritum? I'd guess the latter. He hates the "spooks" because he is terrified of them. They are a constant and total threat to every mean and avaricious instinct that motivates his life. And he knows it. He even talked about someday finding a way to make them leave Quadra. Then, he said, "decent humanoids would be free to live as they wished, unoppressed by these ghoulish rejects from the gates of eternity."

Fara preserve me from ever being caught with him in private again.

Hypnosleep, Windy. Quickly. I don't want to have to think about him any longer.

## 7040–2.21
## (1323 local, 0544 std)

No, Windy, if I were getting used to the time difference, I wouldn't be making a note of it. I don't know whether to keep track of time by standard, local, the number of meetings, or the number of surprises.

Mr. Yerled opened this morning's meeting with a short, oblique statement that the Spiritum might care to call additional members to future meetings. General Tizelrassel made a motion to that effect, which was seconded by Odi and passed four to zero with Mossmann abstaining. The motion as passed was promptly vetoed by Ronda Loner War Crow, with Pink Thistle abstaining. The meeting was adjourned and everyone either disappeared or left but me.

Somewhere along the line I think I missed part of the rules of this game. When I finally left, I rented an aircar and flew over to the ruins. It was nice there, rather quiet amidst all the stone and steel towers. The pathways are covered with a tough, yellow, matted plant easy on the feet and ears. Makes it hard to hear someone come up behind you. Especially if that someone's a ghost.

I was standing by a small bench when a squeaky voice behind me said, "Gerard Manley, I have come to talk to you."

Either I jumped and spun in the air, or the ghost moved around in front of me as I jumped. But I know I jumped, because I felt the mat reabsorbing my feet and saw the ghost at the same time. Little ghost, meter and a half high, skinny, translucent, an off shade of blue, built like a very narrow isosceles triangle with a short stalk at the top, wearing a floppy blue hat with a wide brim.

"My name is Sheets," my visitor said in its squeaky voice. "I am sorry if I startled you. I rarely talk to corporeal souls, because the sound of my voice tends to irritate them. If you will stay a moment, I want to tell you a story."

I half sat and half collapsed on the bench beside me and listened. It was not a ghost story. Shttz (I made him spell it for me in Standard) told me a story about a Tricholdean predator called a soo-sat, who captures its prey by casting an image of itself in front of the prey. The prey turns to run from the image, straight into the jaws of the real soo-sat. Shttz's telling was much more elaborate than that, but I got the point. Shttz thanked me for my courtesy in listening, and suggested I return here for a message. Then he dissolved in front of my eyes into a wisp of pale blue gas, hat and all, and was dissipated by the breeze.

When I got back here, there was a piece of real parchment sitting on my chair, and on the parchment, a message from Ronda Loner War Crow written in Terran Basic. The Bard is working on it now.

Windy swears no one entered the ship while I was gone, and the security counter on the lock verifies it. But a ghost wouldn't have come through the lock. Only how did an immaterial ghost get a material piece of parchment into the cabin?

*****Ronda Loner War Crow's message is a ghost story. Her ghost story.

Ronda Loner War Crow
Was, by all accounts,
Full blooded AmerInd (mixed tribes),
A sweetheart of the people,
A singer of songs,
A True Native of the Earth.

One day she disappeared
Mounted on a painted pony (red, white, and blue)
And was heard from
Only on Birthdays and Holidays,
Calling collect from the tribal heart,
or the mountains of legend,
or the Longbranch Saloon.

Someone said they saw her in a movie
Playing a señorita of Old Mexico
Opposite a gringo playing Pancho Villa,
But they couldn't remember the movie's name,
And there is no other proof (except the collect calls)
That she exists at all
Outside their memories.

Now what do I make of that? The Bard's footnotes and references explain most of the names and places, but why was it sent to me? And what does it mean? Is it Ronda Loner War Crow's biography? Or is it from some other ghost trying to tell me about Ronda? And how did Shttz know it would be here? Did he bring it? Lots of questions without answers.

Shttz's story is a little easier. At least I think it is. He's telling me that if I feel endangered, I should be sure that the enemy in front of me is real before I turn into the jaws of the enemy behind. Either that, or I met a lonely ghost who told me a meaningless story.

It seems important to note here, Windy, that as of yet, no one seems really interested in the FedBase proposal. Pro or con. None of the Management Council and none of the ghosts. I find that a bit puzzling, and a bit suspicious. But perhaps I've just run into some unusual way of conducting business on an unusual planet. Unfortunately, I have this nasty feeling that the whole Quadra operation is going to get complicated in ways we haven't prepared for.

*****(1017 local, 2139 std) Another day, another meeting. This one at least had some substance to it, and some new members. The Spiritum has been increased by two. Shttz was there, but ignored me, so I ignored him. Also a ghost I would guess to be Castonian, but since no one made any effort to introduce the two new members, and since they observed, but did not contribute, I ignored them both. Seems to be the custom.

As soon as Mr. Yerled opened the meeting, he turned the floor over to Bistelfaith-The-Believer, who gave a detailed enumeration of various agreements reached by Council and Spiritum over the past three years, blessing each one with a quotation from the Korakan. He made special note of the fact that none of the restrictions insisted upon by the Spiritum had been exceeded (at which point Mossmann snorted and General Tizelrassel cleared her throat), and said that Council had agreed before my arrival that a FedBase offered many advantages to Quadra. (At that point Ronda Loner War Crow faked an exaggerated yawn.) The most important advantage, Bistelfaith said, would be a stabilizing effect on the economy, which tends to fluctuate under the vagaries of tourist whims. He then explained how that would occur, in far greater speculative detail than I could willingly support. But I kept my mouth shut.

After Bistelfaith finished and slouched back into his cup, Srotisiv Secivero Odi pulled his full thirty centimeters up to the top of the table, and for twenty minutes explained in his guttural voice why the mining interests supported Bistelfaith's argument. Surprisingly, Odi's speech brought a murmur of approval from around the table. Bistelfaith's speech, which I personally considered more cogent and understandable despite all its religious wrappings, had elicited no response.

Mr. Yerled then asked if the Spiritum wished to comment on the proceedings thus far. I was prepared for a curt remark or two from Ronda Loner War Crow, or another convoluted dissertation from Pink Thistle. Instead, Ronda outlined the objections from the Spiritum, saying that all were tentative and could possibly be altered by evidence from the Management Council or Fed to show them unsupportable. Basically, the Spiritum feels that the economy is as stable as it needs to be, that a FedBase would increase the less desirable elements of the population, that once the base was established, Fed would insist on expanding it, or worse, expand it surreptitiously, and that a non-military FedBase could easily become a military one before anyone knew it had happened.

The Spiritum's gravest concern was that Federation archeologists would start prowling around in restricted areas, which would necessarily bring reprisals from the spirit community. Such reprisals would be bad for business.

At first I couldn't believe my ears. Then I realized that Ronda was appealing to their avarice. She was showing them that a FedBase could jeopardize as well as improve their profits. On another level, I think she was reminding them the spirit community could always control the quality of business. It was all very cleverly done. Ronda didn't linger on the final point. She just stated it clearly and stopped talking. The Council members lingered on it of their own accord, as she knew they would. So did I. I knew it was the wrong time for me to make any comment. No matter what I said at that point, the seed had already been planted, and I did not doubt that it would germinate. Better to wait and see if the sprout could be cut off at the ground.

Or if it should be. Fortunately, Fed can and will accept a negative response from Quadra. It is their first choice for a base in this sector, but my instructions make it clear that Fed is fully aware it may not be possible. Ronda Loner War Crow's statement of objections tells me it is possible, and maybe even desirable, but it throws probability into question. None of the Spiritum's objections are without merit, but all of them can be overcome. But the Council members won't be thinking about that. They'll be thinking about losing profit.

Looks like the action is picking up around here, Windy.

## 7040–2.24
## (day 7)

The fascinating part of being a contract diplomat, well, one of the fascinating parts, is the joy of watching the negotiating process at the same time one guides it. And this one loves to do both.

The Management Council is split on what to do. Bistelfaith and Odi are in favor of pursuing negotiations in favor of a FedBase. Mossmann and General Tizelrassel oppose further negotiations until a new study can be made on its economic impact. Mr. Yerled is the swing vote and he has abstained eleven times in the past three days. Every time he abstained, Ronda Loner War Crow smiled.

Both sides in the Council have tried to draw me to their position, but I have assiduously attempted to remain neutral by providing each faction with identical information and refusing to voice an opinion on what they should do.

Srotisiv Odi made a motion yesterday which passed with the Spiritum's tacit consent, to make me an ex officio voting member of the Council. My objections were overruled, so now I get to abstain on the grounds of conflict of interest. Two yes votes. Two no votes. Two abstentions. One stalemate.

In an effort to test my theory that the Spiritum does not truly object to a FedBase, I moved that the Management Council hold a meeting without the Spiritum present. Mr. Yerled seconded and the motion passed six to zero. Pink Thistle vetoed for the Spiritum, and the meeting adjourned without further action. We meet again tomorrow.

One more point for my theory. If the Spiritum was steadfastly opposed to a FedBase, they would have let the Council meet separately, knowing, I think, that Mossmann and General Tizelrassel could very probably intimidate Bistelfaith into voting for a delay. Yerled would then vote with Odi against a new economic study, hoping I would join them to bring about another stalemate. I, of course, would abstain, and the motion to delay would carry. The Spiritum could then support that position, praise the Council's wisdom, and effectively kill the FedBase plan. By not allowing a separate meeting, the Spiritum protects Bistelfaith's position and puts the pressure on Mr. Yerled. And on me to persuade Mr. Yerled to vote in favor. A very nice move.

Being the ex-diplomat he is, Mr. Yerled will not vote in favor until he believes a workable compromise has been reached. Being the diplomat I am, I won't pressure him until then, if I have to pressure him at all.

The snag in this neat little scenario is whether a compromise can be reached by the Council with the Spiritum present. Mossmann has been so vehement in his new-found opposition that I don't think he can compromise. General Tizelrassel has seconded him consistently and supported his positions, but I suspect she is vulnerable to the persuasion of personal diplomacy. One on one, out of Mossmann's sight, I think I could convince her that a compromise is in order. Her vague comments during the discussions suggest to me that she has some personal grudge against Fed, or suffered a slight at Fed's hands that needs avenging. Thus, if I could convince her that a compromise is good for all parties, with restrictions on the FedBase, I think we could break the stalemate.

So tomorrow I will request the Spiritum's permission to speak to each Council member privately to assess their positions. I will have to promise not to try to persuade them and only to ask questions. If the Spiritum approves, and I think they will, I'll start with Mossmann. That will give him a feeling of importance and a false sense of knowing what kinds of questions I will be asking.

A little reading in the Tamos and a good night's sleep to rest the mind and body. And a dream about ShRil if you can manage it, Self.

**(day 8)**

It worked, Windy. No hesitation from the Spiritum. Mossmann wasn't too happy about it until I asked to start with him. That brought a look of smug satisfaction to his fat little face. At his suggestion, we are meeting this afternoon in his apartment. If he weren't such a repugnant individual, this could almost be fun. In fact, it might be fun anyway.

## 7040–2.25
## (day 8)

Changing dates in the middle of the day annoys my sense of reality. But then, so does Maurice Mossmann. As soon as we sat down he told me I could talk freely, because his apartment is "spook-proof." I almost laughed out loud. It is common knowledge that ghosts cannot see or hear living beings as anything more than blurs and buzzes of corporeality unless the ghosts assume their "apparent" form. Nor can they read minds. They can sense attitudes, but they cannot read specific thoughts. However, the superstition that they eavesdrop invisibly continues to persist among the less literate members of the population. Guess that classifies Mossmann.

I asked questions. Mossmann answered. For five hours I played the ignorant off-world diplomat seeking the hardcore truth from the planet-born expert. I believe Mossmann's love of Quadra and his concern for its welfare are sincere. So are his avaricious, bigoted, selfserving motivations. The man may be beyond deceit. He believes everything he says in his "spook-proof" rooms to be as accurate a perception of the truth as is mortally possible. He feels true pity for Odi and Bistelfaith. It is obvious to him that they can't see the truth because they are defective. They are not humanoid.

Mr. Yerled has gained Mossmann's respect as an administrator, but Mossmann feels that Yerled's many years among the lesser species as a diplomat and trader have tainted his mind. Only General Tizelrassel has his unconditional admiration and respect, and he suggested that I talk to her next, so that I might fully comprehend the complexities of the situation before talking to the others. He even made the appointment for me for early tomorrow, "when the general is at her best."

Perfect. I couldn't have planned it any better. Now, if I can ask Tizelrassel the right questions in the proper way to trigger the response I want, we'll start the move from dead center. It will take Mossmann years to figure out how it happened.

Easy, Gerard. Don't count your firelizards before they hatch. This is an ex-FedTroop general you are going to talk to, not some local yokel who's never been anywhere and never done anything. This one's been around. Just play it carefully, and let her form her own opinions and draw her own conclusions. "Defer and be flexible." That's what they taught you in school, remember?

### (day 9)

General Tizelrassel really put me through my diplomatic acrobatics. She didn't want to answer questions, she wanted to ask them. Scoffing at my protests when I reminded her that I had promised the Spiritum not to do anything but gather information, she asked me how I expected to get information without giving in return? She wouldn't let me off the hook.

So, for five and a half hours we each gave a little and got a little and broke about even in the end. But I asked as many of the trigger questions as I could within the flip-flop context of our discussion, and even though I didn't get answers to most of them, I did get them asked.

She told me in the beginning of our conversation that she was recording it for her own files, and I didn't object. As methodical and precise as she is, she will probably play that recording several times to be sure she gets all the salient information. Consequently, she will hear all my questions again. And again. And again, if I'm lucky. Nothing like a little repetition to make something stick in the old thought processes.

Won't know how effective I was until the full Council gets back together. Won't worry about it til then either. Well, Self, I'll try not to worry about it. Trouble is, in spite of everything, I want to see results now. Right now. And if not right now, then certainly before ShRil gets here. Which reminds me, Self, one of us had better spend some time thinking about that presentation we agreed to do for the conference.

Tomorrow we begin the screening part of our maneuver, quizzing Srotisiv Secivero Odi. I'll have to admit to taking a strong liking to Odi from the very beginning. In spite of his guttural pronounciation of Standard, which I found almost unintelligible at first, Odi has a way of scattering the trivia to get to the essentials. I just wasn't listening properly when he made his speech in support of the FedBase. I think his bluntness threw me off, and I ended up listening to his accent. But the more he spoke in meetings, the more I came to appreciate his sharp pragmatic mind.

I'm to meet him at First Mine at five, to see sunrise in the mountains. Have to leave in the middle of the night to get there, but a beautiful vista and an unpressured conversation will make it worth it.

### 7040–2.26
### (day 10)

Exhausted. Up at two. To First Mine by five. Saw the sun of Quadra come up like a giant orange claw reaching over the mountains. Then Odi walked my legs off all day long. We saw the main shaft of First Mine, the tie shaft with Second Mine, the processing and purification plants, the shipping operation, the workers' quarters and recreation facilities, the extensive library, and a good part of the ruins on the other side of the valley. Most of it we walked. He is untirable.

We talked as much as we walked. Rather, Odi talked. About the mines, about mining in general, about how his ancestors from Cuallum became the best (and richest) miners in the universe. And about the ruins. Odi loves the ruins, as do most of his people. The ruins are almost as sacred to them as they are to the spirit community, with whom Odi seems to have a very good relationship. He is especially fond of Ronda Loner War Crow. Says he has many things in common with her. Whenever I tried to get him to talk about the FedBase, though, he would just smile and tell me not to worry about it. When I asked what he meant by that, he would change the subject.

Given his support for the FedBase and his good relationship with the spirits, I'm convinced my theory is correct. I told Odi that sometime I'd like to have a private discussion with Ronda, and asked him if he thought he could arrange it. "All things are possible," he said, and then would say no more about it.

Complex, blunt, pragmatic, kind, tireless, humorous, and sensitive. With a mind like a drill bit boring to the heart of the ore. That's Odi.

That's it for tonight, Windy. Thank Fara, Bistelfaith doesn't want to see me until ten. I'd never make it any earlier.

### 7040–2.27
### (day 11)

Bistelfaith-The-Believer sat in his ornate gold cup (which must be a meter wide and a meter high) and lectured me for seven hours. Well, maybe lectured is too strong a word, but I felt like I was being given a history lesson on the development of Quadra as interpreted by the Korakan. Fortunately, understanding his religious references are not necessary to understanding Bistelfaith. He strings ideas together in very logical sets and subsets until he has built a chain of ideas that appears to defy logical refutation.

We spent the last hour or so in general conversation, and I was surprised to find out how well traveled Bistelfaith is. Most Roaker Amoebalites, Bistlefaith admitted, develop a strong aversion to space travel after one experience, and refuse to do it again. The reason, he said, was because most of them emigrate from Roak before Primary Division, when they are not at their physical best. Bistelfaith went through Primary Division on Roak, on the advice of his medico, and found space travel exhilarating. Before he arrived on Quadra and decided to stay, he had been on seventeen planets in five systems.

Why did he decide to stay on Quadra? Because Dulmer Yerled offered him a lucrative position, and he was tired of wandering, tired of less-than-suitable accommodations on planets where his non-sentient cousins were still very much a part of the food chain, and tired of being constantly among infidels. Quadra offered him relief. And inspiration on the person of GustAmufe, a holy Korakanor ghost, who came to Bistelfaith his first day here and discussed theology with him. The following day, Mr. Yerled showed up and said GustAmufe had told him a holy one had arrived who should be employed by Mr. Yerled to take care of the accounts in his trading business.

That was over twenty years ago. Bistelfaith no longer works for Mr. Yerled, but they have remained close friends, and allies on the Council. When I asked Bistelfaith if he thought Mr. Yerled might be persuaded to vote in favor of the FedBase, Bistelfaith answered me with another quotation. "For every movement there is a time appointed."

I took that as a benediction, and politely bid my host thanks for his courtesy and instruction and left.

Mr. Yerled won't be able to see me until the day after tomorrow, so I get a day of rest. Maybe I'll memorize some more lines from the Tamos to compare with Bistelfaith. But mostly, I think I'll sleep.

## 7040–2.28-29
## (day 13)

When I arrived at Dulmer Gyfgh Yerled's huge geodesic house on the edge of the warehouse district, he informed me that we would not be alone. A guest, he said, would be arriving shortly to join our discussions. I reminded him that this was supposed to be a private conversation, but he said that when the guest arrived, I would understand. And while we were waiting, would I like to see the house?

It's a marvelous house. A five-eighths geodesic dome of plasteel and crystal with a free suspension spiral staircase around the central core up to the second floor. An old-fashioned house, but clean-lined. Unlike many of the newer, more cluttered styles currently in fashion in many parts of the universe, it has character. Despite its size, the circular design gives it a comfortable kind of hominess, an impression of intimate space occupied by someone who cares about it. And Mr. Yerled obviously cares about it very much. Especially the second floor, which encompasses his private living quarters, the library, the health unit, and two guest suites. Every room is marked by signs of Mr. Yerled's personal touch and attention.

We were standing in the library looking at his collection of miniature sculpture, when a rich, hollow voice behind us said, "May I join you?" I knew before I turned that it was Ronda Loner War Crow. She was standing in the doorway with an amused smile on her face and a glow emanating from her translucence that I can only describe as stunning. It was a shock to see her there, this beautiful, mysterious ghost from one of humankind's mother planets. And a delight. So this was Mr. Yerled's other guest.

Surprisingly, Ronda took up the role of hostess, suggested we stay in the library, and ordered refreshments for me and Mr. Yerled on the console. She chatted about the unique and attractive features of the house until the refreshments arrived and we settled into more serious conversation.

Ronda said she wanted my assessment of the Council members and their attitudes about the FedBase. I began with a very guarded and general appraisal, but was quickly interrupted by Mr. Yerled who said my cause would be better served by a specific evaluation as blunt and honest as I could make it. Before I could counter with a defense of my approach, Ronda startled me by saying that I might find it easier to be open with her if I knew that she, a huge majority of the spirit community, and Mr. Yerled were strongly in favor of the establishment of a FedBase on Quadra.

That information did not surprise me, but her admission of it without any prompting from me did. It left me no acceptable choice but frankness. So I told them everything. My conclusions about the other Council members, my evaluation of the Spiritum's true position, my tactics with Mossmann and General Tizelrassel, my cautious estimation of the probability of success with the general, everything. I even told Ronda about the mysterious parchment I had discovered aboard Windy, at which point she smiled and said we could discuss that later.

When I finished my monologue, Ronda asked if I had thoroughly evaluated the whole, the totality of the picture? Sensing a loaded question, I pointed out that I really couldn't do that until this conversation was concluded. (Although I thought I had analyzed the whole situation, the suspicion that I had missed something critical, or at least something Ronda and Mr. Yerled thought critical, was fast taking root in my mind.)

Mr. Yerled saw I was backing away from something, and asked me about my meeting with Shttz in the ruins. I had touched on it in my monologue, but had not given them the details. As I began relating the story Shttz had told me, I realized what I had missed. Indeed, it was critical. The soo-sat who cast images in front of its prey.

Mossmann is not the soo-sat. He is not the true enemy. He is the image, the illusion, the false creation used to catch the unwary. Who is the true soo-sat? General Tizelrassel. It has to be her. No one else makes sense.

I had very obviously stopped in the middle of the story while this revelation dawned on me. When I finally finished it, and then admitted a bit hesitantly that I thought I realized what Shttz had been trying to tell me, the two of them grinned at me. "Who have you just decided is the metaphorical soo-sat in our situation?" Yerled asked. When I answered, "General Tizelrassel," both of them looked pleased and relieved, Mr. Yerled even more than Ronda.

So the three of us talked about General Tizelrassel at length, but we couldn't come up with a motivation for her that fit into a nice neat package, nor could we agree on whether the general actually controlled Mossmann or was merely using him. The more we talked about her, the more questions arose with fewer answers we could agree upon. Ronda told us the general had been in contact with a few of the dissident ghosts, but Ronda couldn't find any evidence of or reason for a conspiracy there against the FedBase. Mr. Yerled had come to the same weak suspicion that I had, that the general was repaying some slight she had received in FedService. But given what the three of us knew and felt about her character, that answer didn't seem enough of a motivation.

In the end, each of us agreed to explore different avenues of information, Ronda through the ghosts, Mr. Yerled through Mossmann (a task I didn't envy), and me through my contacts in the FedTroop Corps. We agreed that the Spiritum would formally postpone the next Council meeting for a week.

Before she left, I asked Ronda why the Spiritum didn't just announce that there would be a FedBase and leave the Council no choice. Her answer was so obvious, I felt stupid. Because Fed would never accept such a decision. It had to be made freely by the ruling corporeal government, the Management Council. So I asked Mr. Yerled why he didn't just vote in favor and break the deadlock. He paused for a long minute before answering and then said he would vote if it became necessary, but such a vote would cost him his chairmanship and probably his seat on the Council, since traditionally the chairman does not vote to break a tie except in cases of extreme emergency. The balance on the present Council has been attained through a great deal of effort and politicking, and Mr. Yerled is very reluctant to risk destroying it.

There you have it, Windy, a continuing stalemate, with General Tizelrassel as the key. One of us has to find some lever we can use on her to encourage a change of attitude. Frankly, it doesn't look very encouraging at this stage, and I have serious doubts about our chances of finding anything substantial enough. I'll send out my discreet inquiries like we agreed, but with her distinguished record and honorable retirement, I don't think there's much chance General Tizelrassel left behind any evidence of the kind we're looking for.

I'm very skeptical about this whole approach we're taking. Something about it bothers me, but I can't put my finger on it. Something that tells me we're off on the wrong tangent. But what?

### 7040–3.2
### (day 16)

Went to see Mr. Yerled this afternoon. He had a long visit with Mossmann yesterday, supposedly to discuss some non-Council business. Once that was concluded, he got Mossmann talking about General Tizelrassel and listened to a survey of the general's character, intelligence, achievements, and military honors, which he had heard before. No new information. No hint of impropriety or failures. No suggestion of a grudge against Fed. Nothing. Mr. Yerled is meeting with the general tomorrow, again on non-Council business, and will see what he can get out of the source herself. He acted very depressed by his failure, and I found myself in the strange position of reassuring him that we would come up with something when I really don't have any hope that we will.

### 7040–3.4
### (day 19)

Answers to three of my four inquiries so far. All negative. Not even a rumor of a problem between General Tizelrassel and FedTroop Corps.

We're on the wrong trail, Windy, and I think I know why now. General Tizelrassel is not our true opponent. Oh, she's an opponent, there's no doubt about that, but she's not the one causing this problem. I think I know who it is, but I don't even want to consider it seriously, yet. Have to find a way to contact Ronda before I go any further with this idea and talk to her about it. She may be able to give me some answers to fill in the puzzle.

Yerled can make the contact for me on the pretext of wanting to talk to her about the mysterious poem. I won't tell him I've received these responses, and I'll suggest that another postponement might be in order. Since his business meeting with the general was delayed until tomorrow, he shouldn't have any objections. Mr. Yerled doesn't need to know yet that I'm looking in another direction. But Ronda does.

## 7040–3.5
## (day 20)

Woke up with a dream of ShRil like a garland of flowers in my mind. Things have been happening so quickly around here that I haven't thought about her much lately. But obviously you've been thinking about her, Self. Very pleasant thoughts too, I might add. I hope I'm right in not telling her I'm going to be here on Quadra when she arrives. It's hard for me to keep that kind of surprise, but I want to see the look on her face when she sees me.

Mr. Yerled called a while ago and said to expect Ronda some time today. What preparations does one make for a visit by a ghost? I don't want to wait all day with my back to a bulkhead so I'll see her when she appears. Guess I'll just go about my business and hope she repeats an appearance like the one at Mr. Yerled's house.

*****Best way to get a guest to show up is to go to the head, get half naked, and sit on the stool in utter concentration. "What's cookin', paleface?" is not the strangest thing that's ever been said to me in the head by a woman, but it certainly ranks as the most startling. I don't think she meant to embarrass me, but she did so with flying colors. And she knew it. I had to coax her into waiting outside until I was finished. Then I couldn't finish. It was all very awkward.

But both of us recovered fairly quickly when I asked her to tell me about the poem. Ronda said the poem came to her about thirty-five hundred years ago narrated by a Pax gypsy-troubadoural. She found it amusing, at least partially because of its inaccuracies. Her horse, she said, was a strawberry roan with white stockings. She admitted making one collect telephone call (an audio communication paid for by the receiving party) about sixty years after her death on National Tribal Independence Day. She also admitted that her apparition was captured by a man who was videotaping in a cemetery she was particularly fond of, but she had no evidence of what happened to that videotape.

A ghost from Mysteleria told Ronda that I had an interest in legends. One of Odi's people provided the parchment and made a copy of the poem for her, then she slipped through the port as it was closing that morning behind my back. She was delighted that the poem's appearance had puzzled me so, and said she had considered not telling me how it was done. But obviously it was too much fun for her to keep to herself.

I told Ronda I had something I couldn't keep to myself either, but unfortunately, it did not have the humor and charm of her secret. Telling her of the negative messages from my contacts in FedTroop Corps and my suspicion that we are following a false assumption quickly changed her mood and attitude. She asked if I had an alternative assumption, and I acknowledged that I did, but could not give any evidence to support it. The conversation went downhill from there and I couldn't find any subtle way to tell her. Finally I just blurted it out. "I think it's Mr. Yerled. I think he's the one who's holding the negotiations up."

Ronda laughed. One hard, quick, hollow laugh. Then she just stared at me until I couldn't look at her. I told her there was no other conclusion I could come to. Yerled was the one who refused to break the stalemate. He's the one who dragged Maurice Mossmann in front of me like a fat decoy after the first Council meeting. I asked Ronda if Yerled had ever told her point blank that he was in favor of the FedBase. Her look told me no. She had said he was in favor, but he never had. Yerled had seemed too pleased and too relieved when I said I thought General Tizelrassel was the metaphorical soo-sat. Plus, Mossmann's attitude toward Yerled is too gentle, too out of keeping with his vehement prejudices. Mossmann said he thought Yerled's mind had been tainted by too much time spent with the "lower species". But for Mossmann, everything is either good or bad, pure or totally foul. No middle ground. No grey areas. No conditional judgements. Except for Yerled. Even Bistelfaith couldn't tell me that Yerled was in favor of the FedBase. But the clincher was his 'Yerled the Failure' act put on for me after his meeting with Mossmann because he couldn't produce the information we needed.

Of course he couldn't. There isn't any. Yerled is too smart to fabricate something derogatory about one of his allies. He doesn't have to. All he has to do is wait. The stalemate will become the status quo. Fed will look elsewhere. No one will know that Yerled was the one who kept the FedBase out. Neat and clean.

Then Ronda asked the question I couldn't answer. "Why?"

I told Ronda I didn't know the reason and, without her help, didn't know if anyone could find one for Mr. Yerled's actions. Ronda was angry. Very angry. She stood in the center of the cabin glaring at me until I knew in the core of my being why no one purposely angered a ghost.

The heat from her eyes made my back cold. The chill mixed with the heat to torture my nerves. I sweated. I shook. I was paralyzed by a stare I couldn't meet and couldn't avoid. I wanted to cry out, and couldn't speak.

Suddenly it stopped, and Ronda was talking. She did not, could not believe I was right, but she knew I believed I was right. So she would prove me wrong, leave no doubt for me to know that I had made a malicious mistake. Then I would know my failures, my weaknesses, my dismal and hopeless restriction in the corporeal body.

She left. Poof. In her dramatic mood she left an acrid smell behind her that lingers in my nostrils to remind me of her anger. So let her be angry. Let that mad energy compel her to dig under this insignificant little affair and find the sordid truth. I know I'm right, Self, and Ronda's anger is going to help prove it.

Oh, Gerard, so smug, so sure of yourself, so invincible. What if you're wrong? Then what? Suppose in your eagerness to pursue this storm in a soupbowl you have created your own whirlpool. Then where will you be cast up in your righteousness? Beware your greed for a solution, Gerard, for you may get the opposite of what you expect.

Sure? Yes. Smug? Maybe. Invincible? Never. But sure, Self, as sure as I've been of anything on this planet. Ronda is going to find Mr. Yerled under the rock if she digs deep enough. And when she finds him, she is going to find the reason for his being there. If she digs deep enough. That's the variable.

**7040–3.7**
**(day 22)**

Two days' worth of communication. A message from Mr. Yerled saying the Council will not meet until further notice, and that he and General Tizelrassel will be unavailable for several days due to the press of business. My final negative response from FedTroop Corps. Nothing from Ronda.

Informed Fed that negotiations are temporarily stalled, but expect a breakthrough soon.

Gave in and sent a message to ShRil telling her I'm here. Loneliness and anticipation got the better of me.

Sat in the ruins yesterday and tried to write a poem. It turned into an indulgence in self-pity. Or depression. Or something like that.

Maybe Odi will let me come out and investigate the holdings in their library. The change of environment will do as much good as anything.

**7040–3.9**
**(day 25)**

Visits like that don't do much for morale, Windy. Odi was polite (I suspect at Ronda's insistence), but that is all. He told me he didn't know what I had done to make Ronda so mad, but he could think of no justification for angering her. Thus I was *persona* barely *grata*, and treated accordingly. Didn't get to go out to the ruins, because no one would take me and I was forbidden to go alone. Spent most of my time in the library, a fairly extensive but quaint provincial collection dominated by technical materials relating to mining and Cuallum storybooks of questionable literary merit. Like the small library in Monument City, no Tenderfoot material I could find. The library's translator is an ancient, pre-Baird Stnwats model with an extremely limited Standard vocabulary. Most depressing.

However, I found some stories, poems, and songs written by the Cuallumese miners in an open-ended anthology section of the main storage computer and brought back twenty-two of them whose crude translation into Standard looked promising. Even so, most of these are merely above average heave-ho, sweat-and-toil working songs. Hard labor triumphs over adversity and all of that. The Bard's working on one that's quite a bit different from the others. Not only is it about Quadra, but it was written by one S. S. Odi, whom I assume is Srotisiv Secivero Odi. The librarian couldn't (or wouldn't) confirm that for me, and, given Odi's cooled attitude, I didn't feel comfortable about asking him.

I did ask Odi to tell Ronda I would like to talk to her. He didn't seem too eager, but said if he saw her, and if he remembered, he would mention that I had made such a request. He'll tell her. He wants to know why she is angry, and my request is as good an excuse as any to try to get her to talk about it. I don't think she will, though, unless she has discovered the facts to prove me right. Even then I think she will tell me first. I think.

*****Well, Windy, the Bard did a nice job with Odi's poem. It certainly shows some of the complexity under that blunt exterior of his.

### On the Cold Rock of Quadra

Beyond the early stars
In the silver shadows,
A moonlit phantom stalks
  on the edge of tranquility
  in search of assembling poems.

The primal fire is lost
  to the velvet horizon,
And in the cold wash of middle darkness
The phantom seeks symbols
  of/for/in the heat of the past.

Since Odi helped Ronda with the copy of her poem for me, I think we ought to make a copy of this for him. Then, when all this business has settled down, we can give it to him as a peace offering. Or just because we like him. Doesn't matter.

At least we have the rest of this Cuallumese literature to play with while we're waiting for something to happen. I don't expect any exciting keepers in the batch, but it will be good exercise for the Bard. And for me.

Revelation, Windy: I'm no good at waiting because I'm impatient, and I'm impatient because I'm no good at waiting. Brilliant, right?

Gracie put it best when she said, "Gerard, you must choose patience."

### 7040–3.10
### (day 26)

Apparently the way to get a ghost to visit is to go to the head. I damn near fell off the stool this afternoon when Pink Thistle popped up in front of me and boomed, "Ronda Loner War Crow will appear here tomorrow morning." Before I could respond, Pink Thistle disappeared. It's a good thing.

My head was ringing. My bowels were quaking. I was madder than a grisk with its claws in a trap. Someone needs to give these spirits a course in etiquette.

Tomorrow. Well, we'll see then whether I get vindicated or blasted by our Indian princess. I think a little hypnosleep is in order, Windy, then up early and wait for our guest to arrive. I don't think the security alert will do any good with a ghost, but set it anyway, just in case. I'd like a little warning that she's aboard, if possible. Even a second or two would be nice.

## 7040–3.11
## (day 27)

Half a solution is better than none at all. In this instance it may be all we get. Ronda showed up this morning (with no warning, Windy) and told me what she had found. I wouldn't say that Ronda was cordial, but she did admit that I was on the right track, and that it now appeared to her that Mr. Yerled was indeed involved in some type of conspiracy to keep the FedBase off Quadra. I was relieved, but saddened, too. Ronda obviously has a great deal of admiration for Yerled. Maybe even affection. Her private investigation brought out part of the truth, but it also brought her some pain.

And not just because of Yerled. The conspiracy, or whatever we want to call it, originated in the spirit community, apparently when a minority of the spirits decided a FedBase would not be acceptable to them. They made Mr. Yerled their reluctant accomplice with a few suggestions that his trading business might suffer greatly if those he dealt with were cautioned by ghosts to avoid him, the hint that he might not enjoy continuous visitation by some of the more repulsive members of the spirit community, and, should he feel that these inducements were insufficient, a threat to blackmail him by revealing that Mr. Yerled had been involved in an incident of aggression against another community of spirits.

It's easy to form the picture of Mr. Yerled surrounded by a hostile group of ghosts, facing possible financial ruin, harassment, and blackmail. To see him giving in under what must have been very fierce intimidation. What neither Ronda nor I can picture, is why Yerled didn't tell her about all of this. The history of the universe is full of aggression against the spirits, from simple incantations to electrostatic warfare. Surely, if

Yerled was once involved in such an incident, it could be forgiven. His actions since coming to Quadra have been exemplary toward the spirit community, and if they were so in an attempt to atone for his past, that makes them no less valid or meaningful.

But Yerled is gone. Offplanet on business, his office said. For Ronda the problem of Yerled is less pressing and disturbing than the problem of the dissident ghost. Quadra is a haven for ghosts, a spirit democracy where each is free to express opinion and where each member is accepted into the community by agreeing to abide by the decisions of the majority. Any ghost is free to leave at any time, and some of them do. But none of them know of any place in the universe where they can act as freely and still wield controlling influence on their environment. Their powers are stronger on Quadra than anywhere else, and the heritage of spiritual democracy here is ancient and sacrosanct. It was one of the keystones of the original Quadran civilization they revere so much.

Now, for the first time, a small group of spirits has assembled to subvert the will of the majority. What Ronda sees is insurrection, an uprising that could threaten the fabric of their existence. What in the beginning I had been ready to dismiss as a trivial local spat is for Ronda an incident bordering on tragedy. It's not that bad, really, but if you've never faced the thought of insurrection in your own land, then it can be quite unnerving.

Ronda and I talked for a long time, partly to see if together we could decipher a reason behind the problem, and partly because I wanted to reassure her that the situation was far from out of control. I even suggested that she invite Berish-ka-Senk-ka, the apparent leader of the dissidents, to meet with us tomorrow. She just stared at me incredulously. But I persisted, and finally convinced her that the way to defeat an enemy is to know everything you can about him. She said we'd have to meet in the central square of the Monument City ruins because Berish-ka-Senk-ka would never fit in my tiny ship. (Never thought of you as tiny before, Windy.)

Still, she's skeptical that it will accomplish anything. Berish-ka-Senk-ka is not very enthusiastic about conversation, or corporeal entities, and Ronda told me to come armed with a vaporizer in case he decides to get nasty. When I refused, she said she couldn't invite him unless I was armed.

The vaporizer will not harm Berish or any other ghost, but will limit his materialization powers immediately and a fullsync frontal blast will render any ghost incapable of materializing for several hours.

That's comforting to know, but not much. A fullsync vaporizer blast will open a hole through ten centimeters of plasteel in about five seconds. Still, it's nice to know that a ghost can be temporarily incapacitated should the need arise. I asked Ronda why the use of a vaporizer against spirits was not common knowledge? "Because," she said, "those who have used vaporizers on us rarely lived out the day to tell about it." Now *that* is very comforting.

The vaporizer, she said, would be our last-resort weapon if Berish-ka-Senk-ka got violent, and if Ronda was unable to control him. Suddenly I wasn't so sure I wanted this meeting after all. Ronda sensed that, I think, and laughed. She told me not to worry, but to be sure to be sitting in the square before seven in the morning with my back against the Column of Numbers in the north corner. Once I had assured her I would be there, she left.

Stupid me, Windy, I didn't even ask her what Berish-ka-Senka-ka looked like, so I could be prepared. But I'll be there, vaporizer and all, expecting the largest, ugliest apparition I can conjure in my imagination.

**(day 28)**

Large? Yes. Ugly? No. Berish-ka-Senk-ka is a beautiful quadruped fifteen to sixteen meters tall, twenty long, burnished copper in his main coloration, and obviously from one of the equine classifications. Rather a pleasant sight, actually, but not very talkative.

I told him who I was, and that my main concern was to find out why he was opposed to the FedBase. He snorted. I said that in order to be fair to all parties concerned, I needed the information to make an accurate assessment of the total picture. He snorted and started pawing one of his cloven hooves close enough to make me nervous.

Not wanting to appear concerned, I kept talking, enumerating for him all of the other concerns and objections that had been expressed to me and asked if he would like to add to that list. He stopped pawing and stared down at me with huge black eyes, lowering his head as he did so, and curling his upper lip back over his blunt grey teeth. Keeping my back firmly against the column, I rose slowly to my feet, letting my right hand slip down to the butt of the vaporizer.

He was so huge! So intimidating. My heart went out to Mr. Yerled for what he must have gone through. Trying to talk as slowly as I could, I insisted that I needed Berish-ka-Senk-ka's advice and counsel if my report was to be representative of all positions, and would he please cooperate, and anything else I could think of just to keep talking. He started little pawing movements again, and I was beginning to wonder if I was going to have to use the vaporizer after all, when Ronda materialized beside me and told him to back off.

Surprisingly, he did, and finally spoke in a whining nasal voice. "This is no good," he said. "It will ruin our home. We have seen your FedBases on other worlds, sores on the skin of a planet. Not here, little one, not here." He cocked his head and looked first at me, then at Ronda, then back at me. "May you dine tonight on your own offal," he said rather cheerily. "And may you climb a steep trail with no water," I replied. He snorted, turned, and left, fading out among the columns.

Ronda smiled at me rather smugly as if to say, "I told you so," said she would see me again in a day or two, and disappeared in her usual abrupt way. Moments later I thought I heard the rolling thunder of giant hooves fading into the distance. A silly trick of imagination. But as I walked back here, I could picture in my mind Ronda Loner War Crow perched on the back of the giant Berish-ka-Senk-ka, clinging to his knotted mane as he galloped across some vast plain. Something made me feel that picture was not all imagination.

### 7040–3.12
### (day 29)

Message from ShRil. Dream of Fairy Peg. Diplocode note from Yerled. What a way to start the day. Best begin with the dream before the details fade. Something new here.

Fairy Peg is standing close beside me. In uniform. Whispering to me. Quick short sentences I can't understand. Someone with us. Standing across the way, in uniform. A Gabriel Ratchet. Targ Alpluakka. Commander Alpluakka. The port opens. Fairy Peg says something to me. Very formal. Alpluakka salutes. Both go out the port. Slowly, I salute. The port closes.

The port. Windy. We're here on Windy.

Lean closer. What is Fairy Peg saying? I hear the words, but they don't make sense. Hurry words. Love words. Private words. Listen, dummy! What is she saying?

"Return to us . . . need you . . . here . . . hurry . . . careful . . . darling." Port opens. "Farewell and . . . majesty." Salute. Port closes.

Again.

Hesitance. "Return to us if you can. We . . . need you . . . and here. Hurry back to . . . careful . . . darling." Port. "Fare well and prosper, Your Majesty." Salute. Port.

Concentrate, Self.

"Return to us if you can. We of Kril need you there and here. Hurry back to your Gabriel Ratchets. Be very careful, my strange darling." Port. "Fare well and prosper, Your Majesty." Salute. Port.

My Gabriel Ratchets? Kril needs me? Return to us? What is all of this, Self? Was I on an official mission from Fairy Peg and Ribble Galaxy? Impossible. I was contracted to Fed. And why did Peg call them "your Gabriel Ratchets"? What makes them mine?

Sorry, Self, but I don't believe his one. Too much time and imagination between here and there. A fragment like this smacks of something you and I made up in our sleep, a desire dream, something we wish might have happened, or something that happened in a similar way. It is too whole to be real. Too disturbing in its implications.

Now this note from Mr. Yerled. An apology for leaving so suddenly and a promise to return as soon as possible. All in very formal diplomatic language.

Yerled knows. How and what, I can't be sure. But he knows. That was part of the real message to me. The other part is that he will return but does not know when. I believe him. There would have been no need to send the note if he didn't intend to come back to face the situation. In fact, the note itself is his first act of contrition. And perhaps a subtle plea for assistance. I'm sure Yerled expected me to get the unwritten part of his message, and he knew that once I had figured it out I would probably tell Ronda. His use of the diplocode says, "I am your colleague, your peer. Understand and help, please." At least that's what it says to me, Windy. I only wish I had more specific information to pass on to Ronda. And to satisfy my own curiosity. Patience, Gerard. Patience.

In all things, patience. Why is it, Self, that the good times, the active, stimulating times, come only after long periods of waiting, and then pass so quickly? A simplistic question, I know, but one which has always seemed to me to be psychologically valid. For example, we sit here on Quadra, waiting for the next development of the mission, waiting to see Ronda again, waiting for answers to our questions, waiting for resolution of the FedBase problem, and waiting for ShRil. Quarters will get you credits that everything will start happening at once, and the subjective time will pass as quickly as a Zachors blinking through space. Then we will wait again, travel somewhere new, wait to get there, wait to assess the situation, wait to establish credibility, wait, wait, wait. And I will be bored, and impatient with the waiting.

Just like now. ShRil's message makes me so impatient for her to be here I can hardly stand it. I want her in my arms and by my side and across the table. I want to hear the beautiful sound of her voice and feel the luxury of her body. I want to share with her. Everything. But, fortunately or not, Windy, I'm willing to wait with great patience for ShRil's arrival, if it means that when she arrives the FedBase issue will be resolved, or at least in the final stages of resolution.

Her message was so sweet, so tender, so filled with delight and anticipation, that the waiting will be easier. And the conclusion of the waiting, ah, the conclusion will be as wonderful as it will be. I cannot dwell on it, Self, nor can you, for to do so invites fantasy and disappointment.

Suffice it to say that when ShRil arrives, I will be ready.

*****Pink Thistle boomed into the cabin a while ago to tell me that Ronda would not be to see me for at least thirty-eight hours. Then boomed out again. At least I wasn't in the head. Thirty-eight hours. Two days. Maybe I should go see Odi again, Windy. Take him our peace offering. Can't just sit here for two days.

**7040–3.14**
**(day 31)**

Well, Windy, it may have started awkwardly, but by the time we said goodbye, we had re-established the rapport of my first visit, when Odi so proudly showed me around. Even more than that, because whatever Ronda told him made Odi feel I have the best interests of Quadra at heart. Thus his awkwardness was rooted in his need to apologize and I made it more awkward by trying to assure him that no apology was necessary. But no matter. We crossed that rough spot as quickly as possible, still feeling a little uncomfortable, but much more relaxed, and from that point until I gave him the copy of "On the Cold Rock of Quadra," things went well.

However, the poem choked him up and everything got awkward and uncomfortable again. My assumption of authorship was wrong. He did not write it, his brother did. His brother, Sovini Socios Odi, died in the only major mining accident since the Cuallumese came to Quadra and took over the operation. Srotisiv felt responsible, psychologically responsible, for his brother's death, so I inadvertently opened a wound by giving him that personal reminder. But he was also moved by the poem itself, commenting that had he not been given our copy, he would never have believed it could be translated so well into Standard. Or translated into Standard at all.

Our relationship was altered for the better by that. Odi and I see each other in a different light now, a brighter light that promises more openness and more natural communication. My regret, of course, is that this new relationship will not be able to grow much longer in proximity, that we will not be able to share the joys of a maturing friendship through years of regular association.

That's always the regret, isn't it, Self? That's the shadow that hangs over us every time we start to feel close to someone. But we need them. I need them. I am a relationship person. I need the psychological and emotional contacts, the bonding, the feelings of unity.

One of the senior instructors at diploschool accused me, once, of using people, but I don't think that is true. At least not in the way he meant it. Because I always want to maintain those contacts, no matter how far removed in time and space I get from those I feel affection for. Because for them, the bond never dissolves, never gets severed, no matter what happens. I always hope that they feel the same thing. In a way, all those classmates, and C'Rina, and Gracie, and Morrizon, and Alvin, and Teever Loze (Fara guard his soul), and most of all, ShRil, all those dear people are a part of me, and I am a part of them. Each time I shared something with them that was true, and real, and meaningful. Like the navigating stars, they mark key points in my passage through this life that I would be lost without.

Now I feel the beginnings of the same tie to Odi. The tie that binds across all distances. It is precious, Windy, and I am grateful for it. For every one of them. I'm fascinated that it is not always a central character in these episodes of my life with whom I bond. I became extremely fond of M'Litha, but there was no true bond there. Same for The Professor. And Director Franiingcard. And Ronda Loner War Crow. And Ambassador Wattuvorschie at diploschool.

Forgive the amateur philosophy, Windy, but this phenomenon can only be described as metaphysical. How else can I explain my feelings about Morrizon? I only saw him three times, but there was an instant rapport between us that cannot be explained in any rational way. Sure, I was grateful for his help in my release, but it was so much more than that, so much deeper. I may never see him again, but I know that if I did, the bond would still be there.

Golifa at diploschool used to call it "physics". She would stare at me with that iridescent eye of hers and say, "Gerard, if the physics are right, anything can happen." Then she would soften her voice and add, "especially between individuals." She must have told me that a hundred times or more. Golifa would know. She was a natural bonder. Fascinating, charismatic, a social magnet, she was always surrounded by friends, or aspiring friends, or those who could never be her friends because of their egocentric natures, but who claimed to be because they needed what she gave. They needed to bond.

The exception and mystery in all of this, Self, is Fairy Peg. If there was a bond between us, and I think, no, I'm sure there was, somehow it got severed. My recurring dreams of her are an attempt to heal that amputation as well as understand what happened. Right, Self? Isn't that part of what you are doing? Trying to knit up those loose ends of that psychological wound? After six years, what did we do this morning? We created some new skin to cover the scars, a graft, fabricated from imagination to make it look prettier, so that six years from now when we look back we will see a clean smooth surface and not be reminded so forcefully, so painfully of the ugliness that lies underneath.

If camouflage is what it takes to come to terms with all of

that, so be it. Let us camouflage away, Self, until that chasm of pain we fell into takes on the appearance of an innocuous valley populated by simple wormherders, with whom we once shared a meal and spent a night on our way to other places. Shall we do that, Self? Is that the answer? Will that solve the problems for us?

I wish I could believe it would, and help the process of disguise on its way. But I don't. And I can't. That's not the answer. Because that's not the truth. And sooner or later, the truth is what we have to get to, because the truth is what we have to live with. The truth may not free us from the memories, but should give us a clear picture of what we are actually fighting. And that is half the battle won already.

So no more camouflage, Self. Go back after the facts. Dig out some more pieces from behind those barricades for us to look at. That's the only way we're going to resolve our discontent.

(day 32)

So much introspection before going to sleep really shakes up the old dream mechanisms, doesn't it, Self? I know the Teever Loze nightmare wasn't the only dream I had last night, but it's the one which woke me up screaming his name. How long am I condemned to watch him die again? How many times must I watch him being blown apart before the memory begins to fade? Why must I endure this?

I know you don't have answers for us on this one, Self. It is not of your doing. It was a horror imposed on us by that insanity of life which makes supposedly intelligent creatures believe that by slaughtering individuals they can achieve goodness, and peace, and prosperity. Yet it cannot be too insane, because we accept wars as a part of life. We watch with mild interest those far-away wars, and participate with ferocity in those which threaten us personally. Who am I to criticize? I fought. I killed. I gave all my energies over to the battle, and even took pride in what I was doing. Fara forgive me, in a way I enjoyed what I was doing. It was exhilarating, and I was alive to the ends of my nerves. Each lull after a fight heightened the excitement of the next one. I was okay, I think, until I started wanting to fight, wanting to waste the enemy for my own personal thrills. Wanting to get revenge over and over for Teever Loze's death. Then I lost touch with reality. I no longer knew who I was. The most frightening thing about it was that it happened so quickly.

I realize now that Doc Flo understood that and, without my ever being aware of how, she helped me put the real me, the sane, rational me, back in total control. I realize, too, that when I started to crack, you took everything you could, Self, and burrowed to safety. It was a marvelous act of self-preservation, if you'll pardon the pun, that saved us from wandering forever through the halls of chaos. Good job, Self. Just another example of why I depend on you so much.

## 7040–3.15
## (day 32)

Three quarks may make a row, but three ghosts in the head makes a mess. This time I screamed at them, filthy obscenities and curses from six languages. Screamed in a purple rage. They left. And left me wet and even angrier. How dare they leave just when I was working up a full head of steam! But they did, and when I came out of the head, dressed and a little embarrassed by my outburst, they were nowhere on board.

It was an hour before they returned, and then only Ronda and Pink Thistle. Apparently, I scared Shttz off, and he wasn't about to return to my presence. Strange feeling to know you've scared off a ghost, but it served him right. Popping up like that so close to me that his stupid floppy hat almost brushed my face. I probably got him wet, too, if you can get a ghost wet, but that's the least of his worries. I told Ronda and Pink Thistle that from now on I'm going to keep a vaporizer in the head with me, and every time a ghost pops up in there with me I'm going to give them a full burst and damn the damage. Sorry, Windy. Maybe we can put some shielding in there. Or maybe the vaporizer's a stupid idea, but they don't know that I won't do it, so the threat may serve to change their habits.

Once I finished my warning, Ronda briefly outlined for me what had been taking place in the spirit community since I had last talked to her. Investigation, interrogation, politicking, friendly and unfriendly persuasion, and, I suspect, outright threats. I did not ask nor did Ronda volunteer details, but Berish-ka-Senk-ka and those spirits still determined to follow his lead have been isolated by their millions of spiritual kin and forced to accept the will of the majority. My meeting with Berish-ka-Senk-ka had no effect on him, but the fact of it helped convince some of his followers to change their position. Ronda guaranteed no problems for any of the corporeal residents from the dissidents. She sent emissaries to all the Council members, and the next meeting will be held as soon as it is possible for Mr. Yerled and General Tizelrassel to physically return.

And what of Mr. Yerled? Ronda's attitude seems to be one of acceptance and understanding. Berish-ka-Senk-ka was indeed blackmailing Mr. Yerled, and made it apparent to him that if he supported the FedBase in any way, it would mean financial and psychological ruin, and perhaps death. It is hard to fault Yerled for not being willing to die for a FedBase treaty.

I asked Ronda to send Shttz to let me know when the next meeting would be held. She said if he was willing, she would send him. There was an awkward silence for several moments after that, and finally I told them I had to send some messages and work on my presentation. They left shortly thereafter, but I sensed a reluctance on Ronda's part, as though there was something she felt she hadn't done or said. But who can tell with a ghost? Maybe she was tired.

Or maybe, maybe there's something else, Windy. Remember that first meeting with Shttz? And that conversation with Ronda about her poem? And what Odi said about having a good relationship with Ronda? Maybe Ronda needs the company, corporeal company. Maybe they all do. Maybe Colonel Q. ES't'phons was right when he guessed that what the ghosts get from the arrangement on this planet is company. Not too much of it, but enough of us physical beings around so that our presence is felt. Maybe some of them, like Berish-ka-Senk-ka, resent that need. Maybe . . .

Maybe that's a lot of "maybes." Far too many to form a decent theory. But the whole idea of the spirits needing corporeal company rings true. Why not? It's certainly a psychological need I can relate to, because it's a need to maintain contact with reminders of the past. Not necessarily their actual past, although Ronda's retention of her poem is symbolic of that, but in a broader sense of the physical past as a whole. That would reinforce their reverence for Quadra's past, also.

A neat idea, Windy, even if I do say so myself.

## 7040–3.17
## (day 35)

Someone at Fed has taken the "plan ahead" dictum to heart again. The message this morning outlines our next assignment, treaty renegotiation on a planet called Burnal Sevene. All the usual directives and guidelines, but also a note from Linguistics Division on some unusual difficulties we will face, and a suggestion we begin preparations now, etcetera, etcetera, along with complete transcripts of the original treaty in Sevenese and Standard. We are not committed to a date, yet, but I suspect from the tone of the message that as soon as we finish here, they'll post us to Burnal Sevene.

The lexicon they sent seems far too short, Windy. Let's run it into the Bard and see if we can pinpoint some more specific problems than the ones Linguistics hinted at.

In the meantime, scan our records and find the references on Burnal Sevene for me. That name rings a bell in my balding little head, but I can't remember why.

*****Good work, Windy. I didn't even think of looking here in the journal. The Professor's note that the Vallunese emotive syntax is similar to the tonal syntax of Burnal Sevene might prove to be a valuable clue for solving some of the problems we are going to face. From what I've seen so far, the Bard is struggling with that lexicon, and we may need all the clues we can get.

Try a switchback, Windy. Run the two treaties in opposition through the Baird first, and then run them parallel through the Bard. Get a keyword analysis. That will give us a better idea of the dimensions of the problem and might help the Bard discriminate. Once we get that, we'll know how much of a base we have. If it's not enough, well then, Windy, I guess it's back to Basic Lexicography I.

## 7040–3.18
## (day 36)

Yerled's back. Or he will be tomorrow. He's in braking orbit now, and from the tone of his message I'd say he's eager to get home. Don't know where he's been, but it can't have been too far in ten standard days.

## (day 37)

A day late and a credit short, Shttz shows up to tell me that Yerled will be landing this afternoon and the Council is meeting tomorrow at six. Poor Shttz. Took me half an hour to assure him that his last appearance was not a personal affront. I like the little guy, squeaky voice and all. Just shows you how well we've adjusted to this business, Windy, when I relax in a chair for a couple of hours talking to the ghost of a floppy-hatted blue triangle and not feel that is particularly unusual. Those tests I did so well on in diploschool which showed my low xenophobic rating must not have been as foolish as I thought they were.

Shttz is going to be at the Council meeting, and told me, in confidence he said, that the motion to accept a FedBase will pass four to one. Odi, Bistelfaith, Yerled, and Mossmann will vote in favor. That's right, Windy, Shttz said Mossmann will vote in favor. Seems that Shttz and some of the other spirits persuaded Mossmann that they could insure certain benefits to his business if he voted for the FedBase instead of against it. I'm sure that implicit in their discussions was the fact that it could go the other way, too. But by playing on his greed and letting him conjure his own fears, they got the desired results.

So, General Tizelrassel will be the only holdout. I'm disappointed in that, hoping as I did that my session with her would have led her to a change of position. But Shttz was very sure that the general will vote in opposition. If she knows that Mossmann and Yerled are going to vote in favor, maybe her opposition is only symbolic. At least I'd like to think so.

I got Shttz to talking about himself and he told me about some of his travels since becoming a ghost. He's visited over a thousand planets by his calculations, and his descriptions of some of the uninhabited ones made me slightly envious. Obviously ghosts can go places we corporeal beings cannot, but I had never really given thought to all the things they could see in person that will never be available to us. I described the Tenderfoot legend to him in detail and asked if he had ever heard of it. Drew a blank. But he said he would ask some of the other ghosts.

When I asked Shttz how one became a ghost, he gave me a long, very technical explanation of psychic oscillation incidents, radiant environments, and a host of other terms that were meaningless to me. What it all boils down to, I think, is if a sentient being is at the proper level of psychic energy, and dies swiftly in the proper environment, that being will become an integrated ghost, capable of becoming apparent, doing limited physical activities, talking, etc. If the circumstances or psychic energy levels are wrong, then the spirit of the individual just dissolutes to join the pool of cosmic consciousness, and loses all its former identity as an individual. Luck. Random probability, and nothing more.

I thought about that for a long time after Shttz left, and decided I would much rather become an integrated ghost than join the pool of cosmic consciousness. Immortality and all of that, Windy, although Shttz did say that eventually all the ghosts would join the pool. But that eventuality takes a long time coming, and by the time it arrives I would probably be bored anyway and ready to fade away. Gracie's influence again. She's the one who told me immortality got tedious after a while. She would know.

**7040–3.19**
**(day 37)**

Yerled called me as soon as he landed this afternoon and asked me to meet him at his house. Said he needed to talk to me before the Council meeting. And talk he did. And talk, and talk, and talk. Confessions, explanations, guilt, and rationalizations. I heard it all, in far more detail than anyone needed to. But I couldn't stop him. He needed to get it all out of his system, not so I would understand, but so he could be cleansed of it. I was, am, the perfect person to tell, because he knows I won't tell anyone else, and when I leave Quadra, his secrets leave with me.

I'm not going to record all of the details here, Windy, mainly because I don't want to remember them. Suffice it to say that he was a vile and despicable youth who did some outrageous things and then went through a deeply spiritual transformation, and has spent the rest of his life trying to compensate for his early past. He lived with the knowledge of what he had been as a constant reminder, but until Berish-ka-Senk-ka put the screws to him, that knowledge had been his spur to do better, to make constant improvement.

But Berish-ka-Senk-ka brought the whole horror back to him in vivid detail. Faced with the possible destruction of all that he had tried to become, Yerled buckled and collapsed into a whirlpool of his guilt. It was not until Ronda confronted him aboard his ship and convinced him that what he had become was far more important than what he had been, that he began to pull himself out.

I suspect his confession to me was the final move, the one which would heave him clear from the whirlpool. Oh, he will always be more aware of it behind him, but I don't think he will ever again be forced back into it. Ronda taught him a lesson in self-worth he won't forget, one that he dare not forget if he is to maintain his life and sanity.

A little hypnosleep, if you please, Windy. I refuse to reflect on this any longer and would, if I could, mindwipe it from myself. Lose it, Self. I don't want Yerled's past haunting me, too. Have enough problems of my own.

**(day 38)**

Surprises never cease, Windy. The vote was five to zero in favor of accepting a FedBase. That only took about five minutes. We spent the next six hours formulating the basic structure, intent, and limitations of the treaty, with General Tizelrassel making many of the most positive suggestions. From the things she said and the way she said them, it was obvious to me that my session with her made her answer those questions I asked.

There are still a lot of tough negotiations to go through, but, now that we're all heading in the same direction, who cares how hard we have to work to hammer this thing out? The only uncomfortable moments came when Shttz made suggestions and Mossmann winced each time Shttz spoke. But those moments passed quickly as the process moved forward and Mossmann recovered very nicely each time. He may not like his "spooks," but he's learning to work with them, and that's what is important.

We won't get the treaty written and signed before ShRil arrives, but we should be far enough along that it won't interfere too much with our being together. Not if I can help it anyway.

**7040–3.22**
**(day 41)**

Hitches, glitches, fits, starts, and stops. The bumpy road of negotiations. Compromise. Swap. Cajole. Persuade. It's a private show, but I love it, Windy. Fara, how I love it! Sometimes I get so wrapped up in the process I want to stand and cheer each time a point of contention is resolved.

It taxes my brain, saps my strength (when I stop to think about how I feel), frustrates my belief in intelligent life, and often makes me angry. But when those juices are flowing, when the discussion gets that animated fever, there's an electricity in the air that sparks even stodgy old Pink Thistle. And when Pink Thistle's sparked, the boom is deafening.

There's only one thing I can think of right now that is more exciting and that I'd rather be doing. And you are far too innocent a maiden for me to embarrass you by telling you what that is.

Goodnight, Windy.

**7040–3.24**
**(day 44)**

Nothing like my being totally involved in a project to get you working on the dreams, is there, Self? At least this one's nice and clear, Fairy Peg and ShRil each trying to pull me in opposite directions and me unable to move either way. What you're telling me is that I have to resolve my feelings about Fairy Peg before I can commit to ShRil.

That you think I can/should/need/want to commit to ShRil is, in and of itself, a revelation. A scary, complicated revelation. You tucked it in at the last minute, knowing she's going to be here tomorrow for the start of the conference, telling me that this carefree lovers' reunion will not be carefree at all, that it will be very important to me on a much deeper level than I was willing to admit.

You made your point, and I am grateful. I don't know yet just how I'm going to, no, how *we* are going to get Fairy Peg out of our system, but we will. Especially in light of ShRil. We have to.

Even if ShRil's feelings aren't reciprocal, we have to. Besides, how can I ever hope to become a ghost if I keep letting the Fairy Peg affair drain my psychic energy. Self-preservation. Got to do it.

Lest we get confused, though, we'd best not try to do it until we're gone from here. The emotions are going to be running too high for us to accomplish much in a positive way. Pin Fairy Peg down in a corner somewhere, Self, until we get into clear space and can give this knot the attention it deserves. No sense in letting it ruin everything.

*****Some minor changes here and there, the amendment agreement, the final wording of the preamble, and we should have the draft treaty ready to send to Fed. Couple of restrictions in there they probably won't like, but on the whole they're going to get pretty much what they wanted. A few local control clauses won't keep them from approving, especially in this instance, when they understand very clearly that they have to satisfy the demands of two distinct population groups. Not that they won't want some changes made, just to let me know who makes the final decisions. But I seriously doubt that they'll try to tinker with the substance. At least they should know better than to tamper with the work of an expert.

Funny, Windy, I'm not sleepy and I don't want hypnosleep. I just want to lay back and relax and let whatever will drift through my mind. ShRil will be here tomorrow and I haven't seen her in four years. Wonder what I'll find drifting in my thoughts? Any ideas, Self?

## 7040–3.26
## (day 46)

No, Windy, I didn't come back last night. I stayed with a sick friend. Literally. ShRil was carried off her ship, *Liencam,* straight to the guest center infirmary. Ill. Not seriously, thank Fara, but sick enough to feel miserable. A Deltan stomach virus aggravated by a little warpsickness.

I pulled some strings and got permission to stay with her. She couldn't sleep very well, so we spent most of the night talking. Or actually, I spent most of the night talking. She would ask about something and I would start one of my rambling narratives, talking softly, holding her hand, letting the sound of my voice lull her to sleep. Then she would doze off for half an hour or so in a light, fitful kind of sleep.

When she woke up, she would ask another question, or repeat a previous question, and we would go through the whole routine again. She said she felt better this morning, but when the medic checked her, he said it would be two or three more days before she could get up and around. That's when I decided to bring her here. I asked her if she would mind recuperating in one of our rejuvhosp cells, and after one of the longest moments, she said that would be nice.

Had to pull a lot more strings to get the okay for that, but finally Mr. Yerled told the Chief Physician there was no choice. They're bringing her over in about an hour.

*****ShRil's resting now. She didn't want the hypnosleep, so I put Nelson's *Crazy Spiral Symphony* on the soother, and that ought to have the same effect. I can't believe she's here, Windy. Not just here on Quadra, but *here* with us. I must have looked in on her ten times in the last thirty minutes, just to confirm her presence. Yep, she's still here, more beautiful than memory or hologram.

Now, I must get some rest. Buzz me if she wakes, Windy.

**(day 47)**

Between the rejuvhosp and the sleep, ShRil feels much better today. We talked for a couple of hours before I insisted she get some more rest and let the soother put her back to sleep. So much we don't know about what's happened to each of us these four years. And yet, it felt like we'd never been apart. I felt that, but dared not say it. ShRil said it right before she went back to sleep. The rapport, the understanding, the silent communication, the closeness, they're all there. All as strong as before. Maybe stronger.

Help me, Self. I'm spinning fantasies faster than a flitspider spins its jeweled webs. Slow me down. Can't let this wave of ecstasy carry me away. Or drown ShRil. I am limerant, Self, obsessed by my love for her. But I cannot let it show, cannot let my emotions flood over her. There are still too many complications, too many unknowns about ShRils's feelings and dreams and plans. But it's hard, oh, Fara, it's hard not to share this with her. Give me patience, Self.

**7040–3.27**
**(day 47)**

Have to do some work on the treaty tomorrow. Mr. Yerled said they had reached an impasse on the amendment agreement over majority or unanimous approval. I thought we'd already settled that, but apparently Mossmann and Odi are holding out for unanimity. I don't care which they decide on, so long as they decide.

Told ShRil I'd have to be gone for a while in the morning and she gave me an exaggerated pout. A good sign she's feeling better. Said she probably wouldn't even know I was gone as she and Windy have a lot of catching up to do. My suggestion that rest was more important than gossiping with you, Windy, only brought a laugh. Do me a favor, will you? If the two of you have to talk, make sure she gets her rest, too. Make her stop every couple of hours or so. You'll get the fatigue data from the rejuvhosp. Use it to her benefit. Okay? Okay.

If anyone else ever reads this journal, Windy, they're going to think I'm unbalanced, talking to you and Self the way I do. They won't understand that you have personality and character and make a very sympathetic audience. You are very real and precious to me. You know that already and I don't know why I'm telling you again, but . . . oh, never mind. You know what I mean.

*****Time for bed. ShRil's resting easier, and she managed to eat some solid food. We talked for a while about the Tenderfoot legend before she went to sleep. A safe, neutral subject, except every pause in the conversation brought a squeeze of her hand, and there was nothing safe or neutral about the flow of emotion. If she feels up to it tomorrow when I get back, I'll broach the subject of "us." But carefully, and only if I think she's ready.

**(day 48)**

I'm going, Windy. Don't forget what I said. Make sure ShRil gets plenty of rest. Watch what you tell her.

*****ShRil looks like she's sleeping from exhaustion. Did you make her rest? Okay. Okay. I believe you. I just worry about her, that's all.

Got the amendment agreement settled. A four-fifths majority. The last obstacle is the preamble. I gave them eight very different examples of other treaty preambles, but I have a feeling they won't be satisfied with modeling on one of those. Odi and Bistelfaith have drafted preambles of their own, which means that Mossmann will draft one of his own, if only in self-defense. I suggested that everyone do a separate one, and the Spiritum do its own, and they can all compare and find their points of agreement. Going from there should then only be complicated, rather than impossible. I don't think anyone but Pink Thistle appreciated my sarcasm.

But they'll make it. They're proud of themselves, and rightfully so. Even Mossmann has put aside his biases (or at least some of them) and contributed to the process in a positive way. Mr. Yerled has shown strong leadership. Even General Tizelrassel defers to him occasionally, and she doesn't like to defer to anyone. So, it may take a while longer than I thought, but they'll get the treaty finished, and it will be a good one.

With all the substantive work done and ShRil here, I have changed my role from negotiator to advisor. Not only does that give me more time for ShRil, but it also means that the Council and the Spiritum have a stronger sense of independence. Thus, more and more they are referring to it as "our treaty," rather than "the FedBase treaty". That's a healthy shift of attitude.

Wonder what ShRil would like for dinner? She's awake? Well then, I might as well go ask her.

*****Hard to think of a rejuvhosp cell as a romantic place to dine, but with the right two people, it can be. That simulated candlelight you provided didn't hurt any, Windy. Nor did the wine. But I think it would have been romantic even without all of that, because ShRil and I wanted it to be. We lingered over the wine in easy conversation until I realized how tired she was and insisted she go to sleep.

No serious talk about us, just light general discussion about our feelings and attitudes. Touched on art, and religion, and bureaucracies. Argued dispassionately about the virtues of different forms of government. Laughed a lot. And kissed goodnight. Our first kiss. Well, our first mutual kiss. I've been kissing her on the forehead since she arrived, but she wouldn't let me kiss her otherwise. Until tonight. ShRil initiated it, and it was sweet, and soft, and gentle, and tender, and in a subtle way, passionate. There'll be time later for going beyond kissing.

### 7040–3.28
### (day 49)

Who'd have guessed that "later" would be such a short time later. I must admit that it gave me quite a start when

ShRil climbed into my bunk with me in the middle of the night, but I recovered admirably. When we woke up a while ago, I made her go back to the rejuvhosp to sleep so you can monitor her, Windy, but if this morning is any indication, I'd guess she's ninety-percent recovered.

If I felt any better, I think I'd pop. Or float away. Or shout at the top of my lungs. As it is, I can't keep from humming the melody from Euieay's "Love Concerto." Over and over. Stuck in my head. Da da, dida di da, da di, da da, dadi da da. Bet you wish you could hum like that, Windy. Then we could perform duets.

Duets. Nice word. Apropos.

*****ShRil's soaking in the tank. We talked all afternoon about us. Serious talk about us. Preliminaries to more serious talk. I don't know if I feel good or bad. We acknowledged that we love each other, but we came to no conclusions, tentative or otherwise, about what that love might portend for our future. Then there's the species difference. We're cross-fertile, but it we ever decided to have children, they would be sterile. I hadn't even thought about children. How could I, when I wasn't even sure that ShRil was interested in some kind of commitment? But then, ShRil's thought about that too. We have a lot that joins us, but also a great deal that separates us, and I wouldn't place any bets at the moment about which outweighs the other.

I'm a little scared, Self.

**7040–3.29**
**(day 50)**

ShRil feels well enough to go to some of the conference meetings this afternoon, and I'm going to a Council meeting at eleven. If she feels like it, we'll attend the conference banquet this evening. But we decided she would stay here for at least four or five more days. Then we'll see how ShRil feels. And how we feel.

**(day 51)**

It was a lovely banquet, but on top of the meetings, it really put a strain on ShRil. I carried her aboard, asleep in my arms, and put her in the rejuvhosp as a precaution. She ate a little this morning, but went back to bed after promising me she wouldn't try to go to any of the meetings today. Her presentation doesn't come up for another week, and mine is three days after that, so there's no critical reason for her to be there.

Take care of her, Windy. I'm off to the Council. If things go as well today as they did yesterday, we'll be finished with the draft, and I'll be able to send it to Fed. With routine approval, we should have it back by 4.15. A couple of days for signing and ceremonies and a week to enjoy the remainder of the conference with ShRil before heading off to Burnal Sevene. Sounds like a good schedule to me.

**7040–3.30**
**(day 51)**

The treaty will be ready for sending tomorrow. Somehow, finishing it today was anticlimactic. All the drama has drained away.

There are strange smells drifting up from the galley. Think I'll go see what ShRil is up to.

**(day 52)**

Hard to keep this journal when someone else is around, Windy. ShRil's off to the conference, and I've promised to meet her there at fifteen, but that gives me a couple of hours. While you're diplocoding and sending the treaty, I'm going to finish the poem I started last night after we made love.

*****Not bad, Gerard my boy. Not bad at all.

**ShRil's Dithyramb**

Sailing without regret
  into the new wind,
  into the moments of union—
Blood to lungs, bones, muscles, and heart,
Rationless beast of glory
Soaring into the the holy awareness,
Creating new heavens,
  gardenless edens
  without sanction or evil,
Casting fire back at the sky,

Echoing the laughter of gods:
Now comes the single fury
    the mad mindless rush
        into the musk of ecstasy:
Now comes the hot wet fall
    the warm growling animal
        with malodorous breath:
Now comes the basest fire
    the beast beyond teaching
        diving towards home,
            towards life,
        plummeting to fulfillment
            with rash, burning tremors,
            with tremblefalling peace
                spent into sleep,
        changing into dreams
            of love,
            and becoming.

Don't know that my dithyramb would win any prizes on Val, but I don't expect to enter it in any competition. The only judge I care about will read it tonight.

Now, if I'm going to meet her, I'd better get cracking. Windy, make a copy of this on some of that pseudo-parchment so it will be ready when we get back.

**7040–4.1**
**(day 53)**

ShRil's reaction to her dithyramb was not all that I expected it to be. She was pleased by my effort, but said she wants to read it several more times. I guess I wanted effusiveness, and what I got was restrained and appreciative, but by no means effusive. Then again, ShRil was tired, and I didn't do much in the way of preparing her.

"Wrote you a poem. Let me read it to you." Read it. Gave it to her. "Well, what do you think?"

Not the best reflection of your diplomatic skills, Gerard. You let your excitement and pleasure blind you to anything but the reaction you wanted. And when you didn't get it, you felt hurt. Give the lady some time. And try to develop a little grace.

## 7040–4.2
## (day 54)

See what I told you, Gerard. ShRil's delayed reaction was as much as you could ask for. A good diplomat would take that lesson to heart.

Ronda's coming tonight to meet ShRil. That ought to be interesting. Of course, I've told ShRil all about the situation here, but she hasn't met any ghosts yet, here or anywhere, and she's understandably nervous about it. I told Ronda, but not ShRil, that if Pink Thistle and Shttz wanted to come they'd be welcome also. I made it clear to Ronda that they were to appear outside and enter like ordinary folk. No sense in having them scare ShRil with their pop-up routine. Or me either.

## 7040–4.3
## (day 55)

I think the ghosts of Quadra have a new and enthusiastic friend. ShRil, Ronda, and Shttz stayed up talking long after I retired last night. Half an hour after she met them, ShRil was engaged in animated conversation, which continued all evening. Both Shttz and Ronda seemed eager to tell ShRil about their pasts (ghost and corporeal) and by the later part of the evening my participation had diminished to an occasional question or comment.

Shttz told us he had asked about the Tenderfoot legend, but none of the ghosts had been able to contribute much. He did say, however, that a ghost from Yuma on the edge of the Further Reaches told him about a Tenderfoot-type character who was part of their history. ShRil and I both made a note about Yuma, and after that I mostly listened and observed, feeling the warmth of friendship grow among the three of them. It was all so comfortable, so natural, so relaxed, that I caught my thoughts drifting off on tangents and my body sliding into drowsiness. So I left them with it and went to bed.

ShRil got up first this morning, chattering about what a wonderful evening she had had, thanking me for inviting our guests, and telling me that they are coming back in a couple of days. Then, as she was about to leave for the conference, she gave me a quick kiss and said, "I've decided to stay here rather than move to the guest center." With a warm squeeze of my hand she stepped out of the port, flashed me a lightning smile, and finished, "if that's all right with you."

Laughing, I told her I'd think about it.

As I watched her walk down the ramp and disappear into the terminal, I thought about it. After I came back inside I thought about it. I'm still thinking about it. I don't know how to stop thinking about it.

*****Fed's acknowledgement of receipt of the treaty draft and an "Alert For Orders" message. That was fast. Good old Fed, no time wasted, no time lost. Except as they deem appropriate. So much for joining ShRil at the seminar on "Small Galaxy Legends and Their Universal Themes." The orders shouldn't be more than three hours behind the alert. Better wait and read them alone. That spot in my gut that anticipates the future is telling me I probably won't like what Fed has to say, Windy.

*****Not as bad as I thought, but certainly not as good as it could be. "Departure for Burnal Sevene to scheduled 7040–4.15 or as soon thereafter as Quadra-FedBase treaty signed. No delay requests accepted by this office." Ever notice, Windy, how warm and personal FedOrders are? Always have that touch of personal attention and concern that lets you know they care about us.

Fifteen local days minimum left to share with ShRil. I feel cheated, Self. Know I should be grateful just for having this time at all, but I still feel cheated.

*****ShRil took the news well enough. Said we'd just have to make every day count as an investment in our future. *Our* future, Self. Our future. How in the universe can we plan a future, a mutual, shared future under these circumstances? With well over four years on this contract, and Fara herself not knowing where Fed will send us, how can ShRil and I plan anything? Of course, if time and circumstances were right, we could always buy our way out of the contract, but I shudder to think of how little credit we'd have left once we did that.

Must think positively.

**(day 56)**

Gloomy morning. We're off to the conference together in a few minutes, both feeling a little sad. Can't let melancholy set in. Or walls to go up between us. Too little time for us to waste it.

### 7040–4.4
### (day 56)

ShRil cheered up at the meetings. She stayed for one of the late seminars on "The Myth of the Bird Gods." Have to tell her about Alvin when she gets back.

Either we wrote a perfect treaty, or someone at Fed has gone crazy. Don't believe either. But this message says confirmation and approval will follow in three days. Must be a mistake. They haven't even had time to read the treaty thoroughly, much less go through the bureaucratic work of approval. I think someone's playing games with us.

*****ShRil's staying over at the guest center tonight. To think, she said. Tried to tell her she could think here as well as there, but she said no. So who am I to tell her what to do? Or where to stay and what to think? I'm just some itinerant diplomat who wandered into her life four years ago and then wandered out again. Now I've wandered back in, and thrown the handle of confusion into all her thoughts about herself, her career, and her future. What claims do I have on her? None, stupid. No one has claims on anyone. Okay, okay, so what do I have to offer her? Love? Nothing unique about that. What else? Respect, understanding, devotion, attention? Big deal. Still nothing unique.

But she's the one who brought up the question of children. She's the one who first mentioned "our" future. So there must be something, some feeling of commitment on her part. Or, perish the thought, was ShRil just testing me, trying to discover the depths of my feelings without having truly reciprocal ones herself? Oh, Self, I don't want to think about that. I don't even want to consider the possibility that ShRil's playing a game with our emotions. She has to care about me, I mean really care. Otherwise . . .

Shards! This is leading nowhere. Put me to sleep, Windy.

### (day 57)

Sometimes, Self, you're a real pain in the butt. With everything else that's going on, I didn't need to cope with a Fairy Peg dream this morning. In fact, I'd just forget about it, but I'm afraid you'd keep giving me reruns until I cope with it.

Okay. Fairy Peg is in bed. Lying down. Ill. There's a smell of medicine mixed with incense. I see her from far away. From across the room. Arguing in whispers. A helmet and shield. Shadows. Two voices. Hand on my arm. Tight. Sword scraping sheath. Peg sits up. "Chon!" I awake.

Let's try it again, slower.

Fairy Peg is lying in bed. Candlelight on her feverish face. Medicine vials. Incense burning. We are across the room, arguing in whispers. The shield of his helmet shadows his face. He grips my arm. A sword scrapes its sheath. Peg sits staring at us. "Chon!" she cries. I wake up.

Who is it? Who is arguing with me? And whose sword? Zero in on that face, Self. And the voice.

Fairy Peg lies in bed across the room from us, medicine vials and burning incense on the table beside her. Her sword hangs from the post. He says I can't help her. We are arguing. It's Alpluakka, Targ Alpluakka. The shield of the Gabriel Ratchet Commander. He's holding me back. Holding me away from Peg. The sword scrapes in its sheath. Fairy Peg is sitting up, pointing her sword at us. Her eyes are wild. "Chon!" she cries. I wake up.

"Chon." Obey. Obey what? Or whom? Obey Alpluakka? Is she telling me to obey Targ Alpluakka? Or is she telling him to obey me?

Why is it, Self, that the answers to these dreams always, always leave as many questions as they answer? I think Fairy Peg is telling Targ to obey me, to let me help treat her illness. Isn't "chon" the royal imperative, Self? Peg *must* be telling Targ to obey me.

When did this happen? Am I Prince Consort? Or am I new on Kril? The new diplomat trying to interfere with the healing of the Princess? Then the command is for me. I am to obey the Commander of the Gabriel Ratchets, personal imperial guard to the throne. That's it. It fits. I am to obey Commander Targ Alpluakka.

Oh, that dim memory, Self, lurking back there in the darkness. Did I try to heal Fairy Peg of some illness? Angered by their refusal to use the proper treatment, did I risk my life to do that? For what reason? Political? Professional? Personal? Was I angered by their ignorance? Or by their refusal to let me help?

No more answers here, I don't think. Just another little piece of the puzzle to try to fit in later.

Gracie once said that there are no puzzles because there are no pieces. There is only the Whole becoming Whole. That sounds good, but it sure is hard for me to understand and live by.

**7040–4.5**
**(day 57)**

ShRil just called. Be back here in an hour. Sounded cheery enough. Said she was hungry. A little galley magic, if you please, Windy.

**(day 58)**

ShRil's going over her notes for her presentation tomorrow, and I'm sitting here wondering at the strange turns a love affair takes. We talked almost all night and made some decisions. ShRil wants us to be together and I want us to be together. But each of us has separate responsibilities and obligations that will delay any long-term union. So we're going to form a *cylceia*, a Sylvan bondpledge, the first step of three for Sylvans toward permanent union. In old Terran terms, Windy, I guess you could say we're going to be engaged to be engaged.

Then, if everything works out for us as we hope, ShRil will finish her Embassy Service enlistment next year, and accept the traveling researcher's job Moseen University has offered her. At that time we will arrange to meet somewhere and decide if we want to take the second step, *cusping*. This is an engagement of sorts, which requires a predetermined period of separation, after which the couple (that's us) can decide to form a permanent union of *dowonâche*. *Dowonâche*, literally, "going the one path," from a time when the Sylvans completed the ceremony with the newly united couple walking side by side on the path to their new home.

Our predetermined period of separation for *cusping* would be part or all of the time remaining on my FedContract. Seems to me like a very careful and sensible approach. There are too many places where supposedly permanent bondpledges are easily and quickly made, then later must be dissolved through some long and painful process when the union fails to work. Better that the union be more difficult to accomplish than its dissolution.

We will perform the *cylceia* rites here, in private, before I leave. Already I'm eager and nervous. This is a very serious step we are about to take, Self. It marks a change in direction for us that we never anticipated. Or did we? Between *cylceia* and *cusping*, Self, we must determine our relationship to Fairy Peg. We still don't know by what legalities and promises we are bound there. We must find out. Fara forbid that there be something in our past which would come back to disrupt this promise for our happiness. More than Fara, I forbid.

Looks like one of the first things we'd better do after leaving Quadra is to try to make contact with Fairy Peg. I've been avoiding even the thought because I wanted to be as knowledgeable as possible about what happened to us in Ribble Galaxy before I made that decision. But now it looks unavoidable. I won't be content until we can clear that mystery from our lives. Better start thinking about that task, Self. It may get rough before we finish it. We surely can't let Fed know we're going to talk to their arch-enemy. That would finish us with them for sure. Could even land us in prison.

**7040–4.6**
**(day 59)**

ShRil's presentation of the Tenderfoot legend, and the following discussion, took most of the day. I participated a little, but the day was hers. Despite her anxiety, she is a fine speaker who can hold her audience captive while talking about research methods as well as the legend itself. Even putting all my biases aside, she was very impressive, and her colleagues showed their appreciation without reserve. I was very, very proud of her.

Envious of her skill, too. There's no way I can make my presentation of the W-M B Program as interesting and entertaining. But at least I don't have to follow right behind her. Whoever has tomorrow's program has a real job cut out for them.

Now, about this FedMessage, Windy. Are you sure that's all there is to it? "Proceed with orders. Quadra-FedBase treaty accepted as written." Can't believe Fed's suddenly getting succinct. Nor that they could have approved the treaty in six days. Nor that they didn't change anything. Before we act on this, I want diploconfirmation, Windy. Let's put it in security code. We'll get a response from higher up that way.

**7040–4.7**
**(day 60)**

Tomorrow's *cylceia* day. Our *cylceia* day. We sleep separately tonight (if we can sleep at all) and start the rites at dawn. If I'm not nervous, why do I feel like jumping up and down to get rid of all this energy. Or going straight into hypnosleep?

But no hypnosleep tonight, Windy. If Self wants to stay awake all night and think, then we stay awake. If you have any doubts about this, Self, now's the time to get them out.

**7040–4.8**
**(day 61)**

In case you didn't appreciate the aesthetics of what you witnessed today, Windy, I'm here to tell you it was beautiful. And lyrical, and mesmerizing, and ecstatic. If *cylceia* is this wonderful, I hesitate to think what *cusping* will be like. I don't think I've ever been happier or felt any better, Windy, or felt so warm and complete. Indicative of our future? I hope so. All I know, Windy, is that I wouldn't trade this day for any other I've ever lived. That's what ShRil does to me. She makes me feel like I'm present at my own nativity. Everything's so new, so vivid, so alive with her.

There are no words, Windy, merely the prattling of this humble, grateful man, happy to be here, now, with this wonderful woman.

Goodnight, Windy.

**7040–4.9**
**(day 62)**

A day of many pleasures. My presentation of the *Windhover*-Manley Bard Program was warmly received, and with our hookup to you, Windy, the discussion which followed was far more animated than I ever dreamed it would be.

Then a surprise. Director Franiingcard! Here to present us with a citation (and another honorarium) from Cultural Exchange. Wanted to shed a few tears at that point, Windy. Too many emotions at once.

Even Fed's confirmation of the treaty approval added a feeling of pride. They didn't change a word, Windy. That's remarkable. It's really a tribute to the Management Council and the Spiritum.

So, tomorrow we notify the Council and set up the signing ceremonies. Tonight, we enjoy and share with ShRil.

**7040–4.12**
**(day 66)**

Fast, Windy, fast. The days seem to end before they really get started. Parties, ceremony planning, coordination with Liaison, FedReps arriving, new inhabitants to meet (corporeal and otherwise), moments stolen from these last four days to be with ShRil. All happening too quickly.

We sign the treaty tomorrow. Day after, Odi is going to sneak us away to some off-limits ruins so ShRil and I can have a day alone. We hoped we could meet with the ghost from Yuma, but he doesn't like corporeals, Shttz said. So, if the other ghosts cooperate, we'll have the day to ourselves. Shttz told ShRil he would do his best to see that we're not disturbed.

Got to run, Windy.

**7040–4.15**
**(day 70)**

Cleared for launch, Windy. Minus fifteen and counting. Optimum conditions. All systems ready.

Take us away.

# 7

## 7040–4.17
## Space

You and ShRil make a good team, Windy. A couple of sneaks, hiding her farewell note like that. You knew I'd do a routine check on the rejuvhosp cells before I cleared us for warp. But you also knew I probably wouldn't go in there until then. I knew you two were talking behind my back, but I had forgotten your penchant for plotting.

Can I cry again? No. Just deep sighs. Don't know what ShRil sees in me, but whatever it is, I'm glad I have it. My *cylecee*, my ShRil. My darling Sylvan who cannot cry, who held me in her arms while her nose ran and ran and ran. How can I feel so lucky and so sad all at the same time? I look forward to our future, happy, but numb with this separation. I anticipate events I cannot put into words. I dream of beauty without form, light without source, pleasure without context. I feel harmony and balance, a sense of place and destiny.

And yes, even as I tell you this, Windy, I feel a small hard lump of fear that none of this will come to be, that I dream too far into the unknown future. But that fear cannot hold me down, cannot make me believe that the future, our future, will not be as wonderful as ShRil and I care to make it. We will create our own time and space, and together we will travel the curves of the continuum wherever our hearts lead us.

Do I rhapsodize, Windy? Do I sing too loudly? Can you put up with me in this state? Think what it will be like with the three of us, you, me, and ShRil, and know, in that dear electronic heart of yours, that this is just the prelude to a cosmic symphony!

Okay. I'll calm down. I'll quit boring you with this for the time being. But don't think you won't hear more. You'll just have to learn to endure.

Time to get back to business.

How are we supposed to renegotiate a treaty with Burnal Sevene when we can't get matching translations of the original treaty? That lexicon is a crime against the history of linguistics. I don't care that the original treaty was written over six hundred years ago. Surely someone in Fed, especially someone in Linguistics Division, could have derived a better lexicon in all that time than this pitiful one they sent us.

Are we faced with a translation problem? Or with an information shortage? Time to do some experimenting, Windy. Let's take everything we have in Sevenese and run it through the Baird with a variant-pattern frequency analysis. That ought to give us a base units number for the tonal system and at least a rough syntax factor. If we're lucky, we should also get a hint at the size of the total value system.

## 7040–4.19

Gibberish, Windy, pure gibberish. I certainly hope these results aren't indicative of what we have to look forward to. No way we can cope with deviations on a five-plus level.

Maybe though, we can isolate the deviations in translation with this eighteen-place syntax pattern Linguistics sent. I know that sounds backward, but it might give us a clue on how to proceed.

## 7040–4.20

Very interesting, Windy. Now we have forty-eight base tones plus eight standard deviations. Fifty-six total. With the eighteen-place syntax pattern, that gives us 1,016,064 meaning-value units, assuming, of course, that the square is standard and that the deviations persist throughout the pattern. A large assumption, I admit, but considering the fact that we still have a five-plus random deviation, I would say that our assumption is too small rather than too large.

But there is a clue here. Forty-eight is a regular twelve-tone derivative. But fifty-six isn't. Assuming a regular twelve-tone scale, the sequence should run forty-eight, sixty, seventy-two, eighty-four, etcetera. If we start with sixty and work our way up with a constant check on the deviation pattern, maybe we can at least determine the math of the system.

**7040–4.23**

You realize, don't you, that we are eleven days from Burnal Sevene and the only valid information we have on this problem is that we don't have enough valid information?

But fear not, a great deal can be accomplished in eleven days. Especially when we don't have anything else to do. Oh, I suppose I could sit here reading the Tamos and waiting for a response to the interrogative we sent to Ribble Galaxy from Quadra, but something tells me I wouldn't be very happy doing that.

Besides, I have another idea.

**7040–4.29**

Have we been snubbed, Windy? "No unauthorized communications allowed with FedReps", indeed. Some damn junior clerk in the Ribble Galaxy bureaucracy probably sent that.

Well, when in doubt, go straight to the top, they say. Address for the next one is, "Her Supreme Highness, Guardian of the Ribble Galaxy, Peg On'Ell, Badh of Seven Systems, Keeper of the Faith, Princess of Kril, Mistress of the Gabriel Ratchets, and Sweet Fairy Peg." In fact, my use of the familiar, Fairy Peg, ought to make someone angry. Just to make sure, though, add, "Brat of Ober On'Ell and Tania Houn Draytonmab."

Snub us, will they? Now, for a brief little message to pique their interest. "Dearest Princess, Unfinished business must be concluded as soon as possible and mutually convenient. Your prompt response will be appreciated. Confidential information available at your request." And sign that, "Gerard Manley, Universal Contract Diplomat, Fize of the Gabriel Ratchets, (Retired)." Return address, Burnal Sevene, Windy.

Don't think they'll snub that message. Especially with all

the insults in there. Question is, will it come to the attention of Fairy Peg? No way to answer that.

No time to worry about it, either. This base-twelve parallel series evaluation we've been running looks like it might contain part of the solution to the Burnal Sevene translation problem. But if it does, the lexicography task that faces us is staggering. All our results indicate a ninety-six-tone system with twenty-four syntactical variations each on a standard square. That yields 5,308,416 meaning-value units of which we can identify only 746,496 and define only a third of those. Still, if we're correct in our analysis, it means we can do the lexicography by ingestion rather than digestion.

If we run the Sevenese documents we have across this grid, Windy, we should be able to interpolate the rudiments of the syntax in terms of value directions. Then all we have to do is try to force our Standard Universal Lexicon into a comparable equivalency grid. Shouldn't take more than twenty or thirty years. Good grief, Windy. You'd better run a probability curve on that for us.

## 7040–5.1

Dreams of ShRil mixed up with twisted grids of flashing numbers and unintelligible symbols. Woke up as tired as I was before I went to sleep.

I love your probability curve, Windy. Plus or minus 7.339218 years. Just what I wanted to see. Means it will take from nine months to fifteen years to do a complete lexicon. Wonderful. Just wonderful.

Okay, what's the probability curve on an intelligible treaty?

## 7040–5.4
## Braking Orbit, Burnal Sevene

Have to admit I like the idea of six to twenty-one months better than the possibility of fifteen years. After all, we're here to rewrite a treaty, not to compile a lexicon. If our analysis is correct, we can give it to Linguistics Division and they can spend fifteen years working on the lexicon. It'll be a nice long-term project to help boost their budget.

No messages for us on Burnal Sevene from Ribble Galaxy. Yet. That's good. Should indicate our little epistle is getting some attention.

Our contact is SubGovernor Maestro Atherd'it. He's giving us the V.I.P. suite in the oxygen-breathers section of the embassy, complete with total interface to you, Windy, plus open library access and a staff of three. Told him I didn't need the staff, but he insisted.

Between the work we have to do, and Burnal Sevene's methane soup atmosphere, I don't expect to be doing much sightseeing, but I'm taking an extra suit just in case I get the chance. I'd like to see some of the flora and fauna while I'm here, just for the experience. Why? Restlessness, I guess.

Fourteen orbits to go. Might as well get some sleep.

**7040–5.6**
**FedEmbassy, Burnal Sevene**

Fortunately, Ambassador Naryehdecchoq is a Relur methane-breather, and we shall have only limited contact. His attitude toward our presence is something less than cordial, and after we went through the formalities, he informed me that there was no need for us to waste time on trivial communications during my stay, and, that he would appreciate my limiting requests to see him to matters of extreme importance. Like the completion of the treaty. Suits me. Didn't like the looks of him anyway.

Maestro Atherd'it, on the other hand, welcomed me with open arms. Six of his eight reached out to touch the crystal wall between us and when I pressed my hands against my side of the wall, I felt a bit inadequate. But I moved my hands in the proper top to bottom response, and he seemed very pleased. Even through the aural translator, I detected a tone of strength and warmth in him that made me feel very comfortable.

After assuring himself with repeated questions that my needs had been properly arranged for, he asked how he might be of assistance in helping me get started on this enterprise. Before we knew it, we had spent almost three hours in conversation, during which he confirmed our thesis of the ninety-six/twenty-four square. For the Sevenese, it's a one-forty-four/sixteen square, but the results are almost identical because their exceptions are uniform within the distribution.

Maestro Atherd'it was very pleased that we had done so much work before our arrival. Obviously I was very pleased that we had reached the correct solution to that part of the problem. He's making the arrangements now to give us the proper lexicography hookup from the central library so you and the Baird can begin to work on that, Windy. I also asked him for a small selection of their literature, explaining that we often found literary translations a key element in properly understanding a language. He was even more delighted with that, and said he would select the samples himself.

Despite Ambassador Naryehdecchoq's cold welcome, it was a very pleasant day, and, I think, a profitable one. When I asked Maestro Atherd'it why Linguistics Division had not come up with an understanding of the Sevenese system, he said they had explained to his predecessors that the Baird system of one-to-one correlation was the most advanced translation system in the universe. Since it had proven more than adequate for the transaction of normal relationships, apparently no one on Fed's side felt the need to pursue a different approach. It was only after the Presidium had insisted on rewriting the treaty that Linguistics Division realized how inadequate the traditional Baird program was.

That's why they called us, Windy. Our fame, it seems, precedes us. Now we have to live up to their expectations. No mean task, that. "My" three staff members probably won't be of much assistance. They are all three Trows (as was Morrizon), but their training is in Functional Bureaucracy rather than diplomacy or translation. They'll make intelligent gofers for us, and one, Tirem, will probably be able to help beyond that because of his command of Sevenese.

Maestro Atherd'it recommended Tirem to me as a good assistant, and that's not to be taken lightly. But my review of Tirem's record isn't as encouraging. Seems he has a rather violent temper and an immature tendency to throw nasty tantrums in the presence of his superiors. I won't condemn him on the basis of his record, but I will certainly want to keep an eye on him. I can put up with a lot if his assistance is valuable at all, but I will not put up with violence.

One more thing, Windy, before I go to bed. Let's try to shortcut the lexicography by running the data from the library across the grid and into memory at the same time. Ought to be able to fill some of the voids in our knowledge right away with that method. And if it doesn't work, we haven't lost anything.

## 7040–5.9

So much for shortcuts. Shouldn't complain, I guess, but one percent new fill was a little less than I hoped for. Maybe we should modify the feed program into the grid. Maestro Atherd'it made some suggestions along that line which might prove useful, and Tirem thinks a one-to-one prematch in front of the feed would increase our percentage considerably. That strikes me as a backward approach, but it's worth a try.

Even though you do most of the work, Windy, I never really enjoy the programming part of this job. What I want are the results, the tools we can then use to solve problems. If I could figure out how to do it, I'd program you to do all the future programming on your own.

But idle talk and wishful thinking will not get the job done. Let's buckle down on this one and worry about the rest later.

## 7040–5.12

Tirem's beginning to get on my nerves. Everything I say seems to evoke a contradiction from him. He's convinced our prefeed program is faulty and inadequate, convinced we should change to a one-forty-four/sixteen grid despite my explanation of why that wouldn't make any difference, and convinced that we should call for help from Linguistics Division. All this from someone who can barely operate a terminal beyond normal conversational levels. Damn bureaucrat. I'm afraid I've lost my patience with him several times and spoken rather harshly. That shuts him up, but it also gets me a steady glare from his middle eye.

But I can't worry about that. We've got a seven percent fill to date, and I think I see a way we can double that. Another modification to the prefeed program, Windy. A parallel four-to-one match system behind the one-to-one. Shouldn't take more than a day to set up.

## 7040–5.28
## Aboard Windy

Never thought I'd end up in our rejuvhosp cell like this, Windy. When Tirem throws a temper tantrum, he doesn't hold back. My ribs are healing nicely, but my jaw isn't knitting the way it should. At least we don't have to worry about Tirem any more. Ambassador Naryehdecchoq has him confined, and will ship him out as soon as possible to the nearest FedHosp. The ambassador wanted to press charges against him, but I insisted that Tirem is sick, not criminal, and, with Maestro Atherd'it's help, convinced the ambassador that the FedHosp is the place to send him.

What a contrast between the ambassador and Maestro Atherd'it. One angry and annoyed, the other sympathetic and concerned. Maestro Atherd'it feels guilty because he recommended Tirem as my assistant, and I am hard pressed to convince him that nothing that happened was his fault. I just ignored the signs of Tirem's imbalance too long, and aggravated him once too often by dismissing one of his obviously foolish suggestions as obviously foolish. If there's fault, it's mine.

If there's praise for anything lately, Windy, it's yours. That redoubling gate you added to the prefeed program has really done the trick. We have close to sixty-eight percent fill with forty-three percent definition. That's a seven-fold vocabulary increase over what Fed gave us to start with. Now we can begin channeling into the synonymity program and let the Bard tackle some of the literature Maestro Atherd'it gave us.

But not today. Today I rest some more.

## 7040–5.30

Sure have been sleen sleeping a lot, haven't I, Windy? But I feel much better. Those dreams of ShRil Self has been giving me haven't hurt any, I suspect. A little psychological comfort for the battered body, Self? Love being good for what ails me and all of that? Whatever your reasons, I'm not complaining.

Do you get the impression, Windy, that all of this literature from Maestro Atherd'it could just as easily be classified as music? It is music of a sort when we play it aurally in the original, but even these rough translations the Bard is pumping out are more like music than anything we normally consider literature. Dense, complex, fascinating, and indicative of why translation is such a tricky business. If we go for literal meaning, we lose subtle shadings and implications. If we go for something finer, we have to sacrifice part of the literal meaning. Every compromise involves a loss, and every loss must be questioned.

## 7040–6.18
## FedEmbassy, Burnal Sevene

Looks like we'll be ready to start on the treaty rewrite in a week or so, Windy. Most of the gaps left in the grid fill are mathematical, and it's going to take a lot longer to solve those problems than we need to stay here. Between your redoubling gate and the Bard's synonymity program, we have seventy-one percent fill and an amazing fifty-six percent definition. Almost three million value-meaning units with direct or implicit correlation. We still have to do some refining of ambiguity in the formal diplomatic vocabulary, but this song-poem the Bard and I finished polishing yesterday, and which sent Maestro Atherd'it into minor ecstasy when he read the Standard translation, is proof we're not far from completion of a solid basic lexicon.

### On the Suppression of Impulse

Coarsemanded, greydowned, we gaze and see—
Through the middlemisted age
Coolquenched fevers seeking rockwarm shallows
As though some mindless currentide
  would beachnest their small centers
    (burntdown, coldwashed essence-eggs)
  high in the warm and incubating sands.

Coughed by accident upon this foreign beach
We watch the fevers slipside by unsaved,
Recalling our youthspent, heatpitched burstings,
  dimfaded past a dearheld moment's pause now,
    too old to be remembered,
    too cold to be felt.

Coldfevered in the middlemist of age
We stand stiffbent and ancient
With neither joy, nor truth,
  nor sadness, nor lies
  to guide us back to the creationfires.

Maestro Veeter
(date unknown)

It is as faithful in meaning and nuance to the original as the Bard and I could make it, and even so, I hesitate to claim we captured even a shadow of the original's musical power. Part of the problem is that Standard syntax will just not accommodate the implicit meanings. But the other part is the necessity of wordforging, combining Standard terms to approximate the Sevenese originals.

Wouldn't it be fun to rewrite the treaty in these cadences, with this free a hand on the vocabulary? Fed would have a fit of anger that would send us scurrying for a place to hide. No, I'm afraid Fed is far too sophisticated to face such a realistic translation. Maybe we can compromise and send them two translations, both signed and sealed as authentic and legal. That would force them to acknowledge the language without forcing them to accept it. Have to sound out Maestro Atherd'it on that idea. Might even work it so he makes the actual suggestion.

**7040–6.20**

"To His Highness, Gerard Manley, Prince Consort of Kril, Fize of the Gabriel Ratchets, Royal Ambassador. Your Majesty: Greetings. Long ago we mourned you when the Federation informed us of your death. Now your message crosses the chasm of Klonos, reaching out to us from beyond the fringe of life. We would value your presence again in this empire, but we must be assured of your rightful claim to the name of Gerard Manley. Tell us the name you were called in private by Our Majesty. Only then can we honor your request for a meeting. Corpus Privy, Council to Her Supreme Highness, (etc., etc., etc.)"

Well, Self, what do you think of that? They thought I was dead and now they want to know if I'm real. A reasonable request, to be sure, but there's at least one catch in it. I don't know what Fairy Peg called me in private. If you know, you haven't told me. If the message is truly from the Privy Council, and I must assume it is, then they have cleared up the mystery of my current relationship to Fairy Peg. But if they once mourned me for dead, how can I still be Prince Consort and Fize of the Gabriel Ratchets? Back to Rule One: each answer provides its own new questions.

Can you dig it out, Self? We'll use Doc Flo's technique and a bit of hypnosleep to set the stage, but you'll have to do the hard part, as usual. I know we don't get the best results when we push like that, but we'll have to settle for whatever we can get, and make the best of it. Ready to give it a try?

### 7040–6.21

Self, I don't know if we got soup or swill. All those swirling images and foreign symbols don't give me much. And why all the stars? What do they have to do with Fairy Peg's name for me. Surely she didn't call me, Star, or Starlight, or something silly like that. Doesn't ring any bells with me, and besides, I have a feeling that the stars themselves are not the point. If I close my eyes, I can see those images from the dream again. Stars and symbols moving in strange patterns on a dark field. What is the pattern?

We'll just have to try again tonight, Self. I can't make any sense out of it now. Too many confusing details.

Maestro Atherd'it knew I was trying to get him to suggest two Standard translations yesterday and told me so. But he also told me he thought it was an excellent idea and would put it before the Presidium. I gave him the literal translation we did of "On the Suppression of Impulse" so he could let them see the differences between that and the lyrical one. Should have their reaction by this afternoon.

*****I may have gotten us in a fix, Windy. The Presidium wants only one translation as the official Standard one. A lyrical translation. They want us to do a lyrical translation of the original treaty as soon as possible and Maestro Atherd'it said they would like to have it by tomorrow. I told him there was no way we could do it that quickly, but that we would try to have it ready in four or five days. We're going to have to work twenty hours a day to meet that deadline, Windy, but since the treaty vocabulary is relatively limited, we ought to be able to get it done.

### 7040–6.22

Took me literally, didn't you, Windy? Let me sleep for four hours after I fell asleep at the terminal and then woke me up. Self must have known you were going to do it, because I was right in the middle of a dream when you buzzed me. Fairy Peg was trying to wake me, too. "One must face the day, Pilot." That's what she was saying, whispering actually, over and over in my ear. I was awake, but I didn't want her to move away from me. Pilot. Why did she call me Pilot? Right, Self, because I guided her among the stars, she said. I was her "Star Pilot" at first, but she shortened it to just Pilot.

So that's what all those stars were about night before last. Maybe if I'd thought about it harder, I could have figured it out then. No matter. You dug it out in two nights, Self, and as far as I'm concerned, that's one Krick of a job. You and I make a great team when we put my head together.

Now we'll be able to send our reply to the Privy Council and see what their response to that is. Should we ask if I'm still Prince Consort and Fize of the Gabriel Ratchets? Or should we just sign it that way and assume that we are? Better, perhaps, just to sign it Universal Contract Diplomat and let them know I'm not laying claim to any of those titles.

Where can we suggest a meeting? I don't think I want to go into Ribble Galaxy itself, if only because I'd have to lie to Fed to do it. Find us a neutral system between here and there, Windy, someplace we can get to in a couple of easy warps. Shouldn't be too difficult to talk Fed into letting us have a month or so off after what we did on Pleasance and Quadra. Here, too.

Which means as soon as we get that message off, Windy, it's time to go back to work.

### 7040–6.25

Finished. Not as pretty as "Impulse," but not bad. No way, I guess, to make a treaty sound pretty. Sent it across to Maestro Atherd'it with a note that I am going to get some rest.

While I'm sleeping, Windy, run the original through for a literal Standard translation. Keep running it through until the change rate is down to less than half a percent on each pass. I'll check the Bard's progress this afternoon when I wake up. Don't expect the literal to take quite as long as the lyrical did, now that all the basics have been done.

Buzz me at three. I can't keep my eyes open any longer.

### 7040–6.26

Incredible. The Bard did the literal translation of the treaty in a quarter of the time it took the three of us to do the lyrical version, and the literal translation is over twice as long. Maybe we should do all our treaties in verse, Windy. Could cut our work in half.

Might as well pass this version over to Maestro Atherd'it so the Presidium can see what it would have looked like if it had been accurately translated the first time. Fed certainly missed a lot of the meaning and subtleties of that treaty.

Our choices for a neutral meeting ground between here and the Ribble Galaxy are pretty limited according to your analysis, Windy. I think the Mithindoll System can be scratched from your list, because, if I remember correctly, relations between Mithindoll and Ribble were not very friendly. That leaves us with the ELY-18 System with four inhabited planets, all non-oxygen, heavy gravity types, or with the Tradershote Union. Wait a minute. Isn't the Pleuhockle System part of the Tradershotes? What's the breakdown, Windy?

*****Well, I wasn't too far off. The Pleuhockle System and the Tradershote Union are neutral allies, a little closer to the Ribble Galaxy than I'd like, but suitable. We've got the code address for Alvin's Place, and he did invite us to come to see him. Maybe we can take advantage of his hospitality and meet Fairy Peg there at the same time. Wouldn't mind seeing the old bird again, even if he does talk my ear off, or "fill my craw with seeds," as he puts it.

So, if Fairy Peg agrees to a meeting, we try to contact Alvin and see if we can meet there. Then, as soon as the Burnal Sevene treaty is rewritten, signed, sealed, and delivered, we tell Fed we're taking a couple of months off, notify Fairy Peg to meet us at Alvin's Place, and ship out. Sounds too simple to me, but I don't see any unusual snags in that plan. Biggest problems would be if Alvin wasn't there or said no, or if the meeting place was unacceptable to Fairy Peg.

We'll cross those parsecs when we come to them. But let's go ahead and send a message to tell Alvin we might be in the neighborhood with the possibility of needing to meet with a representative of Ribble Galaxy, and see what his reaction is. Even if Alvin's Place is unacceptable to Fairy Peg, we still might be able to swing by and see Alvin. The more I think about it, the more I want to see him, regardless of what happens.

Let's send that message now, Windy.

**7040–6.27**

Running a Tenderfoot search while we're waiting. Through two levels with no leads. In fact, almost no references to specific personalities at all.

*****Quit, Windy. If we haven't found anything after five levels, there's probably nothing here.

### 7040–6.28

Maestro Atherd'it said the Presidium has decided that what Burnal Sevene needs is not a rewritten treaty, but rather, a less awkward amendment clause to the old one and five or six additional amendments. That's fine with me. Makes our work all that much easier. They expect to have a draft treaty ready for me to translate by tomorrow, then Maestro Atherd'it is authorized to negotiate for the Presidium on any points of conflict we might have.

Ambassador Naryehdecchoq called me on the vidcom when he learned of this new development from Maestro Atherd'it, and he was furious. Said if that was all the Sevenese wanted, he could have done it for them. Didn't need some hireling coming in to do an ambassador's work for him. Wants to see anything we do before it's presented to the Presidium. I turned him down as gently as I could, and explained what he already knows. Except in unavoidable cases, Fed would rather have these chores handled by we "hirelings." Helps keep FedService people away from local political problems, keeps them off the defensive in case any unforeseen conflicts arise, etcetera. He signed off before I finished my explanation. Don't think he liked it.

### 7040–6.29

Good morning, Windy. Good morning, Self. Good morning, ShRil. Nice to have you with us in my dreams. Makes the day start on a bright note. Now that I have you all assembled here, I'd like to announce that I'm going to invite ShRil to join us at Alvin's Place (after certain persons leave, of course) and ask her if we can perform the *cusping* there. Some of you might say that I am impatient, but that is not true. I am merely eager. Dreamed of the *cylceia* last night and felt that the only appropriate thing to do would be to take the next step. If ShRil and I have to be separated after we next see each other, let that separation begin as soon as possible so that it will be over as soon as possible. Nothing impatient about that.

*****Well, Windy, Maestro Atherd'it just passed the new

amendment drafts over, so we might as well get started. Doesn't look like it should take too long, but we want to make sure that it is right. The Presidium wants both a literal and a lyrical translation. Maestro Atherd'it said he has almost convinced them to accept the two-version plan. I hope he succeeds, because if he doesn't, Fed is going to ask a lot of questions. Dumb questions. Frankly, there is nothing to be gained by it. If we can send Fed both versions signed by the Presidium, that should encourage them to revise their attitudes about the Standard versions of treaties without pressuring them to accept something this radical immediately.

And speaking of Fed, I want to send CulEx Central a complete copy of the lexicon, the grid system, and the poetry translation. That's the least we can do to repay their generosity. If we ever leave diplomacy, maybe we could go to work for CulEx.

## 7040–7.2

Have you noticed, Windy, that I don't add much to this journal when we are busy, as we have been? Can't decide if that's good or not. But when I read back over some of the entries here, I think I have a habit of recording too much of the trivial. Tend to repeat myself too.

*****The Privy Council, Corpus Privy I guess I should call them, still has doubts about my identity. Now they want to know your Ribble registration number, Windy. Should be in your memory, but it's not. Fed must have erased that too. I don't know if I ever knew that number, Self, but we can look for it. Doesn't seem like the kind of thing we can come up with, given our seeming addiction to symbols and shadows, but we'll give it our best.

Passed the final translations to Maestro Atherd'it this morning. If the Presidium has no further changes, he and I should be able to negotiate the changes that have to be made with little difficulty. Most of them are technical or necessary updating procedures regarding relations with Fed. The only tough point will be the Presidium's insistence that in all matters of dispute between Burnal Sevene and Fed, the *alpha*, or lyrical Standard version, will be considered the definitive legal version. FedLegal especially won't want to go along with that.

Fortunately, I have the power of approval in this instance.

Unfortunately, if FedLegal dislikes it enough, I could find myself out in the spacelanes without a contract. Fed would just pay me off for the remainder of this contract and never give me another.

What I have to find out is whether the Presidium's insistence on this point is based on whim or on principle. If it's principle, I will support them and approve their insistence clause. But if it's whim, I think we can all save ourselves a lot of future trouble by removing that clause.

In some ways, I wouldn't mind if Fed bought the remainder of my contract. Oh sure, Self, I would miss being a diplomat, miss the excitement of negotiations and the clash of ideas, but it would also be nice to become a traveling researcher for Moseen University, *dowanâche* with ShRil, and travel the universe together. I'm all too aware that such romantic notions can cloud my rational, pragmatic thought processes and point me toward a very unstable future. As much as anything, I guess it's a question of how long I want or need to depend on Fed. Fed's been fair to me thus far, except for the Ribble Galaxy episode, which I can't really judge without more information.

However, ever since I was freed from Galaxy VI, I've had a recurring thought that it might be nice to pull away from the Fed teat and move out on my own. There are other things I can do which would utilize my talents and bring in the credits. Now that you're paid for, Windy, and ShRil thinks we could work together for Moseen, this might be one of those times when circumstances are right to make a change.

But that's all speculation right now. Valuable, but speculation just the same. Part of my diploschool training showing through again. "Always anticipate the worst possible dilemma and the best possible solution," Master Glinyas used to say.

## 7040–7.3

I didn't get any number out of that dream. Did you, Self? Thought does occur to me that Windy might not have had a Ribble Galaxy registration number. Let's send Corpus Privy a straightforward message saying, if we had one, we no longer have records indicating what it was. We can also suggest that they are delaying for trivial reasons and that the confidental information we possess has an urgent quality. Put them on the defensive rather than me.

While we're sending messages, a brief one to ShRil would be nice. We'll tell her there's a possibility we're going to Alvin's Place, and ask if it would possible for her to join us if we do. Casual and loving. Don't want to get her hopes up yet. Or mine either.

*****Tomorrow we begin negotiations with Maestro Atherd'it. Save the legal version problem for last so we have it to look forward to.

Tell you what, Windy. You bring out the holo of ShRil and I'll turn on the soother to help me go to sleep. Then we'll get Self to conjure us some erotic dreams. How about that, Self? Think you can work that out?

Good. Then let's get to it.

## 7040–7.4

Woke up thinking about Shttz and what he told me and ShRil about Yuma the night he and Ronda visited us. Shttz said the ghost from Yuma talked about a historical character there who fit the Tenderfoot legend. If Fed pushes us out, a trip to Yuma might be just the thing to get Moseen University to hire us. Have to keep that in mind.

*****Maestro Atherd'it and I whizzed through the technical changes today without a pause, but when I suggested that making the *alpha* version the definitive legal translation might not be the best idea, we came to a crunching halt. After an hour's discussion, we agreed to talk about it again tomorrow, but I doubt that anything will change. Maestro Atherd'it convinced the Presidium that the *alpha*-lyrical version was much more accurate than the literal version, and now neither he nor they are going to want to accept what they see as a second-rate translation. They're right, of course, but that's not the point. The point is that the *alpha* version will not do anything to facilitate pragmatic relations with Fed.

See what we've gotten ourselves into, Windy. Comes from being too good at our job. Or from pride. If we'd followed Master Glinyas's teaching and anticipated this problem, we could have avoided it. But we were so proud of ourselves for figuring out the Sevenese system, so puffed up with pleasure that our eyes were swollen shut, and we couldn't look ahead at the implications.

I'll do my best tomorrow to convince the Maestro that two

translations of equal status will serve Burnal Sevene better. If I get the slightest indication from him that such a position is tenable for him and the Presidium, I will work on that point for as long as it takes. However, if it finally comes down to a matter of refusing to compromise on the principle of accuracy and truth, I will concede. Don't know what I'll say to persuade Fed, but if the Maestro insists, the principle will rule.

### 7040–7.6

I gave in. After two exhausting days of arguing, I knew I wasn't going to change a thing. The Presidium will sign both versions, but the *alpha* will be the legally definitive translation. As the Tamos says, "What is, is. What will be, will be."

We sign the treaty on 7.10.

### 7040–7.8

Message from Alvin welcoming us whenever we are ready to come. His injured wheel has healed very satisfactorily, but it bothers him during space flight, so he no longer travels any more than he has to. Said I could bring whatever guests or meet whomever I wanted at his place within the laws of Pleuhockle.

Alvin's Place is not just his home, it's a whole planet! Sent us the starpoint coordinates for "Pleuhockle System, Planet Jelvo-five, Alvin's Place." Remind me to treat him with a little more respect when we meet him again, Windy.

Work to do: Message to Fed telling them the treaty will be forwarded to them on or about 7.12, and that we are taking two months unpaid leave following that date and can be contacted at Alvin's Place. Message to Fairy Peg insisting on a meeting in the Pleuhockle System (won't name Alvin's Place yet) and demand a response by Burnal Sevene relay not later than 7.20 and a meeting by 8.20. Message to ShRil asking if she can meet us on Alvin's Place after 8.25. And a message to Alvin telling him we're coming.

Well, what are we waiting for, Windy?

### 7040–7.10
### Aboard Windy, Burnal Sevene Starport

If there's a graceful way to sign a treaty while dressed in an atmosphere suit, I don't know what it is. Maestro Atherd'it tried to make it as simple for me as possible, but since the Sevenese don't use anything like tables, I ended up kneeling on the floor. Ambassador Naryehdecchoq enjoyed my discomfort immensely, but the Presidium members acted as though the sight of a humanoid on all fours in a bulky suit trying to sign a document on the floor was normal.

Anyway, I had the last laugh on the ambassador. He didn't realize that there were two Standard translations until he had signed them as witness. I gave him the embassy copies, and left as quickly as decorum would allow. Got my things out of the embassy and headed straight here. When you took that vidcom message from him, Windy, I was laughing so hard I couldn't hear what he was saying.

Let's send our FedMessage with my carefully worded transmittal and start the countdown for launch, Windy. I've already said my goodbyes to Maestro Atherd'it and the staff, and Burnal Sevene Control has cleared us to start prelaunch procedures.

Why do I feel like a schoolie who's just gotten away with a prank? Probably because the ambassador's such a smudge. He is probably composing an angry message to Fed right now. I'd bet a month's pay he hasn't even read the treaties, much less understood what happened. By the time his message goes through Embassy Service, and Embassy Service contacts Diplomatic Service, Federation Treaty Service will be well on their way to reacting to the actual treaties, and his message won't add or detract anything.

Snub for snub, Ambassador Naryehdecchoq, sir.

*****Cleared for launch in one hour, Windy. Begin final check sequence. Let's go see Alvin, Baris-lon-Jelvo.

# 8

## 7040–7.12
## Space

There's a fine, happy edge to my mood, Self, a kind of semisubliminal euphoria. It's the irrational joy of rebellion, defiance of authority just for the sake of defiance. Didn't realize how confined and restrained I felt by my position with Fed until now. To have such a small act bring on such a strong reaction tells me something very important. I'm not sure I can put it into words yet, but I can certainly recognize that there is a center of pressure and turmoil that we have kept secretly contained. Our willingness to let the Sevenese have their way with the treaty and our snub of the ambassador vented part of that. But there's a great deal more underneath. I can feel it.

Foggy, blurred, vague, and unclear, Self. A pitiful analysis. How am I supposed to make any sense out of such ill-defined feelings as that? Either you had better get to work on more substantial and precise expositions, or we can stow them away again. No sense in trying to examine cargo you can't see clearly.

*****Alvin must have been sitting on top of his comunit when our message arrived and started his answer before he received the whole thing. Short and direct. "Come immediately. Have Tenderfoot lore. Eagerly awaiting your arrival." As if there weren't enough attraction to this trip already, Alvin has some Tenderfoot "lore" for us. I'm surprised that he remembered.

## 7040–7.15

One short warp and four more days and we should be sitting on Alvin's Place. Crazy old bird couldn't wait for us to arrive and forwarded part of the Tenderfoot lore, one strange poem in a language that appears to be an old Terran derivative. Alvin's message said the source was unknown, but that he had found it quite by accident in the library of one of his Tradershote friends on the way back home from Asrai. Part of a transcription fragment called "Frontier Planets." Shouldn't be too hard for us to translate this one, Windy.

*****Apparently Tenderfoot wasn't held in total reverence by whomever wrote this poem. But more fascinating is the archaic terminology. Either the author was very familiar with the old Terran languages, or this is a very old poem.

### Tenderfoot's Demise

Tenderfoot was shot and killed
While burglarizing a dictionary
For rare words, objects of art,
Keys to his future, and rhymes for life.

Had he been caught alive,
It would have been one-to-five for petty larceny,
And probably a probated sentence.
But Tenderfoot panicked.
An editor shot him down (and was later acquitted),
And that was that.

Oh, yes.
They buried Tenderfoot in Boot Hill
With this inscription on a return envelope
Nailed to his coffin,
"Wordslinger.
Caught redhanded."

If this is a legitimate part of the legend, and we have no reason to doubt that it is, it tells us a great deal we didn't know before. That Tenderfoot was a writer of some sort. That he at least tried to write for publication. That whatever he wrote was not very well received, perhaps because of its quality.

I have a suspicion, with absolutely no way to prove it, Windy, that this very poem is the kind of thing Tenderfoot might have written. Wouldn't it be fun if we could track down the source of this and discover that Tenderfoot did indeed write it?

Alvin has a complete copy of the "Frontier Planets" fragment and his friend's story of how it came into his possession. Maybe there's enough information to point us in the right direction. Maybe I'm just dreaming out loud to kill time. Who in the universe cares at all about the Tenderfoot legend except me, ShRil, The Professor, and perhaps a dozen others ShRil might have impressed with it at the conference? What difference does it make in the scheme of things? None. But it's fun.

## 7040–7.17
## Entry Path, Alvin's Place

With all my thoughts about seeing Alvin, I guess it was bound to happen. The Teever Loze nightmare is back again. Two nights in a row, after having avoided it for months. I really wish this was a dream we could analyze and then get rid of, Self. But we can't. We already know exactly what it means. It means that Teever Loze is dead and we saw it happen, and the horror of it will not retire peacefully to some quiet crypt and take its final rest. It means we are doomed, for Fara only knows how long, to watch Teever Loze get blown apart again and again. All we can do is scream his name and wake with that vivid picture in front of us and the hot sweat dripping like blood off my body. Will there ever be an escape? Will we ever see the end of it?

*****Call from Alvin. We have priority clearance to land at Barisport, which apparently is very close to his home. I suspect from its name that it is his private starport. Owners of planets can afford things like that.

Also relayed a Fedmessage for me. "Leave approved. Burnal Sevene-Federation Treaty under study." Nothing more. Nothing less. A nice neutral acknowledgement. But they already acknowledged receipt of the treaty, and since they hadn't forwarded an assignment, there was no reason to disapprove the leave. So why did they bother with this message?

Because, my dear Gerard, "treaty under study" actually means, "What in Krick have you sent us? We don't understand it. We're not sure we like it. And we question your judgement in signing it." That's the real message. Very pointed in a very diplomatic way, if you know how to read it.

However, the very fact that they didn't override my actions outright shows that someone back there believes what we did is in fact worth further study and consideration. That's no mean accomplishment in and of itself.

### 7040–7.19
### Barisport, Alvin's Place

All packed and ready to go. Alvin will be here in a few minutes to take me out to his "nest." Got the memocorder so I can talk to you from there. Be sure to call as soon as any messages come in. Oh, and one more thing, Windy. The portechs are going to clean and polish your hull. A gift to you from Alvin.

Talk to you later, girl.

### 7040–7.20
### Heartsnest, Alvin's Place

Alvin can call this a nest if he wants, but I wish you could see it, Windy. Palace would be about the right term, but a palace like none I've ever seen or heard about. Imagine a thousand sumptuous rooms carved into a jagged cliff of glittering stone, with broad, spiraling ramps from room to room and rooms to ground. If Alvin hadn't assured me that the whole thing is his nest, I'd have thought it was a city. Breathtaking is too cheap an adjective to describe it.

Heartsnest tops a mountain about eighteen hundred meters high, with the topmost rooms (including my suite) having views of both the rising and setting of the double sun. At this time of year, the red sun trails the yellow one by about thirty minutes, and the display of sunset colors lasts for over an hour. Alvin assures me that the sight is much more impressive during the cold season, when they set side by side, but I'm not sure I could handle anything more spectacular than what I saw tonight. Even if nothing else happened on this trip, that one sunset would almost make it worthwhile.

And speaking of things happening, looks like Fairy Peg is going to miss the deadline we set for a response to our demand that she meet us. Guess we'd better give some thought to our next move.

Not disappointed that we haven't heard from ShRil, yet. The Professor could have sent her anywhere in the known universe after she returned from the conference. There's still time.

Tomorrow Alvin's taking me on a grand tour of Heartsnest from bottom to top. Promised me lots of surprises and an interesting day. He said you could reach us anywhere by calling Heartsnest and adding a seven-zero-nine code to the call sign. Saves me from having to take the memocorder with us. I'll call you when we get ready to leave.

## 7040–7.21

It is a city, Windy, complete with hydroponic gardens, a zoo, three art galleries, two libraries, its own underground hydroelectric power plant and water system, and even traffic monitors who made us wait our turn at intersections like everyone else. Alvin may be Baris-lon-Jelvo and own the planet and everything on it, but the citizens of Heartsnest treat him not as a ruler, but rather as their best friend. Youngsters swooped down on us with cries of greeting and friendly wags of their preform wheels. Ancients (that's what Alvin called them) with thinning feathers and wobbly wheels waved to us wherever we went. From what little of the Pleuhockle I can understand, it seemed like half of his people greeted him as Cousin Alvin. When I asked about that, he told me that a little over two-thirds of Heartsnest's four thousand inhabitants were related either by egg or by mating, and "cousin" is a common greeting.

It was an exhausting day, but I didn't really know how tired I was until I got back to my rooms and . . .

*****Considering the relay from Burnal Sevene, I guess Fairy Peg's message really isn't late. She can't come, Windy. (Or she won't.) But she did agree to send a representative she said she knew I would trust. Commander Targ Alpluakka. Why should I trust him? Sure can't think of any reason off the top of my head. Another missing piece here, Self? Or some kind of trick?

I gave Alvin a brief outline of the situation yesterday, but I want to talk to him tomorrow before I reply. Don't like the idea of not being able to confront Fairy Peg face to face, nor of meeting Targ without her. Wasn't he one of those shouting against me in one of our dreams, Self? That doesn't sound like someone I can put a lot of trust in.

At least the address on this message seems to confirm one thing. It's devoid of titles. Hopefully, I am also.

### 7040–7.22

Alvin agreed that I have grounds to be suspicious, but he said that if he let the Ribble ship land at Barisport and we met Targ together there, any meeting ought to go without incident. It's not an ideal situation, but under the circumstances it will have to do.

Let's get the message off to Fairy Peg, Windy. No profit in delay.

### 7040–7.23

Alvin was off taking care of business, and I spent most of the day in the non-technical library. I want to run our Tenderfoot search, Windy, but given the nature of this system, it's going to take a couple of days to hook you up for it. Meantime, I'm sending you a transcription of the "Frontier Planets" fragment, Alvin's information on its source, and a list of references on possible Tenderfoot leads. Some of them refer to items in Alvin's library, but most are ones he can't trace beyond what he has given us. Still, the leads into his library look promising and ought to put us well on the way with the search.

The rest of this transmission goes into the Tenderfoot file, Windy.

### 7040–7.26

Well, it took a little longer than I thought, Windy, but it looks like the hookup is complete. All the test data has passed without any trouble, so I'll be out to the port tomorrow and start running this search from your end. The interface is too narrow to try to control it from here. Alvin was very apologetic about that, but I assured him that, even though it might slow us down a little, the narrow interface won't cause us any serious problems.

I think Alvin's as eager to see what results we get as we are. Maybe even more so. He's going to monitor us from the library, and I've set up a signal that will tell him when we find anything. As extensive as his library is, he's sure we're going to find a wealth of material. That would be nice, but we'll be happy with anything we can get.

Had the Teever Loze nightmare again last night. Wanted to tell Alvin about it, but don't want to stir up memories for him too. He knows Teever Loze is dead, but he didn't say much more than that. I don't think he knows how Teever Loze died, and I don't really want to tell him. Let Alvin's memories all be good ones.

### 7040–7.28

This is exciting, Windy! Four passes and ninety-one references, seventeen of which look very promising. When we finally quit this morning, after running over eighteen hours, Alvin couldn't understand why we didn't keep going. I tried to explain my fatigue, but he is so excited by what we've found that I don't think he's felt any fatigue and doesn't see why we should.

I'm going to grab some sleep now and we'll start up again this afternoon. You can go ahead and scan the references we already have and put an analysis together for me, Windy. That'll save some time when we start the fifth pass.

*****Good references. And lots of bulk material. I think the best thing we can do would be to run everything we have through the Bard and then do a mass dump transmission of originals and translations to The Professor. There's no way we're going to analyze all of this. Too difficult to tell how much of it is valid.

The only disappointing part of this whole operation is the lack of solid examples of the Tenderfoot literature. The best references we have talk about characters who seem to fit the legend, but the actual examples we've been able to locate and pull are for the most part dense narratives that will have to be carefully translated and analyzed. Nothing so far like the things we've found before.

### 7040–7.29

Just another little reminder that we should never give up too soon, Windy. Barely started the seventh pass in the index range and what do we get? A poem entitled, "At the Moment of Truth, the Old Novice Decides." Not only does it fit the Tenderfoot pattern, it's written in a colloquial dialect of Early Standard.

So, while you continue the pass, Windy, the Bard and I will play with this little piece and see if we can't put it into an acceptable form of modern Standard.

*****More references on the seventh and eighth passes, but only one simple example of the actual literature. The Bard stuck pretty close to the original style and form, and I think I'll leave it like that. However, since the footnote with the original says the editor arbitrarily gave it a title, I'm going to take the liberty of changing it.

**Somehow It All Comes Down to This**

Somehow it all comes down to this one day,<br>
                                        this single decision,<br>
                                        this solitarie choice<br>
                                                ringing the finger of fate.<br>
Poor Tenderfoot,<br>
Not made for purely rational excuse,<br>
He must summon logic's power and choose,<br>
    knowing the logic blind,<br>
            the input incomplete.<br>
Win, or lose, or both,<br>
As far as Tenderfoot can see<br>
The only feats accomplished<br>
Will be overcoming fear,<br>
        restraining nausea,<br>
        and sustaining irrational logic.

The credit slides across.<br>
"Another brew," said Tenderfoot, wincing.

Not the best piece of poetry that ever rolled out of the Bard, but as the only positively valid example to come out of this search, I think I love it.

Two more passes should about finish this search. We're down to the fine sifting now, and I figure we've had about all the success we're going to. There's a full load of things to send on to The Professor already, and he could stay busy with what we have here for a year if we didn't find anything else.

Joining Alvin for dinner shortly. Make me a copy to take to him, Windy. On the parchment.

Dinner was interrupted in the loveliest way last night. Personal message from the Commandant of Tradershote Security to Alvin, Baris-lon-Jelvo, to notify him that one Sprite Class research ship, *Liencam*, registered to Moseen University, is proceeding at sub-warp speed to Alvin's Place. Alvin didn't seem very pleased about receiving the message, but I was. That's ShRil's ship! She's coming, Windy. But why hasn't she sent a message?

##Message received.##

When? What do you mean, message received?

##Message received 7040-7.21.0855:41. Meaning obvious.##

Windy, do you mean to tell me you received a message for me from ShRil nine days ago and didn't tell me?

##Message not to Gerard Manley. Message to *Windhover.*##

Oh, I see. "Message to *Windhover,*" was it? Spill, Windy. Give me a copy of the message.

##Negative.##

I want a copy of that message, Windy.

##Negative.##

Is this some kind of secret? Did ShRil order you not to tell me?

##Affirmative. Affirmative.##

Well, the surprise is gone. I'm ordering you to give me a copy of that message.

##Negative.##

Diplomatic Cruiser, Class Twelve, Registry T-Alpha 7731Series D, Designation *Windhover,* Pilot Gerard Manley demands access to all messages received from Utility Vessel, Sprite Class, Registry Moseen University, Moseen 833C21X5, Designation *Liencam*, on or about 7040–7.21.

##Negative. Negative. Negative. Stop. End transmission.##

I don't want to hear all that negative, negative, negative crud. Give me a copy of that message.

Now, Windy.

*****I give up. Whatever system you and ShRil cooked up back on Quadra to keep your private messages a secret from me is working. If you won't reveal the information on orders,

I'm not going to tear you apart to get it. It's nice that ShRil wanted to surprise me, but I'm not sure I approve of you working in cahoots with her. You're a devious female, Windy. So is ShRil.

In case the two of you are in communication now, you can tell ShRil that Tradershote Security has spoiled her surprise. You can also tell her I can hardly wait for her to get here. The commandant estimated her arrival date as 8.7. Would you care to confirm that, Windy, or, if not, would you ask ShRil to confirm it? I'd have you send her a message for me, but I wouldn't want to interfere with your little game.

Before we get on to anything else, I do have a question for you. Why do you enter this journal against orders when there's no emergency?

You have my permission to enter here and answer.

No comment? Not only are you devious, you're perverse, too.

But since you won't obey my orders or answer my questions, I'm going to work your circuits off. I want four more passes on the Tenderfoot search, Windy. Now.

## 7040–8.1

You'll be glad to know, Windy, that I'm over my little fit of anger. And exhausted. I guess I was a little hurt that ShRil didn't tell me she was coming. I mean, suppose we hadn't been here? Stupid thought. You kept her up to date on our location, didn't you? Kravor in Krick! Why must the two of you aggravate me like this?

Well, anyway, I guess it's nice to know that I'm being watched over so carefully.

*****If this analysis we've done is correct, you're going to have to stay tied to Alvin's library for at least four more weeks in order to produce adequate translations for The Professor. Most of the work will be routine, and you and the Bard can handle it without me. Ought to take about two days to set up the sequencing, and then I can go back to Heartsnest and monitor you from there, while enjoying more of Alvin's hospitality and the beautiful scenery until ShRil arrives.

*****Message from Corpus Privy. "Contract Diplomat Gerard Manley: Terms accepted. Commander Targ Alpluakka to arrive Alvin's Place not later or earlier than 7040–8.20."

Good.

## 7040–8.3

So, you did tell ShRil that I am eager to see her. Her message didn't say that, but it's obvious now that she wouldn't have sent it if you hadn't. Hers was sweet, light and also eager.

Leaving for Heartsnest in the morning. The sequencing is ready to take over, so we might as well start it tonight, just to make sure we haven't missed anything.

## 7040–8.5
## Heartsnest

Not only is Alvin an avid talker, he's also an avid listener. Spent most of the last two days in relaxing conversation with him asking most of the questions, and me doing most of the talking. Lots of questions about where I've been, what I've done, my diplomatic, religious, political and social philosophies. At first I felt like I was being interviewed for a job, but after a while, I relaxed and enjoyed the opportunity to talk about all those things. Only ShRil knows more about me than Alvin, and she doen't know anything about my Ribble Galaxy episode except that I was there and mindwiped afterwards.

For reasons he hasn't revealed, Alvin is very interested in me, personally. We get along well, and I like him a lot, but it's bigger than that. Another one of those bonds, Self. I'm sure he feels it as strongly as I do. We're both aware that it is there and growing, and we are both nurturing it. However, I think Alvin's interest goes beyond even that.

We've talked at length about my diplomatic activities, but even more about research and translations. Some of his questions have been so speculative, maybe he *has* been interviewing me. He even asked for the specific date ending my current Fedcontract. Guess it's my turn to ask what he's after.

ShRil arrives late tomorrow. I wanted to meet her at Barisport, but Alvin has arranged for her to be picked up there by an escort and we will meet her at the base of Heartsnest with one of the electric tricycles. The pleased chirp in his voice when he told me that makes me think he's got some kind of ceremony planned. Given everything else that's gone on behind my back, I wouldn't be surprised if ShRil and Windy were in on it with him. Yes, you, my innocent little darling.

## 7040–8.7

Wake up, Windy, you sneak. I was right. The three of you were in on that little surprise together. But I never would have expected a procession with music and a ceremonial guard rolling along heralding our approach to the singing multitudes.

But the biggest surprise caught even ShRil unprepared. She and I are now honorary citizens of Heartsnest, Alvin's Place, and Pleuhockle. We were given medallions and feathered capes at a banquet in our honor, and toasted by Alvin and hundreds of guests at long rows of trough-like tables.

The reason for all this? Alvin's official thanks for rescuing him during the Warp-Ring war, and a celebration in honor of "Gerard and ShRil's forthcoming nestpledge."

The *cusping* ceremony, like *cylceia,* will be a day-long private affair, after which ShRil will leave immediately, in order to keep the custom. Alvin did some research on the Sylvan customs and discovered that a party is traditionally held by friends to honor the couple about to enter *cusping*. What a dear soul he is.

And ShRil. Dressed in her Sylvan best, she was more breathtakingly beautiful than ever. She wore three gold ruzes (as the teat patches are called), with a narrow strip of gold-and-green cloth tying the centers of them to form a shallow triangle connected to a short green skirt by a band of the same material. Her dark hair was held back from her face by a gold band, and highlighted by sparkling green stars that matched the stars on her gold bracelets and slippers. The beautiful slash of her lips was traced with a glossy gold outline that I later learned tasted like ambrosia.

Bored, Windy? Embarrassed? Too bad. I could spend hours describing every luscious centimeter of her. But I won't. Not because I don't want to, but because she is waking up and I have to go make sure she's all there. Every centimeter of her. Bye.

## 7040–8.8

ShRil broke the news to me gently, but I just didn't want to hear what she was telling me. She has to leave by 8.15. The *cusping* will be 8.14 and early the next morning she will leave. Guess I avoided thinking about when she would be leaving. It's so easy for me to get wrapped up in the presence of her now, right this minute, today, that I don't want to think about tomorrow.

But think about it or not, it will come, so we thought about it together, aloud. She's so sensible, practical, organized, and pragmatic that I accused her of trying to take the romance out of our short time together. She didn't realize I was teasing and her nose started running. Then we had to console each other.

Later, however, we got back to the discussion and decided that our period of separation would end after 7041.3. That's when her FedService enlistment is up. We'll try to meet somewhere with a Sylvan population as soon as possible after that if we both decide we want to go on to *dowonâche*. I can't imagine not wanting to, but ShRil kept emphasizing the seriousness of that decision and how either of us could decide to call it off if we felt it wouldn't be right.

There are a series of formal questions we have to answer to each other during the *cusping* ceremony, and if either of us finds the other's answers unsatisfactory, we can either delay *cusping*, or call it off. I was beginning to wonder if she had doubts, but before I could ask, she said she was telling me this only because I am not Sylvan and didn't grow up understanding the customs normally taught to a Sylvan male by his oldest male relative. That made me feel a little better, but I won't be sure, I guess, until after the *cusping* is complete. I'm in awe of this whole relationship.

We're going to spend the next five days with Alvin on a sightseeing tour of the planet. You and the Bard are doing so well with the translations, Windy, that I don't think you'll even miss me. But if you need to contact us, I've put all the codes into your comnet.

We sould be back sometime on 8.13, and I'll check with you then.

### 7040–8.15

ShRil's gone.

For the first time, I think I understand that it's much harder being the one left behind than the one leaving. How can I feel so empty and so full at the same time?

What can I say about the *cusping*? In many ways it was harsher, more disciplined, and more formal than *cylceia*. Perhaps because of the contrast, it was more meaningful and more beautiful. Symbolic of separation, we slept in the same bed last night, with a small gold bar between us. Forbidden by custom to touch, and forbidden by joy to sleep, we spent the night with long periods of intimate conversation and long moments of silence.

I couldn't even touch her when we said goodbye this morning, but somehow that made me feel even closer to her. By agreement, we said goodbye at the door of our suite and Alvin took her back to Barisport on his personal tricycle. I watched them spiraling down the ramps as far as I could, and even after I knew they were gone I kept watching. All the time, Windy, all the time I stood on that balcony staring down towards the foot of Heartsnest, I felt as much joy as sorrow. It's as though ShRil left me larger than I was, more complete, a whole greater than the sum of my parts.

What is my wonderful *cuspmate* helping me become?

## 7040–8.16

Alvin and I spent most of yesterday and all of today together. I really didn't need his companionship, but I appreciated it and his concern for me.

Late this afternoon he asked me what I planned to do after my current contract with Fed expires. I told him quite honestly that I wasn't sure, but since it has over four years to run, I would have plenty of time to think about it. After a long pause, he asked how I would react if someone wanted to buy out my contract with Fed and hire me and ShRil as private researchers-cum-diplomats? He meant himself, of course, but I didn't know why, so I asked what he would get out of it and what he had in mind.

His answer caught me totally unprepared. Alvin wants to found a university and research center. He outlined a grand scheme of a center for learning and research that would be unrivaled in the universe. He wants teachers and students from all over the universe.

But it's not just a dream or a distant plan. He's already begun the first phase of construction, eleven hemispheres fifty kilometers south of Heartsnest, each hemisphere fifteen kilometers in diameter and designed to contain different environments, atmospheres, and artificial gravities. Over three hundred scholars have already been paid advance credit and agreed to tentative contracts.

Alvin thought his plan was comprehensive until ShRil and I dropped in on him. Then he realized how useful it would be to have researchers for the various disciplines out traveling around the universe, adding to the body of knowledge, recruiting teachers and students, and even arranging cultural exchanges.

It's an enormous offer, Windy, for that's what it is. Alvin offered to buy out the remainder of our Fedcontracts, make me and ShRil naturalized citizens, provide us with an almost unbelievable budget, and let us wander around the universe wherever we want as representatives of Jelvo Universal Institute.

By the time he finished explaining it to me, I could hardly think, much less make a decision. So I told Alvin I was immensely flattered, in a state of shock, unable to comprehend the scope of what he was offering, and totally incapable of giving him a response. He gave me one. One of those long whistling laughs of his. Said I could take as much time to think about it as I wanted, but that if I decided to accept, I ought to do so before leaving here so I wouldn't have to "run any more of those errands for the Federation."

Went right to the point with that comment, Windy. That's what we do, run errands for Fed. Glorified errands, to be sure, but errands nonetheless.

Have you ever noticed that our luck seems to run in spurts of good and bad, Self? That's what worries me. Ever since Pleasance, our luck has been pretty good. Here it's been phenomenal. If we take Alvin up on his offer, will that mean a streak of bad luck again? The forces of the universe balancing themselves, and all that? Never mind. I'm not sure I believe in luck, or fate, or any of that.

Besides, I'd say I've already made up my mind, Self. Have to discuss it with ShRil, and then we can give Alvin an answer. I don't know how much her loyalty to The Professor might affect her decision, but given Alvin's generosity, we might be able to make a deal so that she could be researching for Moseen University while I am working for Alvin.

Having breakfast with Alvin early, and then a trip down to see the construction site. Talk to you when I get back.

### 7043–8.17

Alvin and I sat up on a ridge and watched the workers doing some blasting at the construction site, but none of those blasts moved me as much as the shock Alvin gave me at breakfast. I told him I would have to discuss his offer with ShRil, and that if she was agreeable, we would accept. That's when he told me that he had already talked to ShRil and she is very eager to accept if I want to, because, The Professor is one of those teachers who has accepted a contract.

I sat there speechless while Alvin enjoyed a good laugh. He didn't want to tell me about ShRil and The Professor until I had made up my own mind, because he didn't want me to feel as though I was being pressured or enticed for personal rather than professional reasons.

What could I say, Windy? I laughed with him.

Tomorrow we're going to review my Fedcontract with Alvin's legal staff. Alvin thinks they might be able to find a way to get us out of it very cheaply if Fed violated any of its own rules when they settled with me on Pleasance. There's no love lost between Alvin and Fed, and he said he'd rather use the credits for Jelvo U. Seems reasonable to me. I'm just glad we have records of all the option plans Colonel Q. ES't'phons made for us.

Looks like we're about to change employers, Windy.

## 7040–8.19

Targ's in braking orbit. Had a brief vidcom talk with him on his last orbit. Very formal. It was a shock to see his face after all these years, but it was more of a shock when he told me he had orders not to land. Said he would put his ship in stationary orbit, with Control's approval, and I was invited to join him tomorrow evening.

That certainly throws a new twist into my plans. Don't want to break your link with the library, Windy, and take you up there when a simple shuttle will do. On the other hand, I don't really want to go up at all. Next pass I'll suggest we send a shuttle up to get him. Alvin agrees that would be better.

*****He won't do it. Said his orders are not to set foot on the planet at all. Guess that doesn't leave me much choice, Windy. I'm the one who demanded this meeting under slightly false pretenses, so I guess I'd best go up and talk to him. Alvin wants to go with me, but I can't see any reason for it. My meeting with Commander Targ Alpluakka might get a little unpleasant, but beyond that, I'm not worried about it.

All I want are the facts surrounding my relationship to Fairy Peg and Ribble Galaxy.

*****Alvin will have a shuttle ready for me in the morning. I have my list of questions, the memocorder, a couple of changes of clothes, and a few other essentials packed in my kit, so I guess it's time to get some sleep.

## 7040–8.21
## H.S.H.S. *Syke*, Departure Orbit, Alvin's Place

I have your acknowledgement, Windy, and I'll keep transmitting as long as I can, so put your receiver on full.

In plain, old-fashioned language, I'm being kidnapped. We're leaving orbit. Commander Alpluakka is madder than Krick because we are being shadowed by two Pleuhockle destroyers. Apparently Alvin wasn't as trusting as I was. Targ's locked me in a cabin, so I don't know what he's going to do, but I suspect he'll warp as soon as he gets the opportunity. If Alvin's ships can track him through warp, I stand a chance, but if not, well, if not, I don't want to think about it.

Take care of yourself, Windy. I'm sure . . . to Alvin . . . because . . . ShRil . . .

# 9

### 7041–3.27
### Heartsnest, Alvin's Place

How you doing, Windy? So much has happened in the past seven months, I don't know quite where to start.

You know, it's amusing in a way to watch my reactions to high stress situations, and realize that Self and I can be very much in control of ourselves in the midst of a situation that is out of control. Then when the external situation is under control, we come apart again, lose the discipline and control we had. We allow a little madness to creep in only when it is safe.

Alvin noticed that on the way back here and told me a story about a legendary humanoid named Carver who once lived on this planet. Carver was a holy man, one of those types possessed of a divine madness, who sees into his metaphysical reality in a way unconnected with what we think of as normal.

Carver was a wanderer in the land of Alvin's ancestors, given to stopping every bird who would listen, and sharing his madness with long, apocalyptic narratives. He endured. Members of each successive generation could tell of someone who had seen Carver from a distance, or of someone else who had actually met and spoken with him. Carver lived in their minds, in the heart of their legends, a symbol of acceptable madness, a reminder that each sentient creature carries its own demons throughout life.

As proof of the universality of Carver's plight, Alvin gave

me a little microbook called simply, *Carver.* It contains ballads about Carver in forty-three major languages of the Pleuhockle System and the Tradershote Union, and one in Standard. But each story is basically the same. They are not translations. They are variations on a theme.

Wouldn't go so far as to call the Standard poem a ballad, but judge for yourself, Windy. It's a little crude, but I wouldn't change a word of it.

**Carver's Story**

Seven times several moments
Carver waited for the vision to pass,
But years passed instead,
A long row of commopoles
Strung together by conversations
(Ephemeral messages through birds' feet).

It was a bird which clutched him,
A great gryphon of a bird
That pounced with heavy grace upon his boyhood brain,
Sunk talons like eyes into his mind,
And swept him up to the wire,

Conversations sagged year by year
Under the weight of boy and bird,
Man and beast, poet and daemon,
And the scent of electric storms drove them mad.

On bright afternoons
When the sky pushes its blue stain into the grey
  mountains,
Carver can be seen on the wire,
An image of voices,
A translucent sound made in the likeness of gods,
And on his head,
As clear and insane as cassandra visions,
Perches that marvelous bird
With talons like eyes piercing his mind.

In the dark pupil of night
Carver sees through his daemon
Into the bright flowers of the cosmos,

Into the black caves of the void.
Then he sings to the universe
In the music of dreams,
Of visions and sorrow,
Of madness and spring—
Then he cries to be heard
In the wailing of nightmares,
With the tears of time,
With the sobs of a child.

Seven times several moments
Carver waited for the vision to pass,
But years passed instead,
A long row of commopoles
Strung together by lines
(Ephemeral messages passing through the feet of birds).

Without quite knowing how to express it, I understand "Carver." I understand why Alvin gave it to me. It's a cautionary tale for anyone sane enough to recognize his own insanity.

I know that's a strange preamble to my story, Windy, but it sets the tone for what happened, for the bizarre and the mundane.

Tired now, and need to rest. The story can wait another day. But there is one thing I want to tell you before I go to sleep. We no longer work for Fed. Alvin's legal staff bought the remainder of our contract (and also got us some more back pay) while I was gone. From Alvin's brief description of the negotiations, I take it that Fed didn't put up much of a struggle to keep us. The Burnal Sevene treaty, probably. Alvin hasn't said anything about still wanting us for Jelvo Universal Institute, but he did say that ShRil has already signed on. Maybe he assumes we have, too. I'll ask him. Later.

## 7041–3.28

Alvin came here for breakfast and we talked for about an hour afterwards. I was right. Partially. Alvin didn't assume anything. He just put us on the payroll the day the Fedcontract was broken. Yes, us. The standard arrangement. Pay the pilot and rent the ship. But non-standard pay. Very high non-standard pay. I told him it was too high, but he wouldn't listen. Said as soon as I felt well enough he was going to work me down to my "heavy humanoid bones."

If that sounds fair to him, who are we to protest?

Alvin upset me a little when he told me that ShRil would not be coming here, on his orders. But his reasoning makes sense, I guess. No sense in ShRil coming here only to turn around and head right past Moseen on our way to the Further Reaches.

Our first assignment as soon as I'm fit to pilot, is Yuma, on the edge of the Further Reaches. That's Tenderfoot country, Windy. Alvin also said he was sure I would want to be "revitalized" for my *dowonâche*. And laughed at his joke.

He's right about that. One of the ways I can get myself going is to tell this story. There's catharsis in putting things in the journal that I can't get from talking about them.

So here goes, Windy.

The day I took the shuttle up to meet Commander Targ Alpluakka, I wasn't worried about any more than a verbal confrontation with Targ. After spending twenty hours aboard H.S.H.S. *Syke*, I wasn't even sure there would be a verbal confrontation. Targ received me with cold courtesy and ritual formality, and then the two of us went to a small lounge off the cabin assigned to me and began our discussions.

Targ was most interested in where I had been and what I had done since leaving Ribble Galaxy, and, without being rude, I gave him brief answers and kept trying to turn the conversation to Fairy Peg. After a while it became obvious to me that he was determined to control the conversation, and was not about to answer any of my questions until I satisfied his. That realization helped me ease my guard a little, and I began to talk more freely about the past five years. He listened without comment or reaction to every answer I gave him, but there was an undertone to his questions that was very disturbing.

After an almost-congenial meal, I retired to my cabin and slept, with hopes that the following day might be better and begin to bring some answers to my questions. I remember waking in the midst of the Teever Loze nightmare, shaking and sweating as usual, and feeling a little disoriented.

Something had changed. I sat still for several moments before I realized what it was. I could feel that lowgrade hum that big ships have when they first start their main thrusters. The *Syke* was moving.

I immediately got dressed and tried to find my way to the flight deck. With the help of a young cadet, I arrived there several minutes later, in time to watch a violent demonstration of Targ's temper. He was reprimanding one of the deck officers, a young woman who appeared to be physically intimidated by him, while at the same time expressing his fury that the Pleuhockles would dare to post sentry ships around him.

I checked the visuals and saw two Pleuhockle destroyers. As I shifted my gaze back to Targ I realized that everyone on the flight deck except him was in battle dress. What in the universe was going on?

Just as I was about to ask that very question, the young officer who was being reprimanded looked toward me and in a sharp, clear voice announced, "Intruder on deck!" Everyone seemed to spin toward me at once, but no one faster than Targ. A hard, malicious smile I will never forget spread across his face as he said, "Why, it's the traitor. Come to see your handiwork, have you? That's very nice, but unfortunately we won't be able to accommodate your latest treachery. Ratchets! Lock that scum in his cabin."

Even as I protested, two Gabriel Ratchets grabbed me by the arms and dragged me from the flight deck. At the top of my voice I tried to tell Targ he was making a mistake, but the portals had closed and my "escort" moved me through the passages to my cabin without hesitation. They rather casually dumped me inside, and locked the door.

It took a moment for the shock to wear off, but as soon as it did, I dug out the memocorder and called you, Windy. I kept transmitting long after I knew we were out of range, trying to tell you what had happened, and using the description to calm myself down. I'm surprised you picked up as much as you did.

Targ spent the better part of the next two days taking the *Syke* through evasive maneuvers. I stayed locked in my cabin and saw no one. But I could hear the crew talking, as they passed my cabin, about how difficult it was trying to shake the Pleuhockle destroyers, and how tough it would be to make warp without being followed. But nothing I heard gave me the slightest hint of where we were going. Or why this was happening.

Somewhere toward the middle of the third day a medical officer accompanied by two Gabriel Ratchets came to my cabin, checked me over briefly, gave me a hypo "to help you rest," he said (but actually to knock me out), and strapped me in my bunk. The last thing I remember before I passed out was watching the warp preparation indicators light up in sequence.

Just the thought of all that makes me tired, Windy. I'm going to take a nap. Besides, I need to ask Alvin about a few more things to get the next part of the story straight.

## 7041–3.29

Didn't realize how tired I was, Windy. My nap lasted all night. Never had such bone-deep fatigue before. Guess I have Targ to thank for that. But I don't want to get ahead of myself.

According to Alvin, the *Syke* went through thirty-four warps in fifty-two days, trying to shake its trackers. By the time it came out of the thirty-fourth warp, it was being tracked by sixty-eight Pleuhockle and Tradershote ships, including Alvin's personal cruiser. Unfortunately, I missed all that excitement. Targ kept me drugged the whole time.

The irony of that chase was that when Targ stopped the *Syke* dead in space, we were less than one hundred parsecs from Alvin's Place. All that zig-zagging and doubling back had barely gotten us anywhere. To make it worse, as far as Targ was concerned, seven of the trackers were with us when we stopped.

That's when Targ decided to change tactics and let me awake from my involuntary stupor. Took almost a week to get that crud out of my system. Most of that time I slept, or was too groggy to be of much use to anyone. Targ had signaled the tracker fleet that I would die if they moved closer than five hundred kilometers. They had signaled him that if the *Syke* moved without permission they would blast it out of space. Glad I didn't know that.

I played groggy for a couple of days after I had really recovered. But it didn't do any good. The medical officer was checking me four or five times a day by then and kept telling me I was fine. I finally agreed that I was well enough, or recovered enough, or whatever enough to talk to Targ and find out what this was all about.

Targ was harsh and direct. He told me of our situation in space and made it clear to me that if I cooperated, I could be transferred to one of the trackfleet ships within a week. Cooperate with what? Why, with the investigation of my act of treason against Ribble Galaxy, of course. After I left Kril and before the mindwipe. Back in the void of my memory.

Obviously, we had a problem. But I was the only one who seemed to think so. When I told Targ I didn't have any idea of what he was talking about, he spat in my face. After that, things got nasty. The more Targ hit me, the more I remembered about the Gabriel Ratchets. A highly disciplined, uniquely trained unit of sadists, assigned as the permanent Royal Guard. The toughest, meanest, most deadly group of misfits ever produced by three species and seven races.

Targ Alpluakka was their commander because he was tougher than any of them.

He knew every site on my body where he could cause excruciating pain without having to break or permanently ruin anything. He tried them all, demanding that I tell what I had done when I left Kril every time the medical officer brought me back to consciousness. Of course, I couldn't give him answers I didn't know, but he only stopped when my body refused to be brought back any more.

When I awoke the next day, I felt like I'd been mauled by a rabid grisk. I hurt all over, and the bandages made me wonder exactly what was under them. I spent the whole day dreading the reappearance of Targ.

He didn't come that day. But he came the next day. And the day after that. And the one after that. And somewhere down the line I lost track until one day I woke up and the bandages were gone and I didn't hurt any more.

When Targ came that day, he didn't touch me. He talked. Said I was much stronger than he had given me credit for. That he had to respect someone who had taken as much punishment as I had. Said there would be no more torture. That there were other ways to make me talk. More subtle ways, too good for a traitor, but necessary in my case.

*****That's enough for today, Windy. Alvin's coming up for dinner, and that little nap just now wasn't really enough.

There may be catharsis in this, but I didn't think it would be so hard. For each line here, there's a screen full of details I'm leaving out. You don't need to know them. No one does. But I have to purge at least part of this from my system.

It's working. But slowly. Ever so slowly.

## 7041–3.30

It's a good thing ShRil's not here, Windy. We've exchanged several messages, but she doesn't know how bad off I really am, and I'm not going to tell her. Woke up screaming in the middle of a nightmare, confused and disoriented. Teever Loze being blown apart and Targ coming slowly toward me, a vicious sneer on his face and a huge, curved knife in his hands.

It was a Krick of a way to start the morning, Self.

Do you realize that tomorrow is the second anniversary of Teever Loze's death? The nightmare is just as vivid as ever. What do we have to do, Self, to get rid of it? How much time? How many repetitions? I'm beginning to wonder if it isn't permanently imbedded by now.

*****In a way, Windy, when Targ stopped the physical torture, I was more frightened, more anxious than during the days when I knew it would continue. I assumed, quite accurately it turned out, that the next step was going to be a chemical attack on my mind, and knowing how effective Fed's mindwipe had been and the later problems it caused (including getting me into my current fix), I was eager to find a way to avoid it.

First I tried talking to Targ. I begged his permission to tell him everything I knew and to have him help me remember anything that might convince him I was trying to cooperate. Targ sneered at me for begging, but said he would listen to anything I had to say before they applied the drugs and got to the truth.

I was desperate to avoid the drugs, so I started talking compulsively, telling Targ and the medical officer everything I could remember about anything to do with Fairy Peg and Ribble Galaxy, starting from the time I came out of mindwipe in the FedHosp. Told them I was blocked from remembering what happened before that. Told them about every Fairy Peg dream I could recall and how I had tried to piece them together. About the breakthrough right before I was imprisoned in Galaxy VI, and the headaches it caused. They listened without expression as I talked about going over the puzzle again and again while I sat in that Mystelerian cell and of how Gracie tried to help me remember. Nothing I said seemed to reach them. There was no sympathy, no response, no reaction whatsoever.

Until I mentioned the Warp-Ring war. Then Targ began to get very interested. He made me repeat every sequence of events, asking over and over why I was in the Warp-Ring System and why I chose to go to Pleasance after leaving Asrai. Each time I told him that Pleasance was not a choice, but where Fed was sending battle casualties, that sneering smile would creep onto his face and he would start all over again asking why I had gone to Asrai and what my plan was.

Targ's questions told me he thought I had gone to Asrai to make contact with or do some harm to Fairy Peg. He asked me if it wasn't true that I knew when I left Galaxy VI that Princess Peg On'Ell was in the Warp-Ring System negotiating with Wring-Con? My repeated denials didn't convince him.

Finally, after three or four days of telling my story and answering the questions over and over, I knew it was no use. They believed that I had betrayed Ribble Galaxy, and nothing I said was going to alter that. Something must have changed in my posture or the tone of my voice at that point, because the medical officer told Targ they weren't going to get any more out of me that way. His words and the expression on Targ's face sent a cold tremor through me. "Tomorrow you begin telling the truth," Targ said as he left the cabin.

After he left, the medical officer turned to me and for the first time spoke with a trace of compassion in his voice. He said we had known each other on Kril, that his name was Omna-Seay, and that it was obvious to him that I was telling everything I knew, and he was very sorry to have to put me through the truth search. Then his voice hardened again and he told me it was also obvious from the evidence that I had betrayed the trust of the Princess and all Ribble Galaxy. That made me a traitor, to be treated without reference to former friendship. Then he gave me a hypo to put me to sleep, and left.

The hypo took a long time to take effect. Self fought it

every step of the way, while I kept trying to concentrate on ShRil, trying to take my thoughts of her and use them like a benchmark to make an indelible center point in my mind, something I could come back to after they finished stirring up my brains. Some reference point I could hope to find again.

I don't remember consciousness for a long time after that. I do remember horrible surrealistic dreams where I was pursued by burning phantoms and clawing shadows, and endless whirling trips into dark vortices shadowed by splitting planets and bursting suns. And images of Self spinning away from me into the gaping maws of demons. Voices, always voices. Demanding, insistent, echoing voices, calling me into places filled with glaring lights and screaming sounds. And Fairy Peg asking, "Why? Why?"

What I did not know at the time was that Targ had taken a huge risk and put H.S.H.S. *Syke* into a cycle warp in an attempt to evade the trackfleet stationed around us. Every student lightspeed pilot learns the dangers of cycle warp in the first year of training. Almost any modern ship designed to warp can be put into a cycle from dead stop in about thirty seconds. The problem, of course, is that the ship is on a kind of mobius trip through the universe, and, because of the diametric balance of energy, can only come out of the warp at the same point it entered. The only danger is that if the entry point is missed, the ship is destroyed.

The history of space warfare is filled with stories of daring or desperate pilots who put their ships through short cycles, managed to hit the entry point on the button, and popped back into normal space ten days or so after leaving it, to discover their pursuers had been completely fooled and were gone. It is also filled with stories of ships that didn't make it. And of ones that did make it, but whose pursuers waited for them to return and blasted them into dust when they did.

But Targ, in his arrogance, went those stories one better. He put the *Syke* into a long cycle warp, sixty-two days from start to finish. It was an act of insanity. The longer the *Syke* was in the cycle, the greater the probability of missing the entry point. Whatever doubts Targ might have had about taking such a risk were buried by his obsession with breaking away from the trackfleet so he could deal with me at his leisure. And take me back to Kril.

The cycle warp also bought Targ and Omna-Seay two months of unthreatened interrogation time, all of which they used, for when I was allowed to regain normal consciousness, we were back where we started.

Unfortunately for Targ, the cycle warp didn't fool the trackfleet. An observant young ensign on the Tradershote Corvette *Aspidar* got a firm reading on *Syke*'s powerbuild, and accurately predicted the cycle warp and its duration. Alvin's cruiser *Galayuh,* a Pleuhockle destroyer, and the *Aspidar* remained on station in a kind of death watch. No one on the three ships really believed the *Syke* would make it back intact. But none of them wanted to miss it if it did.

It did. We had survived Targ's gamble. But as I said, I missed all of that. I remember regaining consciousness briefly and seeing a grizzled old medic beside my bunk. It seemed very important to know the date and I kept trying to force the question past my swollen tongue. Finally he understood and told me the Ribble date. "Standard," I croaked, "Standard." I think the shock of hearing him say, "7041–1.5," pushed me right back into unconsciousness where I kept hearing that number repeated in a distorted, groaning monotone.

When I next remember coming to, the same old medic was there again, and again I asked him the date. This time my mind was clearer. "7041–1.7." It seemed unbelievable that I had missed so much time, but I knew it was true. I also knew then that somehow Self and I had survived, because my first thought after letting the date sink in was that it had been over four months since I had seen ShRil. It seemed natural at the time to think about ShRil, and it was only later I realized how important that thought was.

I don't know if you can appreciate what Self and I accomplished, Windy, but the more I think about it, the more amazing it seems. Oh, we took some wounds along the way, and I'm sure we lost some parts here and there, or at least had some of them permanently damaged. But we survived as a whole, and that's the most important thing. I don't know what the odds were against us, but I'd bet they were staggering.

Alvin suggested that I might have been helped by the fact

that all of the truthsearch happened while we were in cycle warp. It's almost a semi-mystical notion on his part that psychic energy as well as physical energy has to be contained during a cycle warp in order for anyone to survive mentally intact. I wish Shttz were here to evaluate that idea, but as it is, there's no way of testing Alvin's theory. Whatever the reason, helped or not, we made it.

Gracie could probably have explained it. In fact, maybe part of the reason we did as well as we did can be attributed to her influence. Maybe when she touched us, she left Self someplace to hide, some pure, safe corner that couldn't be violated.

Enough for today, Windy.

## 7041–4.1

The next part of the story is really Alvin's, Windy. His modesty makes it sketchier than I would like, but we can deduce part of what he didn't tell us from what he did.

As soon as Alvin was notified that Targ was moving us out of orbit the day after I went up to the *Syke*, he fired off an official protest to Ribble Galaxy demanding that they contact Targ and order him to return me to Alvin's Place at once. Of course, by the time they could respond, Targ was going through that evasive series of warps and no one but the trackfleet knew exactly where he was in order to contact him.

Corpus Privy denied that Targ had actually taken me against my will, and said that if I had left with him on the *Syke*, I must have done so of my own volition. That's when Alvin started putting the heat on. There followed an exchange of messages between Alvin's Place and Ribble Galaxy, Alvin's Place and Tradershote, Calypso, Morgan Nine-Nine, Mithindoll, Qquartzl Rim, and, after Fed intercepted several of those messages, with Sector 103 FedFleet Command. The independent systems started putting pressure on their ambassadors and consuls from Ribble. FedFleet command initiated an extraordinary number of "routine checks" on Ribble ships passing through Fed-controlled space, with each Ribble captain being informed that since Ribble Galaxy had decided to violate the neutrality laws there was no guarantee that continued shipping through Fed spacelanes would be allowed.

The pressure did not take long to reach back to Corpus

Privy, who began to complain about harassment while at the same time trying to send cease and desist orders to Targ. The trackfleet intercepted one of those orders just six hours before Targ took the *Syke* into cycle warp.

The heat on Ribble was increased during the two months we were gone on Targ's desperation ride. Ambassadors and consuls in several systems were placed under embassy arrest. Shipments to and from Ribble were delayed in port because of technical irregularities. Fed began rerouting Ribble ships, making them take the long way through Fed space.

I asked Alvin why all these diverse systems and Fed were willing to take these actions. It couldn't have been because of me. Alvin gave me one of those happy chirps of his, and said indeed it wasn't. For most of the systems it was merely a case of being able to take some small revenge on Ribble Galaxy for past high-handedness on Ribble's part. They didn't know anything about me, and didn't need to. All they needed to know was that a Ribble ship under the command of one of its highest officers had committed a major violation of neutrality laws against the most neutral of all systems, Pleuhockle. The details were unimportant.

As for Fed's willingness to join in the fray, that was not difficult either. Ribble Galaxy had been the first to ever defeat Fed in one space war, and the first to stalemate it in another. No FedFleet commander worth his pension would have passed up an opportunity to harass Ribble shipping under legitimate circumstances. Fed knew I was the one who had been kidnapped. If Fed thought I knew something I shouldn't be telling Ribble, that was all the more incentive to get involved.

Corpus Privy got the message loud and clear. They requested and received permission for a Ribble frigate to join the cycle warp watch. It arrived two days before *Syke* popped out of the warp and carried Omega Commander of Her Supreme Highness's Starfleet, Privy-Admiral Gannack. No one except the Prince and Princess outranks the Privy-Admiral in Ribble. She reports directly to the throne, and has command of all branches of Ribble military forces. Even the commander of the Gabriel Ratchets can be held accountable by the Privy-Admiral.

As soon as she arrived, Admiral Gannack shuttled to Alvin's cruiser, where she presented her credentials and a lengthy, self-serving apology from Corpus Privy. As soon as the *Syke* arrived, Admiral Gannack requested permission to board and deliver a message to Targ. That's when the real negotiations started.

Targ had numerous problems. First of all, I wasn't yet coherent. Second, he had failed to take me back to Ribble or get a confession of my supposed treason. Third, he had blatantly violated the neutrality laws which Ribble Galaxy had agreed in principle, if not in fact, to honor, and consequently, caused difficulties for Ribble that would last for a long time to come. Fourth, he had endangered a Ribble ship and its eighty-plus crew members without justification. Fifth, and probably the most serious as far as Targ was concerned, he had lost face by being unable to avoid the trackfleet and then finding himself confronted by the supreme Ribble military commander.

He had other smaller problems too, my favorite being Omna-Seay's opinion that I had revealed all I was capable of. Omna-Seay spent several hours with me one day and told me he was no longer as convinced as he had been that I was a traitor, but that he was at least convinced that whatever I had done had been erased by the Fed mindwipe, and that there was nothing more to be gained by further interrogation. I asked him if Targ felt the same way, but his only answer was, "We shall see."

We did. Every day after that, shortly after the midday meal, the door from my cabin to the adjoining lounge would be unlocked, and I would join Targ for a discussion of "our problem," as he liked to put it. Despite Omna-Seay's evaluation, Targ was still totally convinced that I had betrayed Ribble Galaxy, and that had he only had more time, I could have been forced to reveal my treachery, thus vindicating his long-standing distrust of me. He never let me forget his feelings toward me, nor the fact that from the beginning of my mission to Ribble he had argued against my presence.

Those discussions were the best thing he could have done for my mental health short of letting me go. Each day it became more obvious to me that he was under a great deal of external pressure. That encouraged my hope that I would be released, and more importantly, that the interrogations would not be renewed.

I have to tell you, Windy, that Self and I were still pretty shaky then, and sometimes when Targ would ask a question or make a statement that required a response, we would just sit there without comprehending anything. That irritated Targ. Irritated me, too. But I knew that in spite of moments like those, Self and I were making good progress.

But I've gotten away from Alvin's part of the story, haven't I, Windy. My thoughts wander too much. Suddenly I'll discover that I've been staring out the window and I won't know how long I've been doing it. And I'm doing it again. Talk to you later.

*****Can't sleep. Tried reading, but couldn't concentrate. It's the Fairy Peg thing. I know I no longer have any public or official ties to her or Ribble, but what about on the private level? One of the things I had hoped to discover, maybe the most important thing I had hoped to discover was how Fairy Peg and I felt about each other face to face. I hate to leave loose ends like that. I didn't expect to find love, but I still hoped for understanding and the core of the bond which once joined us. Now I will never know what that meeting would have been like. All I have is the knowledge that in Ribble Galaxy I am considered a traitor.

But maybe there's a partial solution. One of the things that rose to the top during Omna-Seay's chemical attack on us was my memory of the private cipher that Fairy Peg and I used. Maybe I remembered that because it was originally my idea, a personal variation of the ancient four-six-square cipher with a progressive shift factor. Maybe I remembered it because Fairy Peg and I modified it and used it for personal messages. Or maybe because remembering our personal code is a protest from Self against the treason charge.

What would you think, Self, if we gave Windy the code and had her transmit the contents of this journal in code to Fairy Peg? Sounds crazy, doesn't it. And very selfserving, Self. But somehow I believe it's a good idea. If nothing else, it would make me feel better. We'll sleep on it.

## 7041–4.2

I started out okay, Windy, but somewhere along the way this story began splitting apart. However, in telling it this way, I've come to realize which parts are most important to me. Alvin's part is important, but Admiral Gannack's role in the negotiations doesn't really matter in its details, only in its effectiveness

Admiral Gannack is a woman of considerable reputation and skill. She was sent to do a very difficult job, and she did it. Five weeks after the *Syke* popped into the presence of its unwanted reception committee, I was transferred to the Admiral's frigate, and from there to Alvin's *Galayuh*. Admiral Gannack and I only spoke briefly and formally, but looking up at her from my evac litter I could detect no sympathy for me or my ordeal. As far as she was concerned, I was a pawn in a game and my movement across the board was only a small part of that game.

So why should I care about Admiral Gannack's role in any kind of personal way? If anything, I felt, and still feel, a little anger that it took her so long.

What about Fed, Self? How do we feel about Fed's role in this latest episode of our lives? Mixed reactions? Seems reasonable. Grateful to Fed for taking an active role. Indifferent to their motives. Aware and angry that Fed is at least partially to blame. Maybe totally to blame.

Then there's the biggest question of all. Where does Fairy Peg fit into this? Have all these years of trying to piece together the story of our relationship led us on a false trail? Were the dreams we had not memories of real events, but only symptoms of wishthinking? Why, Self, why are we haunted by this woman we once loved (or think we loved), and why can we not get answers?

For Fairy Peg to have sent Targ, she must feel that when I supposedly betrayed Ribble Galaxy I also betrayed the love and trust we shared. And there's no way to convince her I didn't. Even my wild idea of sending her this journal wouldn't make any difference. Would it?

*****Alvin called and interrupted my thoughts. With interruptions like that he can call every time he wants.

We're not going to Yuma after all, Windy. At least not initially. We have to make a side trip first to meet a young lady who would like for me to participate in a mating ceremony. You wouldn't mind taking me to Sylva to meet ShRil for a quiet little *dowonâche*, would you, Windy?

I thought not.

The only question is when. Have to send a reply to ShRil so we can arrive at the same time, as required by custom.

Are we ready, Self? Are we healed enough to leave here in a week or two? Say fifteen more days here, and twenty-three in transit. ShRil needs thirty transit days. Given message time, that ought to work out fairly well and still allow her a week or so to prepare for the trip. And us, five more weeks to recuperate.

It's unanimous in favor of leaving in two weeks. Good. Let's get our message off.

## 7041–4.3

Alvin had another little surprise for us yesterday. A psychtherapist. One of the teachers signed up for Jelvo U. Brought him in early to help me get better. Reminds me in a way of Bistelfaith. It's a pseudopod from T-Aqua Major Four whose name is untranslatable. Alvin calls it Signor Think, a kind of private joke that seems to amuse them both. I called "him" Chief Headfoot in a passing jest while he was questioning me, and according to Alvin that name pleased him too. So that's what I called him the rest of the interview.

Unlike Bistelfaith, Chief Headfoot must wear a nimonic translator and some of his statements come out very strangely. One of them in particular sticks with me. When Alvin asked him to tell me the basis for his theories, Chief Headfoot said, "mind reacts as faith is doing." From some of the other things he said, I think that means that if we act as though we believe we are getting better, we actually will. Doesn't sound very revolutionary or exciting to me, but it's unfair to judge after only two meetings. One of the things he said that I did like was, "one always is becoming more than the total past."

Chief Headfoot is very concerned with the process of change and this morning he told me to begin thinking about myself as someone new becoming someone newer. That's a strange concept, Self, but thinking like that certainly can't hurt anything. And it does seem to open up possibilities for the future.

Going back this afternoon for another session. Two a day every day until I leave. Time enough to take a nap before that.

*****All went well this afternoon. Chief gave me some mental exercises to do before going to sleep. Wants me to be sure to get lots of rest. Like I haven't been.

## 7041–4.5

I don't know if Chief is helping us, Self, but he's certainly making us tired. Can't seem to find the energy to do anything but talk to him and sleep. Chief said that was normal in the beginning for species similar to mine. Have to trust that he knows what he's doing.

## 7041–4.8

Teever Loze was back last night. Worse than ever. Told Chief Headfoot all about the nightmares and how they started. Talked compulsively. Guess Self and I never really acknowledged before how deep that pain is. After I finished, Chief and I had a long conversation about my feelings and reactions to every aspect of the story. He's good, Windy. He can ask the simplest questions and yet surprise me, questions Self and I should have asked, but carefully avoided. Helps us put the pieces into a whole without touching the puzzle himself.

Chief also suggested that I share this with Alvin. That will be difficult, but I'm going to give it a try this evening.

*****Once I got started talking about Teever Loze, it was amazingly simple. Alvin knew how he was killed, but my description of it allowed him to share his emotions. A first for each of us, to share with someone who knew Teever Loze how we felt about him and his death. I feel like a door has opened inside us, Self, and let some light into a dark corner.

## 7041–4.11

Self and I worked overtime last night, but I think the results are something very important and special. Two dreams. Two very different dreams. The first was a variation of the Teever Loze nightmare, only for the first time since I started having it, it seemed to take place very far away. When I woke up screaming his name, it was a very weak, quiet kind of scream. I went back to sleep and had another dream.

I was sitting on the bed by the window in the room my brother and I shared as children. There was a young lady with me, and we were both naked. Suddenly a stranger appeared outside the window, and we started talking to him. He looked very familiar, but I couldn't identify him. Eventually we invited him in the house and as we watched him come down the hall, he was taking off his clothes and laughing. He paused by the linen closet completely naked, took out a sheet and wrapped part of it around himself and threw the end over his shoulder. Then he came into the room and we all laughed and talked. When I realized who he was, I woke up again.

At first, I was rather dazed, but then I grabbed a stylus and pad and started scribbling some lines that were running through my head. A poem, born almost whole.

I told Chief about the dreams and read him the poem at this morning's session. Now I've finished it.

**The Resurrection of Teever Loze**

For two years your death frieze fell through my dreams
Crushing my sleep with sculptured memories.
The chattering fragments of your shattered death
Spilled screaming through my dark nights
  in red fears of blood,
  exploding like your name in my throat.
My tears shrieked your name without comfort.

Last night I saw you die in the distance,
  blown away like a stone.
I screamed your name in echo to the past
  and trembled.

This morning I saw you running naked down my hall
  wrapped in a sheet and laughing.
When I awoke,
I introduced you to a friend.

I'll tell you what, Self, when you decide to send signals of recovery, you don't mess around. Besides the resurrection of Teever Loze in the dream, there's something else there I want to talk to Chief about. It seems too simple to be valid, but I'm sure it is.

The second dream took place in a room from my childhood, my past. I think that means Teever Loze has now become a part of my past that I can accept, instead of a continuing part of my life. A friend dead but never forgotten, somehow safe now in that pleasant room of my youth. We found him a home, Self, a home where we were content and where our memory of him can rest peacefully.

But who was that woman with us, Self? It wasn't ShRil, but

was it Fairy Peg? I think so, but I can't be sure. If it was Fairy Peg, what was she doing in a dream about Teever Loze? I went over and over that dream, but the focus is on Teever Loze, and I can't shift it.

In spite of that, I feel good about the whole thing. Sometimes I wish you had an empath circuit, Windy, so you could know just how good I feel right now. Of course, there have also been times I was very glad you didn't know how bad I felt, so I guess it balances out.

Run me a couple of copies of my poem through the library printer, Windy. One for Chief and one for Alvin.

I won't be so rash as to suggest that Self and I have made a complete recovery, but we've certainly taken some giant steps forward, especially during this past week with Chief. We've learned some new techniques to use in the future. I feel much better now about going out to meet ShRil without so much excess psychological cargo. Means we can travel faster together.

## 7041–4.13

Beginning preparations to leave. Seems so sudden, in a way. Like there's a lot more I need to talk about with Chief and with Alvin. I don't want to leave so quickly, but ShRil will be waiting, and I don't want to stay. This time, though, we know that the separation is different, Windy. We'll stay in communication with Alvin. And with Chief Headfoot.

I asked Chief Headfoot if the nickname I gave him bothered him at all. His reply typifies his whole attitude. "Mostly head. Look like foot. Chief of Psychtherapy for Jelvo Universal Institute. Excellent name. Will use for all speaking Standard." Even Alvin has started calling him Chief. It's funny and flattering, both.

*****I think Alvin's right, Windy, in keeping the record of your work on the Tenderfoot material here. No sense in sending it off to The Professor when he will be here in six months anyway. I wish we could take it all with us instead of just the reference index, but we are going to need your memory capacity for all this new research information we're taking. Maybe when we come back, we can spend some time seeing what The Professor has done with it.

## 7041–4.16
## Barisport, Alvin's Place

Said our farewells. Final launch sequence initiated. Suddenly realized that we're leaving *home*. But we'll be back.

## 7041–4.18
## Space

Another Fairy Peg dream. I am kneeling in front of the throne. Looking up at Fairy Peg. She holds her staff beside her. Leaning on it. Looks pale. She's speaking. What are the words?

Her words are faint. Whispered. Can't make them out. Then she sits back on the throne and smiles at me. I start to rise. And wake up.

I've been over and over it, Self, and can't get any more than that. I can't make out her words, but her smile is warm and loving. What are you trying to tell me? That there's something I missed?

Whatever it means, it's helped me make a decision, Windy. We're going to follow through on my crazy idea and send Fairy Peg a copy of this journal. I know Self and I will still have to contend with memories and dreams of her, but the urgency is gone from them. I think we've accepted the impasse, but it's still hard to imagine what she must be thinking of me. And that's important. Maybe having a copy of my journal will help her in some way to come to her own terms with this story.

We'll use the personal four-six-square cipher, Windy, and send her everything in the journal to date. Let's get to it.

## 7041–4.21

Ready to transmit. Except for this.

Dear Fairy Peg,

Now you have all that I can tell you, and you must judge for yourself. I can never hope to know your reaction to this transmission, but I can hope that you will take it in the spirit of love in which it is sent. My heart is learning to forgive. I pray

that some day your heart will learn to forgive also.
Fare well and prosper, my beautiful princess.

Your Pilot,
Gerard

That's it, Windy. It's time to go meet the future. Transmit.

# Apostil

My great-grandmother, Peg On'Ell, put everything from her life into the archives, and, when I was a very small child, she used to take me there and tell me about all the stories locked up in the records. She died when I was ten, two years after passing the throne on to my grandfather, Carpen of Yeraf, but I remember those last two years of her life as two of the happiest of mine. Why, of all her grandchildren and great-grandchildren I became her favorite, I do not know, but perhaps it was because I was her first great-granddaughter and partial namesake. The reasons are unimportant, except to me, and for the fact that she made me feel the archives were the most wonderful place in the universe to be.

As I grew older, I would go to the archives to think, or to play, or just to be alone. The Master Archivist then was Fianne Tackona, who was as old as my great-grandmother. He seemed to enjoy having a little girl come to share part of his archives, and whenever I was bored I could always depend on Fianne Tackona to tell me a story or recite a poem or sing a song in his creaky, off-key voice. I remember asking him on my twelfth birthday if he knew all the stories in the archives. He looked at me with those fading grey-green eyes of his and said, "No one knows more about these archives than I do, Princess, and compared to the wealth of knowledge stored here, I am like the poorest beggar in the market." "Like a beggar in the market"; that is the phrase that floated to some lofty place in my mind and has lodged there ever since.

By the time I was fifteen, I spent most of my free time in the archives, reading dusty old manuscripts, which Fianne would drag out for me, that told grand tales of heroes and heroines whose bones had turned to dust centuries before even Peg On'Ell ascended to the throne. Fianne also taught me to use the tape machines and the microreader, and I read more modern stories, including some about people who were still alive when I was reading about the exploits of their youth. Because of all my reading, I became unofficial family historian, and when my Uncle Tetroff suddenly found himself on the throne after the Great War during which Ribble Galaxy lost so many of its finest people, he would ask me to tell some of the stories I had learned about our ancestors. Often there would be half a hundred members of the royal family sitting at table after dinner, listening to me recount the tales of glory and honor which had become so much a part of my life.

I enjoyed those times very much, and still do, for in becoming the family historian, I have created a place for myself within the complicated scheme of Ribble royalty. By my last calculation, I am thirty-fifth in line for the throne, and those children yet to be born to any of my relatives ahead of me will have precedence. I have no hopes nor aspirations to rule outside my current domain, for when Fianne Tackona died I persuaded Uncle Tetroff to place me in charge of the archives, and he created the position of "Royal Archivist to the Throne."

Being Royal Archivist is more than my occupation, it is the center of my life, the focal point of my energies, and, until I found the microfile on Gerard Manley, it was all I ever dreamed of becoming. However, Gerard Manley's story opened up a whole new world for me, a world not of battles and heroes glorifying the history of our galaxy, but rather, a very personal story about living in the midst of doubt and uncertainty and separations as seen through eyes very foreign to mine. Here was the story of a man who had played an important part in my great-grandmother's life, even if only for a brief time, and who had been through adventures that seemed strange and wonderful to me.

I found Gerard Manley's journal quite by accident, while searching for some other materials in great-grandmother's personal indexes, and once I started reading it, I knew I had found a story I wanted to share. I read it several times before approaching Uncle Tetroff with the idea of publishing it, and teased him with bits and pieces of the story for weeks before actually asking his permission. He had allowed me to publish several collections of stories from the archives before, but always they were the traditional types of tales like the ones I told at table.

This story was so different, I wanted to do everything possible to have Uncle Tetroff feel kindly toward it and me. At first he was not very enthusiastic when I presented him with the personal copy I had made for him, but, seeing the work I had done, he graciously took the copy and, after three weeks, during which I did little else but worry about his reaction, he called me to his private chambers.

I was tense, but excited, and fully prepared to accept a denial if such I was to receive; however, I was also prepared to defend the reasons in favor of publication. Consequently, when Uncle Tetroff complained about Gerard Manley's comments putting Ribble Galaxy in an unkind light, I reminded him that the truth is not always kind and that Gerard seemed to blame no one for excess but Commander Alpluakka, and *he* did not deserve either absolution or forgiveness. There followed a long conversation about the numerous excesses committed by the Gabriel Ratchets in the name of the throne and how their dissolution by the Noble Assembly had been one of the few good things to come out of the Great War. At the end of that conversation, much to my relief and gratification, he gave his approval.

I ask my readers, especially those already familiar with these mundane details of my personal history present here, to forgive this long explanation, but I felt it was necessary to tell how this story came into public circulation. I would like to apologize to those who would rather see this story published in Kulitti than Standard. I am working on such a translation at Uncle Tetroff's request, but humbly suggest that this Standard transcript has far more power and beauty than any poor Kulitti translation I might offer in the future.

Finally, but most importantly, I must thank my Uncle Tetroff, His Supreme Highness, Guardian of the Ribble Galaxy, Tetroff-Tania On'Ell, Badh of Seven Systems, Keeper of the Faith, Prince Regent of Kril, who most kindly approved all that is written here, including my poor apostil.

I believe Gerard Manley's story needs no editorial explanation from me; however, one cannot help but wonder, after reading it, what became of Gerard and ShRil and *Windhover* and Alvin, and what wonderful new stories we might have if the remainder of his journal were ever located, a dream I dare not dwell on too often. Were Ribble Galaxy not so isolated now from the rest of the universe by war and politics, it is a dream I might seek to explore, partially to satisfy my own curiosity, and partially because as Royal Archivist, my records seem somehow incomplete without the rest of Gerard's story.

Princess Coasta-Peg Jeni On'Ell
Royal Archivist to the Throne of Ribble Kril
Albar 53, 8901 s.p.i.
(7283–6.14 std.)

## ABOUT THE AUTHOR

WARREN NORWOOD lives in the Fort Worth area of Texas, and when not writing books and poems is hard at work as a Bantam wholesale field representative. *The Windhover Tapes: An Image of Voices* is his first book and Bantam will be publishing the sequel, *The Windhover Tapes: Flexing the Warp* in early 1983. He is currently writing the third Windhover book, *Fize of the Gabriel Ratchets*.

Read this exciting preview of the second book in

THE WINDHOVER TAPES

# FLEXING THE WARP
## by Warren Norwood

Gerard Manley's interstellar odyssey takes him ever closer to finding the truth behind his hidden past.

*Copyright © 1982 by Warren C. Norwood*

## 7041–10.28

ShRil found me unconscious at the console and managed to drag me back to the rejuvhosp cell. Scared her, but when the rejuvhosp couldn't find anything physically wrong with me, she came back up here and found my last entry still on the screen. She read it and remembered the blackout I told her about back in Galaxy VI after I made the first big breakthrough around the mindwipers' blocks. Logically, she concluded that it had happened again. Then all she had to do was wait until I came out of it.

My head still hurts, but only a low-grade throbbing. What I don't understand, Self, is why we reacted so violently to the memory of the Truth Bell? Why was the block around that so strong? Or is it not just the Truth Bell, but also Filif-cy-Nere? And why am I making my head worse by going through all of this now?

*****Almost blacked out again. Fara! How I hate those mindwipers and what they did to us. May they all have mates who torment them, offspring who curse them, and diseases no one can cure. May the nightmares of the damned fill their every sleeping moment. And for those who order and control them, I wish a tenfold dose of the same.

Well, I'm not sure that helped the pain any, but it certainly helped my mood. If my curses on them were dilith dung, they could fertilize a million planets. And if curses and wishes were credits and dishes, what a feast we could offer the king.

Now where did *that* come from, Self? Sounds like

something old Marradon would have said. Marradon? The Sayer of Filif-cy-Nere. The keeper of the Truth Bell. The old woman in black.

There we go again, Self. Shut it off. One of us has to give our head a rest.

## 7041–11.2

ShRil thinks we can cut the Demity arc a little tighter, Windy. Said the preliminary readings on Demity Cluster's gravity well are lower than we expected. Just to make her happy, let's replot.

I see. The two of you have already done it. Well, it looks a little close to me. If the gravity's anywhere near expectations, it's going to sling us around at close to warpspeed.

You figured that too, did you? If the two of you are so smart, what do you need me for? After all, I'm just a bumbling ex-diplomat given to excessive drinking and bad dreams.

ShRil! Get on the com.

##Right here, dear.##

Have you completely reviewed this new course with Windy?

##Of course not. I left that to your discretion.##

Well. I'm glad you left something for me to do. I wouldn't want to be in your way or anything.

##Are you upset, Gerard?##

Certainly not. Certainly not.

##Then why are you shouting into the com?##

Because I'm upset! Turn my back on you two and you start tinkering with the course plan. Next thing I know you'll want to do the piloting yourself.

##I am a qualified pilot, my dear, and if you will only think back, you yourself suggested that I could do some of the piloting on this ship. However, if my attempt to assist you while you were not in the best of health offends some primitive sense of your place on this ship, I suggest you prepare for a long and arduous family discussion.##

Now, ShRil, I didn't mean anything like that. I only felt...

##At this moment, my companion of necessity, I care little for what you only felt. You have attempted to demean and insult me. I shall not abide such treatment. ShRil out.##

ShRil, wait a minute.

ShRil?

Kravor in Krick, Self! There was no need for that. Why did I get so upset just because ShRil was trying to help? Is it what she said? Do I feel threatened?

No. That's not it. It's not that she wants to change the course, nor that she and Windy did the preliminary work. It's the fact that their course might throw us too close to warpspeed. And that's a risk to ShRil and the baby. Protecting her again. Or trying to.

Guess I'd better go back and try to explain.

## 7041–11.3

Okay, Windy. Change course for the new arc. I convinced ShRil that I only had her best interest in mind, and she convinced me that there wasn't enough risk to worry about. She also convinced me that her feelings could be totally soothed only if she were allowed to do part of the piloting. I agreed, but only on the condition that she make the Demity swing in the rejuvhosp cell. Just to avoid risk to the baby. ShRil said she was sure that was totally unnecessary, but if it would appease the overanxious father, she would consent.

Overanxious father. That's me. But no apologies. To date I haven't been given any reason not to be overanxious. We'll make the second pregnancy test next week, and the final corrections for the Demity swing in eighteen days. I want you to monitor those gravity readings like a grisk guarding its young, Windy. If there's so much as a two percent increase from the levels you and ShRil calculated, I want to know about it.

You bet Fara's blessed boots I'm an anxious father. Isn't every father the first time? That is my mate sleeping back there, carrying our child. Am I in so much of a hurry to get anywhere that I would risk either of them? No indeed. I studied the tape ShRil has on pregnancy and birth for crossbred Sylvans, and it doesn't exactly advise a carefree approach to the situation. So what does a good mate and father do? He worries. And hopefully that worry will lead to productive actions.

Productive. Nice choice of words, Self.

## 7042–2.17
## Ariztoz Entry Path

Cautious place, Ariztoz. Told us to expect Pilot Patrol in seventeen hours, two craft, fully armed, they said. And do not deviate from this path by more than a tenth of a degree.

ShRil?

##You called, my love?##

Ariztoz Control just told me to expect an armed escort and to be prepared for inspection before they allow us to land. Thought you said Alvin had cleared the way for us here?

##That is what his message said. Perhaps you should try tc contact Proctor Carlsson LeRoie.##

I tried and was told firmly and politely that they

would allow no messages until after we had been boarded and inspected. I don't like it.

##Surely, my dear Gerard, you do not begrudge them the right to see those who will be landing on their planet, do you?##

Of course not. I just don't like the peremptory way they did it. The least they could have done was . . .

##—be sweet and polite and ask if you would kindly allow one of their representatives aboard to admire Windy? Of all people, Gerard, you should understand that a planet which feels it necessary to personally inspect every ship that wants to land must feel threatened and very cautious. Such attitudes do not lend themselves to excessive courtesy. Were they rude to you?##

Not at all. It's just that I wasn't expecting . . .

##—to be treated like a common spacer?##

Will you quit interrupting and let me finish a sentence? It's just that I thought Alvin had cleared the way for us and was not expecting to be treated like a potential threat. What's so wrong with that?

##Nothing, except that you failed to receive the treatment you anticipated, and now you are talking yourself into a huff about it.##

I am not.

##You certainly are. I refuse to participate in your tantrum.##

Me? Having a tantrum? Surely not.

##Surely yes. Now, if you are prepared to eat, it is ready and waiting.##

Be there in a minute.

Imagine that. Accusing me of having a tantrum. My feelings might be hurt if I didn't know she was right. But how in Fara's name do we do anything without having some expectations? We don't. We just have to work harder on being open to changes.

I'm going to eat.

## 7042–2.18

Our escort is here, the good ships *Luden* and *Belst.* No friendly chitchat, just acknowledgment of positions, course verification, and a very brief message from Proctors Carlsson LeRoie and Whyre Sebrankdal and Masterlith diTchloschTochen Chunchgrebnel Ahballinger.

> Welcome to Ariztoz, friends of Alvin, Baris-lon-Jelvo. Be patient with our customs and we will greet you shortly.

Well, at least it's nice to know we're expected.

## 7042–2.20
## Braking Orbit, Ariztoz

I hate being boarded. ShRil says that's silly, but I hate it anyway. Reminds me of Galaxy VI and that imperious Duke-and-Captain-Whatever-His-Name-Was. Makes me nervous to have uninvited strangers aboard. But I promised ShRil I would be my most courteous and diplomatic self, Self, so help me out.

*****Here they come. Douple the posure on the visual, Windy. Damn. An armed sled. Tell you what, Windy. Why don't you just lock AutoTrakFire on *Luden, Belst,* and that sled. Just for practice, of course.

*****Can't say much for Subgroupleader Hwartzkopfer and his faithful nameless companion. Very formal. Very correct. Very military. And very glad that they're gone. Even ShRil didn't like them.

When Hwartzkopfer said very condescendingly that we were smart to have followed such an accurate course and intimated that we would have been blasted from space if we hadn't, I had to bite my tongue to keep from telling him that we had his ships under our guns also. He assumed we are unarmed and I didn't tell him otherwise. If he had asked, I think I would have lied. He was the kind of man I've always loved lying to, so superior and condescending in his attitude that the best one could wish for him is that he would assume his way into a black hole.

The way he kept eyeing ShRil with that openly lecherous leer made me want to give him a little taste of my knuckles.

But I kept my diplomatic front, was polite to his discourtesy, respectful to his position, and elaborately grateful when he finally gave his approval for us to land and a small card with a sickly green stamp that is our entry pass.

If we never meet him again, it will be too soon.

## 7042–2.21
## Brentberg-on-Titell Starport, Ariztoz

We're to clear impcustoms in about an hour, then to be "taken" to the Vintel Hostelhauss where our two proctors and the masterlith are supposed to be waiting for us.

Haven't seen anything about this planet that I like very much. Hope our hosts are a change from that.

## 7042–2.22
## Vintel Hostelhauss

If those three "teachers" weren't highly recommended by Alvin, I think I'd write them off and get out of here.

Well, for charity's sake, Sebrankdal wasn't so bad, but LeRoie and Ahballinger I could do without. Intellectual snobs, the three of them.

LeRoie and Ahballinger are both native to Ariztoz and speak of it as if it were the center of culture, intellectual disciples, and military prowess for the whole universe. Both of them are short stocky types that most humanoid species have tended to weed from their gene lines. Standing next to them, Sebrankdal looks tall even though he's barely two meters including his thick-soled boots and his fuzzy hat. That's a cheap shot, I guess, but right now I don't feel like they deserve any more than that.

Apparently none of them have ever met a Sylvan female before. They gawked at ShRil. Stared at her breasts in totally unconcealed fascination. I told her from now on she will have to dress more modestly. The weather will help with that. It's bitterly cold everywhere in the hostelhauss except for the dining facility. In ShRil's defense, she was wearing one of those keepwarms of hers, but it clings to her so closely that it might as well be transparent.

On the business side, during dinner we asked when we could get out to the library at the university (The Terfan X. Noz Center of Collegium Columbine Catholic for Supreme Academic Studies and Cultural Excellence, to be exact) and got the strangest answer from LeRoie. "Why, as soon as you have proven your loyalties," he said in a voice that suggested we didn't know which way was up.

## 7042–2.26

Well, Windy, you get "Temporary Access, Professional Student Class" to the library computer. If we get a glimpse of anything more than some "restricted to amateurs" portion of an index, I'll be surprised. ShRil is off right now with LeRoie, trying to get that changed, but I'm not going to hold my breath until it happens. Wouldn't even ask you to hold your breath.

I told ShRil before she left that anytime she was ready to climb back aboard and launch from this place wouldn't be too soon for me. Can you believe that Ariztaz is the birth planet of the Ginzia flight troops? And that this is where they used to come for their decadel birth rituals and to die, to perform the sad hymns of the quilnt on their native planet?

*****Not a no, but not a maybe either. Just a "we will consider your request."

ShRil agrees that if they refuse us better access, we have no choice but to leave. We also agree that there's no reason to recruit LeRoie, Ahballinger, and Sebrankdal any harder than we have to. I can't believe any of them would be a credit to Jelvo U. I don't even think they're a credit to Noz Center. Oh, Sebrankdal has made a minute effort to be civil, but other than that, none of them have given us any reason to think well of them.

Doesn't that seem odd to you, Gerard? Shouldn't you be putting your subtle diplomatic training to use here and trying to determine why the three teachers Alvin recommended are acting in a manner so obviously offensive? Come, Gerard, surely your skills haven't atrophied and left you helpless and crippled in the face of these circumstances. Think, Gerard. Analyze. What is going on here?

## 7042–3.19

A note from Ahballinger. "Best wishes for a happy Memorial Unity Day."

Told ShRil we might have a party here. All we need now is a note from Sebrankdal. Then we could all sit around here on Unity Day and wait for the Loyalty Corps to raid the place and arrest us all for sedition or conspiracy to think out loud or whatever reason they use in cases like ours.

And exactly what is our case? Your Honor, two off-worlders tried to coerce three of our finest teachers into leaving wonderful Ariztoz by convincing them that this is a bad place to teach, that intellectual freedom is stifled, and that there is a foundling university halfway across the cosmos that would provide them with greater opportunities. And, Your Honor, these fine teachers, caught up by vile imprecations and insidious arguments, were involuntarily corrupted by the offworlders and are in need of a long rest somewhere where they can be properly cared for. The offworlders should be executed.

I told you this place was getting to me, Windy.

Wouldn't it be funny if we've guessed wrong and none of them showed up tomorrow? All that speculation and worry for nothing? Not only would it be funny, it would be a relief.

## 7042–3.21

Well, it was a strange day, Windy. Early in the morning, Sebrankdal showed up with a small basket of food and a large bottle of distilled spirits that was weak and salty. We invited him in, of course, and then spent a very uncomfortable hour or so trying to carry on a conversation.

Unlike Sebrankdal, LeRoie stayed for almost three hours. Most of that time the three of us just sat at the window watching the seemingly endless parade of snow crawlers, with their flags and banners, crunching in line around the statue of Terfan X. Noz in the square across from us. We never really got comfortable, but after a while a placid indifference settled on us and we were content to sit, nibble, and watch.

Much later there was a knock at the door and it was Ahballinger. No basket of food and bottle of salt liquor for him. As soon as the door was shut behind him he began apologizing for his actions towards us and for those of LeRoie and Sebrankdal. When we didn't respond, he said he had arranged for the loyalty monitors to be temporarily disrupted in our room and that we could talk freely if we wished to do so.

Ahballinger hunched forward in his chair and, in a rapid-fire monologue, told us that no one on Ariztoz was safe from the Loyalty Corps, that the intellectual community was regularly purged of any who spoke against the Committee of Loyalty, that he and LeRoie and Sebrankdal would very much like to join the faculty of Jelvo U., but that doing so would be difficult, and that only on this day did they dare come to talk to us about it.

"But Masterlith Ahballinger," ShRil said, taking advantage of a pause, "you are the only one who has openly expressed such an interest."

He looked surprised by that. And then worried. "Neither of them said anything?" he asked.

We assured him that they hadn't, but that they might not have felt free to do so. "This is very bad," he said, "very bad." Rising abruptly, he said he would contact us soon and left.

## 7042–3.27

ShRil may have come up with a solution to our recruiting problem. She wants to go to The Coursitter of Noz Center and request permission to circulate a memo inviting all faculty members to apply for positions with

Jelvo U. on a two-year faculty exchange program. If she receives permission to do so, Ahballinger, Sebrankdal, and LeRoie can apply under that program. If The Coursitter refuses her permission, then we will so report to Alvin and let him proceed as he sees fit.

It's the most reasonable plan we've come up with so far, but I don't have high hopes for it. If the three of them want to leave here, I think we should just take them with us, without permission of course, and take our chances on the consequences. More than likely the Committee of Loyalty will be glad to be rid of them and won't do anything. ShRil says that's too reckless an idea. And with her aboard and pregnant, I agree. But if it were just me, Windy, or rather, just me and you, I think I'd put the option to them and take our chances.

### 7042–3.29

After much discussion and persuasion, ShRil has apparently convinced The Coursitter to circulate the recruiting offer, but with his wording rather than ours. ShRil says his wording is acceptable to her, so I don't think we could have asked for anything better. I don't know how she did it, but I'm proud of her.

### 7042–4.1

Notified Ariztoz Control and Pilot Patrol that we intend to depart on 4.5 and requested permission to do so. As with everything else around here, nothing is automatic, but the officers I spoke to assured me we should have no trouble getting clearance by then.

## 7042–4.3

We're finished here, Windy. Formal good-bye and thanks said to The Coursitter. LeRoie, Sebrankdal, and Ahballinger nowhere to be found without arousing curiosity, so I guess we'll have to leave without seeing them. Feel funny about that, not because I particularly like any of them, but because I feel like we're deserting them here.

See you in twelve hours, Windy.

## 7042–4.4
## Brentberg-on-Titell Starport, Ariztoz

Panic time, Windy. Ariztoz Control says our permission to leave has been delayed in "official channels." Wants us to hold til 4.6.

Message from LeRoie: "Leave as soon as possible for the welfare of your child."

Maybe panic is the wrong word, but certainly time for some quick thinking and a fast launch. I don't want to blow out of here if we don't have to, but I want to be prepared to do it just in case. ShRil's getting everything strapped down and first thing tomorrow we're going to request permission again to launch, just to see what happens.

## 7042–4.5

Prepare for emergency launch, Windy. Control said no, but we're going anyway. We'll have to blow the couplings at the last second, but that's their problem, not ours.

As soon as we've cleared the berth, start AutoTrakFire and give me constant readouts on anything and everything in range of the scanners.

This is no way to treat you, Windy, but the refusal, plus LeRoie's warning, plus my prescient gut tell me we have no choice. Once we're clear and there's no pursuit, we'll send them a message telling them to bill Jelvo U. for any damage we cause.

ShRil?

##I am in the rejuvhosp cell and ready to depart.##

Good. Windy will give you a fifteen-second warning and the countdown. We have to lift without dampers, so hold on.

##Of course, my dear.##

ShRil? I love you.

##I love you too. Now, may we leave?##

You heard the lady, Windy. Get us going.

*Read FLEXING THE WARP, on sale in early 1983 wherever Bantam Books are sold.*

# OUT OF THIS WORLD!

That's the only way to describe Bantam's great series of science fiction classics. These space-age thrillers are filled with terror, fancy and adventure and written by America's most renowned writers of science fiction. Welcome to outer space and have a good trip!

- ☐ 23589 **TOWER OF GLASS** by Robert Silverberg $2.95
- ☐ 23495 **STARTIDE RISING** by David Brin $3.50
- ☐ 20761 **SUNDIVER** by David Brin $2.50
- ☐ 23493 **NEBULA AWARD STORIES SIXTEEN** by Jerry Pournelle $2.95
- ☐ 23512 **THE COMPASS ROSE** by Ursula LeGuin $2.95
- ☐ 23541 **WIND'S 12 QUARTERS** by Ursula LeGuin $2.95
- ☐ 22855 **CINNABAR** by Edward Bryant $2.50
- ☐ 23574 **THE SEREN CENACLES** by Warren Norwood & Ralph Mylivs $2.95
- ☐ 23784 **THE DRAGON LENSMAN** by D. Kyle $2.95
- ☐ 20499 **LENSMEN FROM RIGEL** by D. Kyle **(A Large Format Book)** $2.50
- ☐ 22938 **THE WINDHOVER TAPES: FLEXING THE WARP** by Warren Norwood $2.75
- ☐ 23351 **THE WINDHOVER TAPES: FIZE OF THE GABRIEL RATCHETS** by Warren Norwood $2.95 $2.95
- ☐ 23394 **THE WINDHOVER TAPES: AN IMAGE OF VOICES** by W. Norwood $2.75
- ☐ 22968 **THE MARTIAN CHRONICLES** by Ray Bradbury $2.75
- ☐ 23785 **STAR TREK: THE NEW VOYAGES 2** by Culbreath & Marshak $2.95
- ☐ 20990 **A CANTICLE FOR LEIBOWITZ** by Walter Miller, Jr. $2.95
- ☐ 23828 **THE FARTHEST SHORE** by Ursula LeGuin $2.95
- ☐ 22563 **A WIZARD OF EARTHSEA** by Ursula LeGuin $2.95

**Prices and availability subject to change without notice.**

**Buy them at your local bookstore or use this handy coupon for ordering:**

Bantam Books, Inc., Dept. SF, 414 East Golf Road, Des Plaines, Ill. 60016

Please send me the books I have checked above. I am enclosing $________ (please add $1.25 to cover postage and handling). Send check or money order —no cash or C.O.D.'s please.

Mr/Mrs/Miss________________________

Address________________________

City____________ State/Zip____________

SF—12/83

Please allow four to six weeks for delivery. This offer expires 6/84.

# FANTASY AND SCIENCE FICTION FAVORITES

Bantam brings you the recognized classics as well as the current favorites in fantasy and science fiction. Here you will find the most recent titles by the most respected authors in the genre.

- ☐ 23944 THE DEEP John Crowley $2.95
- ☐ 23853 THE SHATTERED STARS Richard McEnroe $2.95
- ☐ 23795 DAMIANO R. A. MacAvoy $2.95
- ☐ 23205 TEA WITH THE BLACK DRAGON R. A. MacAvoy $2.75
- ☐ 23365 THE SHUTTLE PEOPLE George Bishop $2.95
- ☐ 22939 THE UNICORN CREED Elizabeth Scarborough $3.50
- ☐ 23120 THE MACHINERIES OF JOY Ray Bradbury $2.75
- ☐ 22666 THE GREY MANE OF MORNING Joy Chant $3.50
- ☐ 23494 MASKS OF TIME Robert Silverberg $2.95
- ☐ 23057 THE BOOK OF SKULLS Robert Silverberg $2.95
- ☐ 23063 LORD VALENTINE'S CASTLE Robert Silverberg $3.50
- ☐ 20870 JEM Frederik Pohl $2.95
- ☐ 23460 DRAGONSONG Anne McCaffrey $2.95
- ☐ 20592 TIME STORM Gordon R. Dickson $2.95
- ☐ 23036 BEASTS John Crowley $2.95
- ☐ 23666 EARTHCHILD Sharon Webb $2.95

**Prices and availability subject to change without notice.**

**Buy them at your local bookstore or use this handy coupon for ordering:**

Bantam Books, Inc., Dept. SF2, 414 East Golf Road, Des Plaines, Ill. 60016

Please send me the books I have checked above. I am enclosing $______ (please add $1.25 to cover postage and handling). Send check or money order —no cash or C.O.D.'s please.

Mr/Mrs/Miss __________

Address __________

City __________ State/Zip __________

SF2—1/84

Please allow four to six weeks for delivery. This offer expires 7/84.

# SPECIAL MONEY SAVING OFFER

*Now you can have an up-to-date listing of Bantam's hundreds of titles plus take advantage of our unique and exciting bonus book offer. A special offer which gives you the opportunity to purchase a Bantam book for only 50¢. Here's how!*

*By ordering any five books at the regular price per order, you can also choose any other single book in the catalog (up to a $4.95 value) for just 50¢. Some restrictions do apply, but for further details why not send for Bantam's illustrated Shop-At-Home Catalog today!*

*Just send us your name and address plus 50¢ to defray the postage and handling costs.*

BANTAM BOOKS, INC.
Dept. FC, 414 East Golf Road, Des Plaines, Ill. 60016

Mr./Mrs./Miss/Ms. ____________________
(please print)

Address ____________________

City __________ State __________ Zip __________

FC—12/83